The Willows
in Winter

WILLIAM HORWOOD

The Willows in Winter

Illustrated by Patrick Benson

HarperCollins*Publishers*

In Memory of
Kenneth Grahame's son
Alastair
1900–1920
to whom the Willows stories
were first told

HarperCollins*Publishers*
77–85 Fulham Palace Road,
Hammersmith, London W6 8JB

Published by HarperCollins*Publishers* 1993
5 7 9 8 6 4

Copyright © William Horwood 1993

The Author asserts the moral right to
be identified as the author of this work

Illustrations copyright © Patrick Benson 1993

The Artist hereby asserts his moral rights to
be identified as the Illustrator of the Work

A catalogue record for this book
is available from the British Library

ISBN 0 00 224353 9

Set in Bembo

Printed in Great Britain by
Butler & Tanner, Frome, Somerset

Contents

· I ·

Into the Blizzard

The Mole sat toasting his toes in front of the fire. The winter wind howled safely outside, sending occasional flurries of soot down his chimney. He was thinking that things were nearly perfect, but not quite.

"I must not be uncharitable," he said to himself, though a slight and uncharacteristic frown showed he was finding it difficult not to be. "I have my health, I have my home and I – I must *not* be unfriendly."

He darted a glance across the hearth towards the smaller and less comfortable chair that was ranged there, looked briefly at the cause of his ill-temper, and looked away again.

"No, I must be patient. My heart must be compassionate. I must put up with it. I must – O bother!"

The wind blew suddenly more violently all round the outside of his house, which was snug among the roots of a fallen old oak tree, and doors rattled, and an ember of the beech log that was burning brightly on his fire cracked and shot onto his rug and smouldered there.

"Don't worry!" said the unwelcome guest who sat in the chair opposite. "I'll move it!"

"I can do it myself, thank you very much," retorted the Mole in a grumbly way, quite unlike his normal good-natured self. "O – O drat!"

He shook his paw in momentary pain at the heat as he sought to pick up the ember and put it back where it belonged.

"Would you like a – ?"

"No I wouldn't!" declared the Mole vehemently. "I would like – I would like – I –"

But he could not bring himself to say what he would like, which was to be left alone and snug in his cosy home, free to potter through the winter evening, free to make himself a warming drink – or not, as the case might be – but certainly free *not* to have to think about someone else.

Free not *just* for this evening, but for every evening to come!

O, how distant those days seemed when he had been alone in his home, and happy! How far off those wonderful days! O yes, winter had come into his life now all right, but it had nothing to do with the snow and sleet that drove against his front door, and the draughts that worried at his paws when he went the short distance between the warm fireside of his parlour and his soft bed. Winter? Such matters as mere cold and ice, violent wind and driving snow were as nothing compared to the bitter loss of his privacy since *he* had turned up.

Mole scowled at the floor, and at the little burn mark the ember had made in the rug, and did his best yet again to tell himself that really he *was* an uncharitable Mole, and deserved none of the many good things life had brought him, if he could not show a little tolerance for a few more –

"Months," groaned the Mole. "The longest months of the year, that's how long he's going to be here. How can I turn him out in this weather? And yet there's absolutely nothing wrong with him at all, *nothing*. It's me that's to blame. I should have sent him packing while I still could."

"Are you all right, Uncle?" asked his most unwelcome guest. "You look gloomy to me."

"Well, I'm not," said the Mole ungratefully.

"Well, you *look* it."

There was a sudden flurry of sleety snow at the door, and a chill blast of air across the room. The fallen oak tree which was the support and strength of Mole's home shook and stressed and both the Mole and his guest

9

looked up at the ceiling in alarm, and at the sideboard on which plates and cups rattled and shook.

"Haven't you got something better to do than *talk*?" grumbled poor Mole.

"Nothing better than talking, especially on a night like this," said his Nephew, leaning forward expectantly.

Then, since Mole was not forthcoming, and thinking to encourage him to talk, the youngster continued after a pause, "Mind you, a winter night like tonight, when most creatures are too weak and frightened to go out, wouldn't worry you! Nothing scares you, I know that. Why, you could walk miles across the Wild Wood itself in the dark and blizzard winds and still save a creature who was in peril, if you had to!"

"How many times do I have to tell you, I am not the Mole you think I am!" snapped Mole in exasperation. "The last thing I or any sensible creature would do is to go wandering off into the Wild Wood tonight. I really am *not* the brave bold mole you seem to have heard about. I am just an ordinary mole, and it makes me very cross when you keep suggesting that I am anything other than –"

"But Uncle, I *know* you are not an ordinary mole. Water Rat told me you were the bravest cleverest boldest Mole he had ever met in his life. Mr Toad declared that if there was one living creature he would want at his side in a time of crisis it was you. And even Mr Badger, and everyone knows how wise he is, said, and I quote, 'There's only one Mole, and no one is braver and bolder and better than he!' So it's no good being modest, Uncle!"

The Mole, who had the good grace to feel just a little flattered, though in his heart he felt that all these compliments were undeserved, wiggled his toes at the flames and thought that perhaps, after all, he ought to try to make the best of things. "Well, I suppose if you have nothing else to do, you could make me a nice hot sloe and blackberry drink," he muttered.

No sooner was it said than his young Nephew was up and at it with that busy, clumsy, exasperatingly energetic way he had, clattering about in the kitchen, rattling at the hob, and, worst of all, humming happily to himself.

The Mole frowned again, scowled and then, finally, smiled.

He stared at the flames and felt his nose all cosy warm. He rested his paws on the arms of his comfortable chair.

Brave? Not he!

Bold? No, not really!

Better? No, no, not so.

"But as for Ratty," he said over his shoulder, "now there *is* a brave animal!"

"What did you say, Uncle?"

"I said Ratty is a brave animal," replied the Mole, half turning to look behind him.

"And Mr Badger too?"

"Yes, certainly Badger's brave, as well as wise. That's quite certain."

"And Mr Toad! He's brave!"

Mole laughed.

"Toad brave? That's not a word I'd use about old

Toad. Bold certainly, foolish definitely, vain absolutely, but never brave."

"But you like him, don't you?" said his Nephew softly, placing the warm winter drink within comfortable reach, together with a slice of warmed bread and butter pudding, dripping with melted butter.

"I really shouldn't," said the Mole, taking it anyway, sniffing at it appreciatively, sighing, and then eating a mouthful.

"No, liking Toad doesn't come into it at all. Toad *is*, that's the thing about Toad. Just as the trees are, and the river, and summer; and the winter. Toad may be the most exasperating creature who ever lived, or ever will live – even more exasperating than you, if I may say so – but at the end of the day, when all is said and done, sitting here in the safety of my home, with the fire burning bright and only memories to disturb our peace and quiet, and with the prospect of a good and deep night's sleep before us – after all of that, I must say that without Toad there would be nothing much to live for at all."

Mole took a sip of his drink, and another bite of his pudding, and stared ruminatively at the fire.

His Nephew studied him uncertainly. He so wanted Mole to talk and tell him of those days when he and Water Rat and Toad and Badger had had adventures along the river and in the Wild Wood. Indeed, it was for this that he had first made the long journey from the Wide World to find his famous uncle, and stay with him for a while.

The Mole had experienced mixed emotions that day

in autumn when the young mole had come knocking at his door and told him who he was, and how his father, the Mole's wastrel and ne'er-do-well brother, had passed on, leaving his son with nothing, and nobody to care for him. How far the youngster had travelled, and what dangers he had survived, Mole was never able to find out, for they were things his Nephew did not talk about. But nothing had warmed his good heart more than to see the look of relief on the youngster's face when he had asked him in, fed him, listened to his brief and sorry tale, and said those fatal words, "Well then, since you're family, you can stay here *as long as you want.*"

If only he had said "Till next Friday morning" or something like it. For "as long as you want" soon feels like a life sentence to a bachelor like Mole, unused to sharing his home with another for more than an evening at a time. Sure enough, the Mole had soon tired of his Nephew, and rapidly found that his constant good cheer and enthusiasm to see and do far too many things were vexing in the extreme.

So, too good, too weak perhaps, to tell him to leave, the Mole had sent him off to stay with the Water Rat for a time, and learn what he could of the river.

"He will not want to come back to me after he's seen the excitements of the river," said the Mole.

But he *had* come back.

"I'll send him to Toad. All that comfort and style will soon make him forget my humble home!"

But he didn't last a week at Toad Hall before he was back once more.

"O dear! O dear!" Mole confided in the Rat as autumn deepened and winter set in. "I know I ought to tell him there's not room enough for two of us, but you see, Ratty, I have a sneaking admiration for him: the way he made his way here from the Wide World, well! And if you had known my brother, who was as weak and hopeless a case as could be, it doesn't seem possible for him to have produced such a resourceful son. But he has, and now, now –"

"Now he's ensconced with you, my dear chap, and you don't like it," said the Rat sympathetically. "Nor would I!"

"Wouldn't you?" said the Mole, a little cheered by this.

"Of course I wouldn't. No one would who lives alone and likes his own company for a good bit of the time. Company's fine only if you can escape it when you need to. You know that, I know that, but the young don't always appreciate it!"

"What can I do?" the Mole wondered.

"I know what I would do – tell him to leave, post-haste and no hard feelings. But we all know that you're not me, Mole, that's your charm, that's your quality. You are kind, and good, and soft-hearted, and –"

"No Ratty, don't say such things, really, I mean it. Just tell me what to do."

"Send him to Badger. I'll be seeing Badger in the next day or two and I'll tell him about your problem. He's the wisest creature living and he's sure to know what to do."

The Mole had done so, confident that with the Water

Rat's support, reinforced by the very frank sealed note he sent with his young charge, the Badger would know exactly how to tell his Nephew that enough was enough and he should now be on his way.

But – he – had – come – back. And neither the Rat, nor Toad, nor the Badger himself would talk about the matter thereafter, except to say useless things like "it will sort itself out". It was almost as if they had conspired not to help him, which if it were so, he could not understand at all.

No wonder then that the Mole had suffered the coming of winter, and with it the chance of his guest leaving dwindling each day, with a gloomy heart. No wonder that he had become fractious and irritable.

The Mole took another sip or two of his delicious drink, the more delicious because somebody else had made it for him, and munched pleasurably at the bread and butter pudding. Was life so bad after all? Perhaps not. Perhaps he could learn to put up with things and make the best of the winter visit. Perhaps it would even do him good!

He stared into the fire, thinking of his friends and feeling suddenly content. His stomach was warm inside and out, his head just a little dizzy, his thoughts drifting into the memories his Nephew had so wanted him to talk about.

"O well," he said finally to himself, "and why not?"

Then, in a warmer voice than he had used for days past, and one that held all his engaging modesty and self-doubt, he began, "Did I ever tell you – ?"

His Nephew relaxed, and though the Mole did not

see it, there came to his face a look of such affection, such admiration, such happiness to be in the company of this Mole of all moles, that his eyes and his nose shone almost as brightly as the fire itself. He leaned forward, hardly daring to breathe, trying his best to be barely noticeable at all. His uncle *was* going to talk after all!

And so the Mole might have done, had not there been a sudden, though weak, rat-tat-tat at the door. Hardly loud enough to be heard over the wind's roar. Indeed, the Mole doubted that he had heard it.

"Just a branch, that's all. Or a fall of icy snow. Now, where was I? Ah, yes, I was about to tell you – "

Rat-tat-tat!

It was a little more urgent this time.

"There *is* someone at the door," said the Mole, glowering, "or some*thing*."

"Some*thing*?" said his Nephew in a thin voice.

The Mole nodded and said firmly, "Whatever it is, I'm not opening the door for it. No one sensible goes out on a night like this. Not a creature with good intent, that's for sure. It can rat-tat-tat all night long for all I care, I will not open that door."

Rat-tat-tat! – but more weakly now, and the Mole, quite put off his stride where story-telling was concerned, glared at the door. The wind positively howled down the chimney; somewhere in the Wood nearby a branch tumbled to the ground.

Then despite all the noise and din, there came through the door, or perhaps from under it, a soft and pathetic cry. Hopeless, helpless, forlorn and lost. The cry of one who had journeyed long through the night, overcome every obstacle and now, reaching at last the only place of help and succour it knew, found no one at home.

Mole's Nephew rose to his feet, finding it quite impossible not to respond to that tragic call. But the Mole responded quicker. He who had been grumpy, then sleepy, then comfortable, and then most reluctant to be interrupted as he began to talk – he became a different Mole. A Mole In Charge.

"No!" he commanded. "Leave this to me! I'm not saying it is, mind, but it may be a trick. A way of getting us to open the door. On the other hand it may be a creature in distress. Whatever it is, take this and be ready to use it if you must! Don't flinch! Don't hesitate! Be bold!"

Nephew was amazed at this transformation in his uncle, still more so when he dived into a shadowy place between the dresser and the wall and produced a solid-looking cudgel.

"A present from Ratty years ago, just in case. Not my kind of thing, but it will have to do. So, stand there, be ready and –"

As a further cry, weaker still, came from under the door, the Mole slowly opened it, while his Nephew stood at his flank, cudgel at the ready. But no great beast or monster loomed there, ready to do mischief; no fiend from out of the night.

Only the sad little huddle of a half-grown otter, his eyes wide and full of tears.

"It's Portly, Otter's son," said the Mole in surprise.

17

"My dear fellow – come – you must –"

But Portly was too cold, too shaken, too frightened to move, and it did not help that Mole's Nephew still brandished his cudgel.

"Put it away!" cried the Mole, as he went down to the little fellow on the ground. "Why, you're cut and bruised; your paws are all bleeding and – and only something very serious indeed would have brought you across from the river tonight."

Then, half carrying him across the threshold, and closing the door against the wind, they led Portly to the fire and sat him down in Mole's own armchair.

"Now, tell me what's happened," said the Mole.

Portly's teeth chattered; his paws shook; his fur steamed; his eyes stared wildly about.

"Try and tell us."

"I – he – you – we – " was all Portly could say, his whole body shaking.

"You're safe with me," said the Mole soothingly, "and you can take as long as you like –"

He looked over his shoulder and saw that his Nephew had already poured a tot of the sloe and blackberry drink, and was getting some food together.

When he brought it over, Portly stared at it as if he had never seen food or drink before. He drank and he chewed; he shivered and he sobbed; then he stopped sobbing and gulped down some more sloe and blackberry drink, and guzzled at the bread and butter pudding, nodding when he was offered more and eating it all up in no time at all, with his whiskers all spattered with butter.

"It was such a long way coming here," he said at last, and most pathetically.

"But what's *happened*?" asked the Mole once more.

But Portly started sobbing again, only stopping when he was given a third helping of the pudding, and offered a fourth tot of the potent brew, which meant that he had had far more than a youngster should.

"It was a very long way which went on and on!" he said suddenly, beginning to calm down.

"You poor fellow," said the Mole, "it must have been hard. Now —"

"Is there any more?" asked Portly.

"Well, my dear chap, I think you had better tell us how you come to be here before —"

All he said was, "I think, Mole . . . "

Portly's voice faded away and his eyes went round in little circles, and he smiled beatifically.

"I think, Mole, *what*?" asked the frustrated Mole. "Please try and tell us, Portly, for it's sure to be important. Portly? Portly!!"

But Portly, his snout and ears now quite pink from the fire, his stomach tubby with the pudding, and his snout squiffy with far too much sloe and blackberry, was sliding towards sleep.

"Yesh, Mole," he said blissfully, "it was very cold out there, very cold, but here —" He yawned, and stretched ominously slowly, yawning even more as he did so, and began to curl his back paws round one way and his head and front paws the other, as only otters can when they are preparing for a very long sleep indeed.

"Who told you to come?" the Mole almost shouted.

19

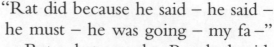

"Rat did because he said – he said – he must – he was going – my fa –"

But whatever the Rat had said, Portly was not now going to be able to report, because with a final weak yawn, and a little shiver, and a smile on his face, he fell into a sleep so deep that nothing the Mole said or did could wake him up.

"What are we going to do?" asked Mole's Nephew.

"Do?" said the Mole with a look of determination and resolve on his face. "Do? We are going to do *something*, of course. Or, rather, I am. You are going to stay here and wait till this wretched and unreliable animal wakes up. Then, if it's not too late, we can find out what he was meant to tell us. Meanwhile I know what I must do!"

The Mole went to the peg behind his front door and took down his warmest, longest, snuggest coat, and a warm, long, snug scarf to match, and put them on.

"Uncle –"

Then the Mole pulled on his goloshes, frowned and took up the cudgel and slipped it through the stout belt he had buckled round his waist to keep the coat tight against the wind.

"If you're going out, Uncle, I –"

But the Mole was silent with determination, and deaf

20

to all entreaties not to go. He wrapped up what little of the bread and butter pudding was left in some grease-proof paper and popped it in his coat pocket. Then he took down the storm lantern that hung by the door, lit it, closed the shutter to the tiniest crack, and checked he had all he needed.

Finally, when he was ready, he took one last look around his comfortable, warm home, shook his head with a look of regret, and opened the front door.

"Where are you going?"

"To Rat's," he said, "where else? Something's badly wrong and I must go and find out what it is since Portly is unable to tell us."

"But the weather – couldn't you wait till the morning?"

"Wait? *Wait?* Would Rat 'wait till the morning', as you blithely put it, if *you* came tottering in and said, 'Mole sent me'? He would not, Nephew. Would Badger? Of course not – even in the winter when we all like to stay snug in our homes. Would Mr Toad!?"

"Well, *he* might, especially in winter," faltered his Nephew.

"Yes, well, he might," conceded the Mole. "On the other hand he might not. No – if any of my friends thought I was in trouble they would forsake all comfort and sleep and rush to my side to see what they could do! So shall I now rush to Rat's! And if it's not him who's in trouble but Otter, then two's better than one in an emergency!"

With that he pulled the door open, only to have the violent wind blast it open still more, sending him reeling backwards. Nothing daunted he drew his cudgel and cried out in a loud voice, "To Rat's!"

With that he battled his way out into the blizzard and the pitch-black night.

"But —" said his Nephew, staring after him with a mixture of astonishment, awe and familial pride, "but, *Uncle!*"

But his uncle, the renowned hero Mole, known up and down the river and far beyond, had gone.

"Cloash the door, thersh a draught," mumbled Portly from the fireside, curling up even more irrevocably in Mole's armchair, and beginning to snore.

The Mole was almost deafened by the blast of wind about him in the wood, and blinded by the stinging snow that drove into his face. To make matters worse, the snow was getting deeper all the time, so that it was a struggle getting his goloshes in and out of it, and harder still to make out the path ahead.

The trees swayed and creaked about him in the night, and if the wind was not trying to rip his coat off his back, the brambles and branches *were*, grasping and clutching and scratching him as he struggled on. And it was dark, dreadfully dark.

His storm lantern was at least some help, for it cast a useful beam of light ahead, and enabled him to avoid veering too much off the path.

"I will not give up!" he muttered to himself, pulling his belt tighter, hunching his head lower, pushing his feet harder, and gripping the lantern ever more firmly. "If it's not Rat himself who's in trouble then it's

Otter. What else could Portly's words have meant? Either way, Rat will need help!"

With bold brave words such as these the Mole kept himself going, grateful for being able to make out the old oak tree, and the rabbit warren, which he recognized as being on the way to Rat's house. He sheltered for a short time near the rabbit warren, and even shouted down to see if anyone was about – but, of course, rabbits can never be relied on, especially when they are most needed, and there was no reply.

Out of the wind, away from the driving snow, he felt his will to go on weakening rapidly, and if it had been any other animal than his dear friend Rat who he felt needed him, he might have taken heed of his Nephew's advice, and sheltered till daylight in the hope that the blizzard might abate.

"I must go on and I shall!" he cried out suddenly, charging out into the blizzard once more, and battling on.

It was only much later, when the dark of night had grown darker still, and the blizzard even more bitter, that a horrible thought occurred to the Mole, stopping him dead in his tracks. Or rather, in his disappearing tracks, for peering behind him through the murk he saw that the snow was now settling so fast that tracks made but moments before had all but gone.

The horrible thought, which would surely have been obvious to a practical animal like the Rat, was this: Rat's house was on the far side of the river, so how was he going to get over to it? The bridge was a long way off, and, of course, Rat's boat was on the far side of the river too.

The answer was that he had no answer, but having got so far, he decided to press on all the same, convinced that it was what Rat himself would have done.

"A solution will come to me!" he told himself.

So it was that, feeling more dead than alive, and with his face-fur all iced up, and his whiskers clogged with snow, the Mole arrived at the river bank. He peered out across the river itself, and though he could not see across to where the Rat lived, in the lurid light of the night he was astonished to see that the river seemed all frozen over. It was smooth and white where snow had settled on the ice.

"Perhaps if I call to Rat he might hear," said the Mole to himself, though without much hope.

"Rat! Ratty! O Rat, please hear me!" he called out as loudly as he could, holding up his lantern as he did so, and waving it about. But the wind rushed and roared around him even more, and snatched his weak words away the moment they were uttered, and scattered them as wildly and uselessly as if they were flakes of snow.

Even worse, the light of the lantern began to gutter, and then, quite suddenly, an extra strong gust of wind blew it out.

"Well then," said the daunted but resolute Mole, putting the spent lantern on the ground, "there's nothing else for it! Frozen rivers are dangerous things, no doubt, but I must try to cross, despite the dangers."

He peered out into the night again, trying to establish if the river was frozen all the way across.

"I could venture out a *little* way," he thought, "and

then I could see the dangers ahead better. Yes, that's what I shall do!"

But no sooner had he scrambled down the bank – O! such a gentle blissful place in summer, but so graspy and slidy and difficult now! – and put his front paws on the ice, than another horrible thought occurred to him. He turned round, clambered back up the bank to a sheltered spot among the surface roots of one of the willows, and scratched his head.

"I must be prudent. I must think of others. It is possible that in trying to cross the river I shall – well, that I shall not return. I must therefore leave my affairs in order and write a message, so that those who come after me will know what my intentions were – so that – O dear! O my!"

The Mole suddenly felt very alone indeed, and tears came to his eyes and rolled down his face, where they began to freeze in his already frozen fur.

"I don't have much to leave behind," he said, "but what I have I like, and I would take comfort as I – as I – *slip away*," (he could not bring himself to use a more precise expression) "to know that my worldly goods and possessions are not only in good hands, but in the *right* hands."

He had no paper in his pockets, except for the grease-proof paper around the pudding, and that was no good. So, finding a suitably large surface root of a willow tree, he did his best in the darkness to scratch a last message for his friends.

It took him some time, but when he had at last finished he felt much better, and stepped back into the storm to admire his handiwork, whispering the words he had written aloud, nodding his head, and feeling that he was now ready to – to slip away, if that's how it must be.

Finally he placed the spent lantern prominently on the path, its handle tilted towards the tree where his message was written, in the hope that whoever found it would look in the right direction, and turned back down the bank once more.

This time he hardly noticed the steep descent, so determined was he to get the difficult crossing over with. Out onto the snowy ice he went, his paws slipping and sliding under him as the wind, clear of the trees and bushes of the bank, came at him in an unimpeded rush. His snout ached with cold, his eyes ran, his flanks shivered, but on he went!

He peered ahead at each step, testing the ice carefully before putting his full weight on it, always checking back to see where he was and that, if need be, he could scramble back to safety. But it *was* hard to see, what with the swirling, driving snow, and the cold – and he *would* feel better if he could only catch a glimpse of the bank on the other side. Even better, if he could see the welcome sight of the Rat himself, standing there, waving to him.

As if in answer to his wish, the wind dropped and for a moment he could see the way clear ahead, right across to the other side. Why, it seemed hardly any distance at all! He could almost reach out and touch it … and then, for the first time, the Mole forgot to look carefully at the way ahead.

The first warning he had that something was wrong was that the ice, so solid till then, trembled and shifted, so that the world about him wobbled. The next was that he heard a new sound, the dull, relentless roar of water, just in front. The last and final warning, and by then it was far too late, was a loud *crack!* somewhere just behind him.

Desperately he tried to turn back the way he had come, his back paws sliding away from him as he did so. As he fell on his face he reached out for something solid and saw to his horror that where there had once been ice there was now a black chasm, and that the ice he was on was moving and wobbling more and more. As it tilted beneath him he felt himself sliding towards the water. He tried to clamber up the ice and right it, but as he did so it suddenly tilted the other way and he found himself slipping unstoppably towards the implacable black race of the water itself.

"Help!" cried the terrified Mole. "O my! O my! Help!"

But this final cry was all in vain. It seemed the night turned blacker still, and then deathly silent, the wind gone, the snow no more, as the cold confusion of icy water was suddenly all about him: below, to right, to left, and he was swept off downstream into the night, clutching at a floe of ice.

Where the Mole had been, nothing was left but the night, the blizzard wind, the river flowing past broken ice; and the first bleak gleams of a winter dawn, shining on a little painted notice on the side of the bank which the Mole had so bravely been trying to reach.

28

"Rat's House," it said.

But no light was there; no Rat; no welcome at all. Only the rattle and rasp of old brambles against each other, and the triumphant howl of the wind.

· II ·

Mole's Last Will and Testament

It was not till the dawn of the third day that the blizzard began to die, and that same midday that it finally stopped. One moment the sky was grey and the trees all bent against the wind, and the next the sky was blue, the sun shone, and all was bright and shining across the meadows, the river, and the Wild Wood, at whose edge the Otter lived.

30

"Rat! Time to rouse yourself! Time to get up!" cried the Otter, scenting at the lovely winter's day, and feeling in need of fresh air and a jaunt.

"Not in this wind! Not in this driving snow!" answered the Rat drowsily from beneath the quilt which the Otter had thoughtfully laid on the sofa to make up a bed for his unexpected visitor.

"My dear fellow!" called out the Otter, "that's all blown over. The sun is shining fit to bust and it's time we got up and about once more. It's as crisp a winter's day outside as you could wish!"

The Rat sat up, rubbing his eyes and eyeing without much pleasure the untidy pile of plates and bottles – all there was left to show for the three days of his enforced rest with Otter.

"All over?" he said sleepily, falling back and curling up again, and remembering what a good time he had had.

"All finished," said the Otter, coming and shaking him by the shoulder. "Time to get up and clear this mess away and then we shall go out and see what damage the blizzard's done. Portly's out already, for I can't see him anywhere –"

"Portly's out?" said the Rat uneasily. Portly was not the kind of animal to get up early.

"That's right," said Otter casually, "and though it's not like him to be up and about before me, I suppose we did let ourselves go a little, old chap – I'll just go and call to him to pop back in again."

The Rat lay listening to his calls, and then to his sudden scurrying about, no doubt to see what signs of

31

Portly there were, till he came back rather faster than he had left.

"No answer and no sign of him," said the Otter with concern, "and no tracks in the snow, as there ought to be!"

The Rat came fully awake with a start. A dark and troubling memory had come to him.

"I know that Portly went out *three days* ago," he said slowly, staring at Otter in alarm. "Or was it four?"

"But he came back," said the Otter, not yet quite fully troubled. "At least I thought he did. *Didn't* he come back?"

"No, Otter, he didn't come back! Don't you remember? I happened by here just as the first snow fell, and you invited me in for some food and drink, and very hospitable of you that was. We got somewhat merry and suggested that it would be nice if Mole were here to join the fun. That – that – that errant son of yours suddenly upped and went off saying 'I'll fetch him!' and then, well, he never quite seemed to come back."

"But if he didn't come back we would have gone to search for him," said the Otter confidently. "We would not have come back till we found him. Therefore, as we are here he must have been here this morning. When, waking before us, he very sensibly – and he *has* been growing up a bit – went out to enjoy the winter sun."

"Except, as you said, there are no tracks."

"None," said the Otter sombrely, his voice trailing away as he looked about his home and saw that Portly's bed had not been slept in.

"No, Otter," continued the Water Rat, "you *thought*

he had come back, because, well, not to put too fine a point on it, we all know that you and your family are rather too partial to that sloe and blackberry drink that Mole makes so well. When I suggested that Portly was not here *you* said, 'If he isn't he soon will be, which is as good as being here now!' or words to that effect. Since when we have both been more or less asleep."

"So Portly's not here now, and you think he has not been here for three days?" said the Otter blankly.

"Three days and three nights. Three very blizzardy days and nights."

"Hmmph!" declared the Otter as the two animals went out onto the bank and looked despondently about.

"Till we know where he is," said the Otter, who was now feeling a lot less bright and breezy than before, "we must conclude that he is missing."

"I hate to disagree, Otter, but I would prefer it if you said 'He is missing *again*'. He's always missing, is Portly. But, as usual, we'll find him before long, and when we do I would wager my rowing boat and sculls that he is somewhere very comfortable indeed."

"Yes," said the Otter, "very probably you're right. Perhaps I ought to just —" He wandered off calling "Portly! Are you there!" rather quietly at first. Then, as he came back, having wandered one way up the bank and then the other, the Rat heard him shout rather more forcibly, "Portly! *Portly!*"

"Well," Otter said rather tersely when he reached the entrance to his home again, "he's not anywhere."

"And there are no tracks in the snow further off?"

"None," said the Otter.

"Which means he *did* leave some time ago," said the Rat darkly, adding, with considerable misgiving, "and, look, the river's almost frozen over."

"You don't think – ?" began the Otter with real alarm.

"I think Portly is capable of almost any foolishness," said the Rat grimly. "The number of times – I mean the trouble he has caused – and not wishing to be hard, but, well, let us be frank. A sensible animal, if he went out looking for Mole, would not try to cross that river. No, he would come straight home. But Portly is not sensible. So – having reached the river, I greatly fear he said to himself, 'Across it I shall go!' "

"We must search for him!" cried the Otter.

"Yes," said the Rat, "I'm afraid we must. He will, of course, be absolutely safe but our minds must be put to rest. It seems to me, Otter, that this must be the last time, and positively the last, that we animals should go searching for your son. He will never become a sensible otter if every time he is scatter-brained we come to the rescue."

"I have spoilt him," said the Otter miserably, "and that is the truth. But bringing him up alone as I was forced to do, struggling to find food enough for both of us, striving to teach him manners and common sense, well, it was not easy. Bachelors like you and Mole and Mr Badger have it easy compared to those of us who bear the full responsibility of –"

"Otter!" said the Water Rat in a commanding way, not liking this kind of talk. "Enough! Let us go and find the wretched animal, and let us hope you will box his ears for him, or something or other that will

34

teach him not to cause his father such concern, and his father's friends such trouble. But don't worry, the sun is shining now and all will be well!"

And yet, as the two friends set off, the Rat could not help feeling that all was not well, not well at all. It was the River that told him this, the River which none knew better than he. What Otter had said was true, he was a bachelor, with few cares in the world. But though he lived alone, he had often thought that it was the River who was his friend and his mate. He knew her moods, he knew her ways, and when she whispered to him, as she whispered ominously now down where the ice stopped and the water flowed, and there where the wind-broken sedges rasped in the winter breeze, he heard a warning voice which said, "Beware! Trouble ahead! All is not well!"

"I think we ought to hurry," said the Rat presently, whiffling his snout at the river wind, "if we are not already too late."

"Rat!" whispered Otter, very much alarmed. "What's wrong? There *is* something wrong, isn't there? The river's not right – I know it's not. *You* know too, for you know it best of all."

"No," said the Rat, "she's not right, not right at all. Come on, Otter, we must make for Mole End as fast as we can, because that's where Portly was going to. Mole will have some news for us, I'm sure."

"We could swim across," said the Otter doubtfully.

"No!" said Rat firmly. "We'll go the long way round. Swimming across is *not* a good idea. We'll go by the bridge."

"But that's miles and miles —"

"It may be," said the Rat, setting off at a rapid pace, "but where the river is concerned, prudence is the watchword!"

The winter's afternoon was already drawing in, and the snow underfoot growing crisp and icy, when they finally reached Mole's little home. The familiar door, the neatly painted "Mole End", the very tree itself about which the Mole's modest place was made, all spoke of comfort and safety.

"But no light," muttered the Rat grimly, "no sign of life at all. It's not like Mole to go far in winter, unless it's to come and see me."

"Maybe he's asleep," declared the Otter. "But look, Ratty! He can't be far!"

The door was ajar and leading from it were what looked like the fresh prints of Mole's goloshes. Rat put his paw to the door and pushed it open, though being a cautious animal he did not go straight in.

"It's not like him to leave his door open. Mole! Are you there?" he called out. "This doesn't look good, Otter."

"It does not, Ratty," said Otter, who was a reliable animal in such situations, as he pulled himself up to his fullest height alongside the Water Rat.

"Listen!" whispered the Rat, peering into the murky interior.

They heard a sniffle, then a snuffle, then a bleat, and finally a sob.

"That's sounds like Portly!" said Otter going straight

in. "No doubt about it!" There was relief in his voice, but consternation as well.

"Where are you, Portly? Show yourself."

The sobbing grew louder as the Rat joined the Otter in the parlour and looked about to see where Portly was.

"You would think that Mole would have had the sense to light a candle or two," said the Otter.

"Mole's not here," said a tremulous voice from the direction of Mole's favourite armchair. "Mole went out and didn't come back."

They found Portly at last, huddled beneath Mole's winter plaid, staring forlornly into a long-dead fire.

"Now listen, Portly," began the Otter in a very stern voice, "something's going on and we want to know what it is!"

Portly began to sob even more.

"Leave this to me," said the Rat, who, for all his fine words about discipline and proper behaviour was a kindly, soft-hearted animal when he saw others in distress. "You light a candle and get the fire going and let me talk to Portly –

"Now, old chap, why don't you tell me exactly what has happened and where Mole's gone, and where that Nephew of his has disappeared to."

"But that's just it," said Portly, "I don't exactly know. You see –"

Then, as the Otter bustled about setting out some candles, clearing the grate and then setting the fire ablaze once more, Portly told his sorry tale.

"So, to sum it all up," said the Rat finally as the Otter

37

offered them a warming drink, "instead of telling Mole we had thought he might join us for the evening – which being a sensible animal and seeing the blizzard on its way he would have realized was not a good idea – instead of *that*, you somehow made him think that Otter or I or both of us were in trouble?"

"Yes," conceded Portly.

"And needed help?"

"Yes," repeated Portly more quietly.

"Then being the Mole he is, which is to say always concerned about his friends before himself, he put on his coat and set off alone into the snowy night *three nights ago*."

"Yes," said Portly, more quietly still.

"Then a short time ago you awoke as his Nephew, concerned for his uncle as all nephews should be, was likewise setting off into the cold, leaving you here snug and safe."

"Not *very* snug," said Portly in a very quiet voice indeed.

"Snug enough," scowled the Rat, who might now have been inclined to be more harsh had Otter not been there.

"He only went an hour or so ago. I *did* offer to go with him but he said to stay here in case you came."

"Sensible," said the Otter.

"He also said to tell any animal that came that he would first go down to the river opposite your home, Mr Rat, because he thought that was the way Mr Mole would have gone."

"Sensible again," said the Otter. "More sensible than some I can think of."

"Very much more so," said the Rat darkly. He frowned and thought for a moment and put down his drink only half finished.

"I think, Otter, we had better be going right away. It's still light outside but the days are growing very short."

"Can I come?" asked Portly.

"No you can't," said the Otter. "You stay here and keep that fire burning. No, on second thoughts, just stay here and don't touch anything."

"It's lonely by myself," said Portly.

"Yes," said the Rat pitilessly, "I daresay it is. Now, Otter, to work!"

The Water Rat was at his very best in a crisis and in no time at all had gathered together all the provisions he thought they might need in the course of what could turn out to be a cold and difficult few hours: some food wrapped up in grease-proof paper; some warming sloe juice; a flint and candles; and some spare clothing.

"The only thing I can't see is Mole's lantern, which he must have taken with him, so we'll have to make do with a jam jar if we can find one –"

Then, with the Water Rat carrying the bag of provisions over his shoulder, the two animals set off once more, giving final instructions to Portly to stay exactly where he was and to keep the candle burning at the window so Mole End could more easily be found in the dark.

It was a route that the Rat had taken many times before – though never in such an apprehensive frame of mind. The way seemed longer than it really was, the hedges and meadows gloomier, despite the snow that lightened their way.

"These are definitely the tracks of Mole's Nephew!" said the Otter, but they were the only words the two spoke almost the whole way there.

The gloaming was already with them, and the trees losing their colour and turning into silhouettes, and the snow all about becoming more violet than white, as they came in sight of the river.

As they did so they saw a figure running wildly towards them out of the dark, shouting and gesticulating. For a moment they thought it was the Mole himself, but it was his Nephew, and in a state of considerable alarm. Indeed, so incoherent was he that the Otter thought the worst and said, "Mole's not –?"

"Worse," said his Nephew. "O, far, far worse!"

"Better show us what you've found," said the Rat, eyes narrowing, as he led the way down to the bank.

"Mole's lamp!" he cried out, pointing out where it stood so conspicuously on the path by the bank.

"But no Mole," said his Nephew. "Gone – gone forever!"

Then he pointed mutely towards the willow tree roots where Mole had left his message before trying to cross the river.

"There are words there; he's scribed words," said his Nephew.

The Rat and the Otter peered at the roots, but the light was now too poor to make anything out.

"Otter," said the Rat grimly, "give me the candle and

flint and that jam jar and let us read what Mole has written here. Mole is no fool, you see. He guessed we might come looking for him, though why he didn't go straight back home after seeing the state of the river I can't – I mean – he couldn't have – he –"

Rat turned to look at the river and the ice that still covered a good part of it, and a thought too terrible to think came to him, and he shook his head and turned back to the tree.

But as the Otter struggled to light the candle in the cold night breeze it seemed to the Rat that the River was speaking to him again, and that what she had to say was bad news indeed. He had never known her splashes so – sonorous; her meanders so – miserable; her normally majestic flow so – final!

"There you are, Rat," said the Otter, giving him the flickering light, "*you* read it, for I've never had much time to learn that sort of thing."

The Rat peered about, looked closer, and was suddenly very still indeed; then, clearly shaken, he put the jam jar down on the nearest flattest root he could find.

"What does it say, Rat?"

"I shall read it aloud," said the Rat in a terrible voice, which he clearly had great difficulty controlling.

"It is headed 'Mole's Last Will and Testament' and this is what it says: 'Before crossing the River, and Knowing I may not return alive, I, Mole, of Mole End, hereby Wish to make the following Bequests: First, my Garden Seat is for Ratty, in memory of the many happy hours we had on it sitting and talking; Second, my Brass Candle Stick is for Mr Badger, as a token of

41

my respect for him and since he needs one, along with those of my books he might choose to take; Thirdly, my bust of Garibaldi is to inspire Mr Toad to better things and remind him of his friend Mole; lastly, but by no means the Least important, I leave Mole End to my Nephew to whom I may not always have been as pleasant and welcoming as I should, but of whom I am very proud. I know my good friends will take his future education in hand till the day comes when he will be a most worthy Mole. Finally, I ask that Portly be kept well clear of my Sloe and Blackberry wine as it goes to his head somewhat. Now –' "

And that was all, nothing more. Not even "Mole".

As Mole's Nephew wept at the unexpected generosity and sentiments of his uncle, the Water Rat read the writing through again and then went down to the river. He peered across and saw the jagged gap where the ice had broken, and the black deep waters of the river that rushed and flowed so cruelly there.

"My friends," he said at last, "I greatly fear that we may not see Mole alive again. He must have been trying to get across the river to help me. He knew how dangerous that would be and yet – and yet he tried. No doubt he went carefully, but Mole was never a river animal and did not understand that of all the River's moods her worst and meanest is when she is covered in ice. Yet alone as he was, and no doubt afraid, on he went in the cause of his friends. Not just for me, Otter, but for you as well."

The Otter sniffed, and a great big tear rolled down his face in the dusk.

"He was the bravest mole I ever knew," he said.

"He was the truest friend I ever had," said the Rat.

"My uncle was the greatest mole who ever lived," said his Nephew.

For a long time they stood in silence as the night gathered about them, the flickering light on the willow root a beacon to light a friend on a journey they could never be part of.

"But isn't it possible he climbed back out onto the bank?" said his Nephew much later.

"Or that he never fell in in the first place but is somewhere on the other side and the ice broke later?" said the Otter hopefully.

"In short, that we have jumped to the wrong conclusion?" said the Water Rat.

The others nodded in the dark.

"Unlikely," said the Rat finally, as he stared at the river, utterly still, his grief total and complete.

Much later still, speaking in a low voice, he said this: "All my life I have lived by the River and I have known her in all her moods. I have shared with her good times and bad. One thing she has never failed to do is to talk to me, though sometimes I found it hard to listen and understand what she said. Today she has been speaking to me but I did not want to hear what she said. You know what I mean, Otter, it sometimes just isn't possible to – "

"To make sense of things," said Otter.

"Exactly. Now, we are all tired and over-wrought and if Mole *is* still alive there is little good we can do floundering around in the dark. We shall go back to

Mole End. We shall sleep. Then tomorrow we shall call on Mr Badger and institute a search for Mole, for I shall not be satisfied till I know what has happened to him one way or the other. Perhaps tomorrow I can try listening to the River once more – by myself – and perhaps it will all make more sense.

"Now we shall put a new candle in Mole's lantern, we shall light it, and we shall leave it here in the hope that somehow or other he will see its light, and know how much he is loved, and how much missed; and how much we want him back again!"

They did this with all due ceremony, standing again in silence with the light flickering on their sombre faces before the Rat led them silently away from the river bank, back through the night to Mole End.

The Water Rat knew a night of shadows and half-dreams in which, try as he might, he could not get out of his head memories of Mole sitting so comfortably on the garden seat in the hot afternoon sun of the summer, reflecting upon life or, more often than not, upon something better still: nothing at all.

"Mole, dear friend," Rat remembered himself saying many a time, "this place is too comfortable, too pleasant, and I feel once more a yearning to get into my boat."

"Ratty, I am not at all surprised," Mole would reply, "and it would be pleasant, very pleasant, to sit in your boat once more, with you sculling, which you do so much better than I, trailing a paw in the placid water, which I do so much better than you.

"Trouble is, we have to get there, and that means getting out of this very comfortable seat."

"It does," the Rat replied sleepily, "it doeszzzzzzz."

Of course, there had been many other occasions when after a day or two of such inactivity, Rat had declared, "If we don't go now we never will, and therefore, Mole, I shall not sit down in that garden seat of yours. No! I shall help you prepare a hamper of food and drink sufficient to last us the whole day through."

"And halfway into the evening, if it stays as warm as this!"

"Exactly! So let's press on!"

And on they had pressed, and off they had gone, though always Mole had cast a backward glance at his delightful nook, knowing that when the time came, when he tired of the river and longed once more for the shade of the trees, and the hum and buzz of the secret fields, it would always be there, waiting for him and his friend.

Such thoughts and remembrances tormented the poor Rat all that night, till dawn came once more, when at last, as often happens after such a night, he fell into a deep sleep.

"We'll not disturb him till he wakes of his own accord," said the Otter later, "for I doubt that he got much sleep in the night at all, poor fellow. The loss of Mole will hit him hard, very hard indeed, and we should let him get what rest he can."

"If Mole *is* lost," said Mole's Nephew.

"It's certainly not like the Water Rat to give up so easily," said Portly.

"Hmmph!" said the Otter. "Make breakfast for us all, you two, and do it quietly!"

So it was that the Rat woke to the pleasant scent of bacon and sausages sizzling on the hob, and the alluring aroma of camomile tea, which sent his spirits soaring and had him sitting up and asking, "Where am I?" before he looked about and saw only too clearly where he was: in Mole's home without Mole, and with no hope that he would ever be here again.

"O!" cried out the Rat, falling back on the pillow – the comfortable pillow it must be said, for it was Mole's own, and in Mole's bed in which Rat lay – "O dear!"

He stared bleakly out of the window, tears slowly trickling down his face, and listened to the quiet bustle of the other three round the corner in the kitchen, and Portly saying, "Do you think he's woken up yet? I'm very hungry and we can't wait forever."

"We'll wait for as long as it takes," Rat heard Otter growl.

The Rat drifted away into a muse, staring at the blue sky – for it was another lovely winter day – and at the drip drip drip of water from the ledge above the window.

"The thaw's set in," he said to himself, "the thaw –"

What was it about that drip of water that had him wide awake in moments and opening the window, and peering outside and all about and scenting at the air? What was it that sent his whiskers buzzing, and made his snout tremble with – with the sense of *things happening*?

He peered out still more, he looked down from the dripping of the water and the trees, down towards – why, towards the very garden seat that Mole had left him in his will. It was glistening with damp, it was waiting, it was –

But before Rat could decide what it was, something else caught his attention, the very thing perhaps that had made him open the window in the first place. His snout had trembled – now it thrilled to the scent of the River come alive once more, too distant for any other creature to notice it. *His* River, across the meadows, through the wood, down the track, beyond the bank, alive and calling to him.

Before he knew what he was doing he had slipped quietly out of the front door without a word to anyone. Then he was off, off down the same path up which he had led the others so dolefully the night before, off towards his beloved River, whose scent was a siren call to him, which, without once looking back, he set off to answer.

· III ·

Toad's First Flight

"Couldn't we just see if he's stirring?" asked Portly, whose mouth was watering at the sight of the breakfast they had cooked.

"Well —" began the Otter, whose good intentions to let the Rat sleep were weakening before the scent of food.

It was enough, and Portly and Mole's Nephew were out of the kitchen in a flash, and gently pulling the blankets from the bed where Rat had slept.

"He's not here!" said Portly. "The door's open and he's gone."

"Gone?" cried the poor Otter. "Gone?"

The briefest of examinations of the Mole's quarters and the open door showed it to be true, and with beating heart and a terrible feeling of apprehension the Otter rushed outside, the others following him.

"O dear! O dear!" he said, pointing at the Rat's unmistakable tracks in the melting snow. "He's gone back to the river."

"But why? And why didn't he tell us?"

"I fear the worst, the very worst!" said the Otter in an anguished voice. "I should have watched over him! I should have thought! Over-wrought by Mole's passing, troubled by nightmares and dark thoughts, there can be no doubt that he has gone back to the river –"

"Well, at least he can swim!" said Nephew practically. "I think we should follow him as fast as we can!"

"That's sensible!" said the Otter, brought back a little way towards reality. "That's intelligent! That's Mole-like! That's what we'll do."

With that all three made their way down towards the river as fast as they could go, slushing through the melting snow and mud underfoot, and looking earnestly ahead as if that might help bring the river into sight all the sooner.

As it was the journey seemed to be endless, but there finally was the bank before them, with the river beyond it, now almost clear of ice.

"Rat's not here!" cried out the Otter. "Too distressed to live without his friend, Ratty has –"

Otter fell silent as Mole's Nephew pointed down the steep bank to the river's edge itself where, among the sedges and detritus of winter, they saw a most remarkable sight.

It was the Water Rat, sitting with his hind paws dangling in the icy water, though he did not seem to notice that at all. His head was high and his eyes were closed and he seemed to be scenting at the air. Then he bent his head sideways and a little lower as if he was listening to the river's sounds; whilst his front paws were gesticulating gently, in little fits and starts.

"What's he doing?" asked Portly.

The Otter stared dumbfounded, signalling to the others to be very quiet. All three sat down to watch and wait in silence, and as they did so the beauty of the clear winter morning, and the gentle gurgle and murmur of the river, running now with snow thaw, and higher than normal, though not yet dangerous or violent, overtook them all.

"I've only seen him doing this once before, and it is a rare privilege for us to be witness to it," whispered the Otter. "This is something you'll be able to tell your children and your grandchildren you saw – Water Rat is communing with the River. She's talking to him and he is talking to her, and I have no doubt at all that it is about Mole they are speaking. Now, however long it takes, we shall stay here very quietly, so as not to disturb either of them."

The sun rose slowly; small white clouds appeared high in the sky; water dripped from the branches of trees high and low all through the wood and, falling in the secret places of grass and fern, withered twig and hidden lichen, turned into a thousand jewels of light which glistened and shone like lights of hope.

At last the Rat's eyes opened and his front paws stilled and stretched up towards the sky. He yawned, shivered, withdrew his hind paws from the water and looked about as if in a daze and uncertain where he was.

For a long time he stared at the flowing water, so dark and dreadful the night before, now filled with the bright winter light of the sky above. He looked upstream to the right and downstream to the left and slowly scratched his head. Then he turned and looked up at the bank where Otter and the others sat so silently.

He nodded and smiled as if to say that he had known they were there, and was grateful they had not interrupted him, yet on his face there was also a look of concern.

"It's Mole," he said at last, "I know now that he's alive, for the River has told me so. But he's not well, and may need our help, so we must try to find him. Now listen, Otter: I think I know what we must do. We must search for him and leave no place along the bank unturned downstream from here to the weir. Beyond that, well – beyond that is the Wide World, and though it may be that is where he is, for that I cannot tell, it is too far for us to search. Now this is what we're going to do."

A new look had come to Rat's face now, a familiar look, a look which told all who saw it that this was the Water Rat Who Got Things Done.

"This is not a task we can hope to do all by ourselves.

We need help and a lot of it. Otter, you and Portly will stay this side of the river and rouse the rabbits, who though foolish owe much to Mole and are his friends. You can get them to begin searching along the bank, starting here and working their way slowly down towards the island." He said this last reverentially, for all knew the island as a holy place.

"Meanwhile, Mole's Nephew and I will go to Badger's house in the Wild Wood, for the time has come to seek his help. Like most animals, he does not like being disturbed in winter, but I am sure that he will not object in such dire circumstances as these. In any case we'll need his help if the weasels and stoats —"

"Weasels and stoats!" declared Portly, frowning in consternation.

"Yes, *them*," said the Rat without remorse. "Badger will order those miserable, conniving animals to help, and though I expect they'll do it reluctantly they'll do it all the same."

"How will we get to Badger?" asked Mole's Nephew.

"Leave that to me," said the Rat. "Off you go, Otter, and remember that though Mole's safe for now he might not always be."

"What about Mr Toad?" said the Otter. "We could send someone up to Toad Hall and ask —"

"Toad?" said the Rat dubiously. "Toad is the last person we need in this kind of crisis. I know he is much improved from the bad old days, but he would perhaps favour us best by staying securely in Toad Hall. So get going you two, and *you* stay here."

With that Rat skipped down to the water's edge,

broke off the last lingering piece of ice, and disappeared beneath the surface of the water, his passage to the other side marked only by a few bubbles that surfaced and were swept off downstream.

He reappeared for a moment to catch his breath and then was gone again till, a short time later, he climbed swiftly up the other side. Then, with barely a pause, he had gone up to his own home, untied his boat and hauled it upstream a little more before pushing it out into the water and sculling it expertly across to where Mole's Nephew stood.

"Catch this rope and hold it fast!" he cried.

Then, without a pause, Mole's Nephew was hauled unceremoniously into the boat and they were off upstream.

"I would have had to move the boat to its winter mooring anyway," said the Rat, panting as he rowed, for the current was strong, "so doing it now makes sense. I'll moor it up by Otter's house. Not far from there there's a special way through the Wild Wood direct to Badger's. He won't mind us using it, I'm sure."

It seemed to Mole's Nephew that it was a long haul and a dangerous one, for the river was growing higher and swifter by the moment, and though the Rat kept them near the bank where the current was gentler, the going became ever harder.

"Not far now!" grunted the Rat. "Not far!"

But it seemed a very long time before they finally reached Otter's house, going a good way past it before the Rat risked turning the boat across-stream and then, with strong and purposeful strokes as the boat was caught by the full force of the current, he pulled it through and over to the other side — right to the mooring itself.

"There!" said Rat with satisfaction. "Now you take the painter and leap out, like a good chap — yes *now* and *quickly*!"

Mole's Nephew did as he was told, but uneasily, for he was, after all, an earth-bound animal and had not yet discovered the joys of the river of which Mole himself had sometimes spoken.

Rat followed him out and together they hauled the boat up the bank and well clear of the water for, as the Rat said, "You can never tell with the river how high it will come, or quite where. Now let's make her fast."

But just as he was about to do so they heard the strangest, most ominous of sounds from somewhere further upstream. A rasp and a roar. Then silence. Then a dull chugging sound. Then silence again. Then a distant cough and splutter, and then a sudden brief roar once more.

"What's that?" asked Mole's Nephew.

"I have no idea," said the Water Rat, "but whatever it is it's up to no good."

"Yes, but —"

"You might well say 'Yes, but —', considering where that sound comes from!" said the Rat.

"You mean — ?"

"Yes, I do mean," said the Rat very grimly indeed. "That sound, whatever it is, comes from Toad Hall, which means that Toad himself is one way or another the cause of it, which in turn means it ought to be

55

investigated. Toad may be altered these days, but I have never been as hopeful as Badger about that. Temptation is a dreadful thing where the weak-willed are concerned, and I hope that ominous sound does not signal some backsliding or other by Toad. I greatly fear he is up to no good, no good at all, but we have a crisis on our hands and for now it is better that we imagine that we have not heard it, and make our way without more ado to Badger's house in the hope that Toad will continue to be good."

With that, and the matter of Toad having so put him out of countenance that the Water Rat quite forgot to make his boat fast, and instead let the rope slip out of his hand onto the grass, the two animals headed off towards the Wild Wood.

It was a very long time since the Rat had ventured into one of the passages that Badger's forebears had made centuries before from what was now his home to the edge of the Wild Wood, so it was no easy task to find where it began.

"Or rather ends," muttered the Rat, as he poked about in yet another clump of damp and prickly undergrowth, "for what we're looking for is really an escape route. Badger said there were several, but the one I'm looking for is the only one I have ever been shown. That was years ago, when I first met Mole.

"When I first met Mole!" repeated poor Rat to himself, remembering those halcyon days when all had been well. He might have yielded to the tears that wished to flow, but suddenly, from the general direction of Toad Hall, that throaty, unpleasant roaring sound came forth again and put resolve and purpose back into the Rat's eyes.

"We *shall* find the entrance!" he said, frowning and searching all the harder.

"Couldn't we go by the surface way?" said Mole's Nephew.

"Not in winter, no. Far too dangerous. There's more than weasels and stoats in the Wild Wood – that's why Badger keeps his escape routes repaired and ready. Anyway, although the snow's melting fast the last place of all where it thaws is in the Wild Wood itself, so the going would be hard in there. No, no, we'll find – here it is! Look!"

He pushed aside some old creepers, dug under some brushwood and dead leaves, and there, well hidden among some ancient tree roots, was the entrance.

They forced their way through the creepers into the cold and musty air of the passage, then the Rat pulled a candle from his bag, lit it and led them along a damp and airless tunnel, from whose arched roof water dripped most ominously.

"Bother," said the Rat, stopping suddenly some time later, "I don't believe I tied up that boat of mine properly. That's what comes of talking about Toad. It's the effect he has on others. Well, we're too far up the tunnel now and finding Mole is more important."

On they stumbled by the flickering light, growing colder by the moment, and soon losing all sense of time and direction. The tunnel seemed to go on forever but at last they reached a stout door with massive hinges set into the enormous roots of an oak, on which the Rat banged as hard as he could.

Bang! Bang! Bang!

How the sound echoed about them, so loud that Mole's Nephew covered his ears when Rat knocked again, even louder.

"Perhaps he's asleep."

"Of course he's asleep," said the Rat, "but Mr Badger will not mind being woken up to advise us how best to find Mole. Mind you, I don't expect he'll be in the best of tempers when he comes, so —"

Suddenly, loudly, even ferociously, the great door was pulled open and a stream of light quite blinded the two animals. As if that was not enough Mr Badger stood hugely over them, a great wooden cudgel in his right paw, and roared, "How *dare* anybody use this — or bang on my — and come —"

"It's *us*, Badger, Rat and —"

" — and Mole?" said Badger.

"Not Mole proper, no," said the Rat. "His —"

"Well, Rat and not Mole then! Don't you know I'm asleep? I'm not to be woken. I'm Not at Home. It's winter, and —"

"Please, Badger, don't shut the door on us!" said the Rat, for the Badger was in the process of doing so, having held his bright lantern in their faces and peered at them severely.

"Can you give me one good reason why I should not close the door and send you packing?" growled the Badger, opening it wider again, and looking at them just a shade more kindly.

"I can and I will," said the Rat stoutly. "It's Mole. He's lost, and perhaps lost forever. He fell through the ice on the river. He — Badger — we — we need your help!"

It was the best that the Rat could do before the tears he had fought back for so long overtook him.

"Badger — I — we —"

"My dear Ratty," said Badger in a very different voice, "and you too," he added to Mole's Nephew, "you come out of that cold tunnel — I must say it was very clever of you to remember how to find it — and tell me what's happened. Come on!"

He guided them into his warm chambers, closed the door and, putting a huge paw on their shoulders, led them into his large untidy parlour where a huge log fire, scented with crab apple wood, burned merrily away.

"Now in a moment I'll get you a drink, but first tell

me quickly what's happened so that I can think about it as I put on the kettle."

They told him what they could and then, as they drank the warming drink he made and their teeth stopped chattering, they answered the many careful questions he asked.

"But to me," he said finally, "the *most* important thing of all that you've said is that you think that the river was trying to tell you that Mole's alive. Every creature hereabouts knows how well you understand the river and would believe as I do that if you say it tells you Mole is alive, then Mole *is* alive."

"Only just alive," corrected the Water Rat.

"We shall institute a search for Mole forthwith, and all the animals of the Wild Wood, yes *even* the weasels and the stoats shall help!"

"But, Badger, I know we need them as well for so great an undertaking," said the Rat, who felt much better for talking to Badger, and hearing all that the wise animal had said, "but they have never been very co-operative and lately —"

"And lately," interrupted Badger, "they have been getting above themselves once more. It is no good relying on their good nature, for they have none that I have ever seen. No, we must threaten them! We must intimidate them!"

Badger banged a gong that stood near the fireside and in no time at all a couple of hedgehogs appeared.

"Go and get the weasel, you know the one I mean, and while you're at it summon that wretched stoat!

"Leave this to me, Water Rat, and in no time at all

they'll be as servile as rabbits and a lot more use!
But don't be weak with them, not for a moment. No,
take as your example the splendid way Mole himself
dealt with them in those days when we had to wrest
Toad Hall back from their miserable paws. Do you
remember?"

"I do, Badger."

Whatever the hedgehogs said to the chiefs among the
weasels and stoats must have been very frightening, for
very soon several weasels and more than enough stoats
were knocking at Badger's door and only too eager
to help.

"Now listen!" said Badger. "This is an emergency,
and although the fearsome Water Rat and myself know
very well that there are some of you who have reason
not to like us, and even less the mighty Mole, remember
that we treated you fairly in times gone by, when we
might have been a great deal more harsh. Now the
Mole is in trouble, and the chance has come for you
finally to redeem yourselves. The first one of you who
succeeds in finding Mole alive and well and brings him
to my home − or to Rat's or Otter's, whichever is
nearest − that first one, *and* a friend of his choosing −"

The greedy weasels and acquisitive stoats slid their
snouts nearer, all the better to hear what the Badger
would offer them as reward. But Badger was rather
stuck for words, for he lived but modestly, and had little
in the way of goods or chattels which were worth
parting with.

The ever-resourceful Water Rat came to his rescue
and said, " − that weasel, or that stoat, *and* his friend

61

shall, as reward, have that which very few creatures in the Wild Wood have ever had —"

"Which is?" hissed one of the stoats, as all the others, weasels and stoats alike, slid even nearer.

"Which is," said the Water Rat grandly, before pausing for full effect, "high tea with Mr Badger himself at his own table!"

There was an awed gasp from most of the weasels and stoats, though not quite all, for one of the boldest of the stoats, scenting advantage, had the nerve to whisper, " ... and?"

"And ..." faltered the Water Rat, desperately wondering what more he might offer, for this surely was concession enough, "and — a letter of forgiveness from Toad for past wrongs!"

There was another gasp of awe, though one last weasel, it seemed, remained unimpressed and held out for more.

"In addition to — ?" he dared add.

"In addition to not being driven out of the Wild Wood!" roared the Badger, at which they all fell back upon each other frightened out of their wits, the negotiations over.

After that, and with so great a prize on offer, the weasels and stoats were putty in the Rat's paws as he, and the Badger, led them to the river bank and began the long search downstream from Rat's house; while Mole's Nephew led a smaller party by way of the bridge upstream to supplement the Otter's work with the rabbits on the other side.

* * *

All that day they searched, leaving no sedge bank untouched, no piece of driftwood unturned, no old vole hole or tiny creek or gully unchecked. Then they started at first light the next day, calling a council to discuss matters only when it became increasingly obvious to all concerned that matters were worsening.

"The river is still rising," declared the Water Rat, "and it will go on rising. We have hardly covered a quarter of the ground and yet if not by tonight, then certainly by tomorrow, all the places where poor Mole might have been washed up, and may even now be lying trapped and calling for help, or perhaps too weak now to call, will be flooded."

"Which means," said the Badger, "the worst!"

The Rat nodded his head gravely.

"It means that our friend, loved by us all," and here even some of the weasels, and one or two of the stoats, looked genuinely sorry, "will be drowned."

But as he said this there was another of those ominous roaring and splutterings which had been coming from the direction of distant Toad Hall for days past.

"What *is* that?" asked the Rat.

Badger shrugged, and the others shook their heads.

"Just Toad, that's all that is. Toad making a noisy nuisance of himself. Best to ignore it, whatever it is. Now, I ask you all, very seriously indeed, to consider very carefully our difficulty and to see if one of us — and there are many of us here — cannot come up with a solution. There *must* be a way of —"

The roaring sound was increasing, and fast.

" — there is certain to be —"

The roaring sound was beginning to shake the very trees.

"There must –"

The roaring sound was coming at them like thunder out of a clear sky, rolling and roaring and shaking and terrible, so that the Badger's words were utterly drowned, and every weasel and stoat there, and many more besides, dived for cover as the Badger, Water Rat, and Mole's Nephew turned their startled gaze up-river.

But it was not up-river that they needed to look so much as above-river, a few feet above-river as it seemed, where a black shadow grew into a dark monster, and that monster into a wild roaring unstoppable rushing thing that flew, and sparked, and shattered its way through the air right past them and just above the swollen river itself.

From which monster, quite unmistakable even above that earth-shattering roar of engines and propellers and wind through wire, came the triumphant laugh of a creature all there thought and hoped they had long since seen the last of: an Ecstatic Toad.

Then Badger and Water Rat, the only two who dared to keep their eyes open – Mole's Nephew yielding to instinct and diving to the ground – saw something more terrible than the braying laughter that they heard: they saw Toad himself waving at them as he roared demonically by, his eyes wide and wild, his mouth open, his hands raised in a salute of unutterable jubilation, as if to make sure that all knew what it was that was rushing by just out of reach, and frightening the wits out of every sensible animal for miles around.

Then he was gone as suddenly as he had come, away down-river, up higher into the sky, the roaring continuing about them after he had gone and then following after him and fading in his wake as he and the contraption which carried him rose in a steep climb into the air, higher and higher, and higher still, till it was nearly vertical. Then, astonishingly, and now out of earshot, it continued its mesmeric ascent till it slowly, magically, amazingly looped the loop and roared off to become a tiny speck.

All was silent when it had gone, and remained silent for a very long time after, as the Badger and the Rat stared open-mouthed into the distant and now empty sky, and Mole's Nephew rose shakily to his feet once more.

Eventually first one and then another, and then a third weasel and stoat popped their cowardly heads out of whatever rabbit hole or bramble bush they had escaped into, or up from whatever tree root or mossy bank they had tried to hide behind.

Badger looked at Water Rat and Water Rat looked at Badger.

"Are you thinking what I am thinking, Badger?"

"I am thinking, Water Rat, that what goes up must unfortunately come down, and that when it does it would be as well if you and I were there to meet it. There to admonish it. And there to permit it to go up again for one purpose only, which is, in the little time we may have left, to help us search the rest of the river bank where Mole may be!"

The Rat could not have put it better himself, nor did

he try to. When the Badger was in this mood there was no stopping him, and no wise animal would have tried.

"You weasels and stoats continue the search," Water Rat ordered, "and report to Mole's Nephew what you find. Mr Badger and I shall go to Toad Hall where —"

" — where," said the Badger very grimly indeed, "we shall requisition this — this *thing* of Toad's, and put it to proper use."

There was no more need of words or orders, for the weasels and stoats were very subdued by what they had seen and the thought that wise Mr Badger and bold Mr Rat might soon be part of it. Without a backward glance, the two determined animals set off resolutely for Toad Hall.

· IV ·

Up and Away

Much as Toad revelled in speed, power and control, there was one thing he liked even more: the opportunity to show off all three at once to his friends. The more awe-struck, admiring, and amazed they were the better he liked it, for though he never doubted that he was a clever Toad, he liked to remind those who knew him how very clever he was.

It had therefore added considerably to the excitements and pleasures of his first flight that fateful

morning that as he roared along a few feet above the
river, at an ever increasing speed, who should he see
below him, and watching with what he imagined was
the requisite awe, envy and admiration in their eyes, but
the Badger, the Water Rat, Mole's Nephew, and an
assorted company of weasels and stoats.

As if this was not enough, his pride ballooned even
more when, moments after waving so regally to his
earth-bound friends, he saw the Otter and a large
collection of rabbits on the other bank. The rabbits,
who scattered in a satisfying way in all directions, were
of little account, but Otter's face was the very picture of
open-mouthed amazement. This was most gratifying,
and encouraged Toad to give him an extra wave for
good measure, before dismissing all else from his mind
but the one thing that really mattered, which was flying
through the air as fast and loudly as his flying machine
would take him.

Or, more accurately, as his *pilot* would take him, Mr
Toad having found it necessary, for this first flight at
least, to allow someone else to take the controls. Yet,
despite this, as the machine roared up into the sky,
leaving his friends so very far behind, Mr Toad could
allow himself to settle back and contemplate with
pleasure the cunning and stratagems that had so
dramatically transformed his dull and trammelled life
into one that at last promised to be worthwhile once
again.

The recent years had not been pleasant ones for Toad,
ever since, in fact, his infatuation with a motor-car
(reasonable), the subsequent trial for theft (grossly

unfair), the long sentence in gaol (horrible), and his escape (brilliant), after which the Badger and the others had allowed him to keep his stolen liberty only on certain strict conditions, the essence of which came to this: that he must be forever more be a Good Toad.

In the long and irksome years since then he had lived quietly on his estate, and been kind and generous to those beneath him, almost to a fault. Nothing had been too much trouble for this new and good Toad, this reformed Toad, if it helped others and – well – *and lulled all those around him, and especially those he was lucky enough to call his trusted friends, into the false belief that his old ways were done, and he was genuinely reformed!*

There had been times when he had believed it himself, for knowing Toad as they did, and being well aware of the silent sacrifices and unspoken sufferings Toad must have endured to remain as sober and good as he had for so long, his friends had been generous in their continuing praise and flattery.

But in the dark of the night, when an animal might be permitted the odd dream or two, Toad had imagined all the exciting things he might do if only he did not need always to be good. Yes, he had dreamed, and he had longed, and he had yearned, for all those things he had given up – but even more for all those things he had never had time to try, or even known about to try, before – before he had become Good.

He might still have been good, and have ever continued to be so, had he not been sitting idly on his lawn one balmy day the previous autumn, expanding on his favourite theme, which was himself, to the Nephew

Mole had sent to him for some education in the better things of life, when, suddenly, far off in the eastern sky but approaching with appealing speed, he had heard the drone of a machine.

"What's that?" he had said aloud, his voice tremulous with anticipation, his eyes widening even as he felt his pulse quicken.

"Can it be what I think it is?" he muttered, screwing up his eyes against the pale sky.

"Is it coming over here?" he whispered, pacing back and forth and staring at the speck that grew bigger and louder by the moment.

It was and it did: a red and yellow flying machine which flew straight over the very lawn on which, but moments before, he had been frittering his dull and fettered life away. It came, it flew, it conquered; and it left in its noisy wake those firm resolutions to be good with which he had wrestled so successfully for so long, all broken and disregarded.

"I must! I shall! I need! I long!" he had cried, dancing about and waving his hands in exultation after the infernal machine which had come from nowhere to titillate and tease him and leave him knowing that he would be forever dissatisfied till he had one of his very own.

"You must what?" asked Mole's Nephew, not understanding at all the change that had come over the great Mr Toad, nor being old or wise enough – as the Mole himself would have been – to see its dreadful significance.

"What?!" said Toad. "You still here? I had forgotten

you were —" and realising immediately the danger he was in, he feigned something like a fainting fit, and muttered, "What must I do? I must not! I shall not! I need not! No, no, you young and impressionable mole, seek not what you cannot have. Be content with the simple blessings that life brings. I long for nothing, nothing at all, but peace and quiet, and — and such *good* things —"

Toad had then subsided into his chair and pretended the very opposite of what he felt and intended, for he knew it would do him no good if Mole's Nephew guessed what was in his mind. He relieved himself of the youngster as soon as he could — claiming to feel ill, which was something near the truth, for he was ill with desire and yearning.

From that day Toad had begun to plot to acquire his own flying machine: first summoning those who knew about such things to Toad Hall and then sneaking away saying he must visit an ageing relative when, in fact, he went to the most exciting event of his life: an air show which concluded with an air race. He returned addicted, and began to plot more feverishly still, for he knew it would be no good simply to acquire a machine and start flying it. No, he must plan!

Plan he had, brilliantly, as he perceived it. His aged relative, now in terminal though lengthy decline, afforded him plenty of excuse to visit that aerodrome whereon the machine he had set his heart upon awaited him. There he had his first ecstatic flights as a passenger, and then, O bliss!, his first lessons, till finally, though not yet competent to fly, Toad acquired the wondrous machine, and arranged for it to be delivered to Toad Hall in the depth of winter, when he knew that the animals along the river would be in their miserable hovels and humble homes, and not interested in prying into his exciting business.

The machine had arrived in parts, to be assembled by a pilot-mechanic behind specially erected and camouflaged hessian baffles and shields in the greatest secrecy. Here the engine had been fired, Toad's pleasure in its glorious noise marred only slightly by the possibility that the Badger and the others would hear it. But they seemed not to have done, and his plans progressed unimpeded by their interference.

He came upon his first real set-back when he discovered that the wretched pilot-mechanic (as he now seemed to Toad) resolutely and adamantly refused to allow him to fly the machine himself till he had had more lessons.

"I order you to!" Toad said finally, after a variety of pleas and threats.

"It would be more than my life is worth, Mr Toad, and yours as well, to let you," was the reply.

"But – but – the *whole* point of having it is that I, Toad of Toad Hall, should fly it and be seen to be flying it," spluttered the exasperated Toad.

"I appreciate that," said the pilot, who had dealt before with other customers like Toad who had more money than sense, and knew just the right combination of firmness and flattery that was required, "I *understand* that, Your Honour, but –"

Toad softened just a little, for he enjoyed very much

being called "Your Honour", though his brow began to furrow almost immediately when he reflected that "Your Honour" was generally used for Judges, and they were a species whose path he had crossed before, and wished never to cross again.

"But can't you make an exception," purred Toad, "seeing as I have very considerable experience with high-velocity motor-cars and − ?"

The pilot slowly shook his head, and leant close to Toad, like a fellow conspirator. "Look at it this way, Your Worship, if −"

Toad softened still more as the wise and sensible pilot-mechanic, a sterling sort of fellow when it came down to it, spoke those words "Your Worship" such as, Toad thought, might be applied to a Lord Mayor or a Bishop, or some such personage of the kind with whom Toad could very easily imagine himself mixing.

"If − ?" whispered Toad almost gently.

"If, as you rightly say, My Lord, if −"

Toad's head swam. Toad's chest swelled. Toad's heart missed a beat as an extraordinary sensation came across him at those potent and wonderful words, "My Lord". No sooner were they uttered than Toad fancied that they were true and that he was, he really was, Lord Toad of Toad Hall, but − but he shivered the sensation away from himself.

Then he sighed, and he sank back into the more sustainable dream that even if those magic words were not quite true, they were almost so. A Lord he certainly was in spirit, just as he felt he had always been. A Lord in all but name, and one day −

" – if," continued the pilot-mechanic, "I were to let you fly this machine without further instruction, and supposing, just supposing, there was a regrettable occurrence, which is to say an accident, then it would not reflect well on you at all. Accidents involving flying machines tend to attract rather widespread, not to say national, interest. All the more so if the personage who is the pilot is well known across the length and the breadth, as you undoubtedly are. There would be –"

Toad's mind swam again, and his hopes and spirits soared. Not so much at the notion of "length and breadth" (precisely what length and which breadth the pilot wisely refrained from saying) as from all the possibilities implicit in attracting the "national interest". Here then, before him, within his reach, though not yet quite within his control, was a way of making rather more of an impression than a merely local one on inconsequential animals such as the Badger, and the Water Rat, and the Mole.

Here, in this shining and beautiful machine, whose sophisticated subtlety and splendid majesty was in such perfect harmony with the notion of *Lord* Toad of Toad Hall, Toad saw his future before him.

Not that he imagined for one moment that the national fame that was surely his due would come as a result of an accident. Rather, he said to himself, if such ordinary mortals as this – this young pilot – to whom accidents no doubt did happen, could talk of fame arising in that way, how much more lasting would fame be if it came about because he, Toad, had achieved something purposeful in his flying machine, like – and in a moment Toad had broken every flying record he could think of for height, speed, distance, endurance, and –

" – and therefore, sir, Mr Toad, Lordship, it would be better if I showed you how to fly it properly before you attempt to do so yourself."

"Tell me," said Toad, in a quiet and conciliatory way, "would anyone on the ground know it was *you* who were flying the machine? Or might they possibly, seeing me in it, think it was *me*?"

"They might very well think it was you," said the pilot judiciously, "especially if you were wearing the proper gear and looked the part and were, so to speak, prominent."

"Prominent," repeated Toad, puffing himself up once more and strutting alongside the machine.

"If you were to sit on a cushion or two, perhaps," said the pilot, "and raise yourself up a bit, and I was to keep my head down as low as possible."

"You low and me high," said Toad eagerly. "You unnoticed and unseen, but I plainly visible, and wearing the correct apparel so that I look the part?"

"Exactly, Your Lordship," sighed the pilot. "You would need headgear, and goggles, and a sheepskin jacket, and flying boots and so on."

"Would this take long to get?" asked Toad.

"Getting it is not the thing," said the pilot-mechanic, "but paying for it is. Such apparel is expensive, though if you are to look the part, and a gentleman like you would only want the best, then –"

"The expense is immaterial!" cried Toad impulsively.

"I'll have two of everything −"

"Well, it just so happens, Lord and Honour, that I have some gear with me that might just be your size," said the pilot-mechanic, who had long since intended to sell Toad these expensive extras. "And a parachute as well −" he added.

At this, some instinct for survival sent a warning pulse through Toad's heart and made him say, "But I won't need a parachute, will I? I mean, *ever*? I have told you before − they worry me."

"Of course you'll never *need* one," said the pilot reassuringly, fearful that his patter had gone a little too far, "but with a parachute on your front −"

"My front?" queried Toad, thinking of his appearance.

"More effective when − or rather *if* it was ever to be used, which it won't be. The fact is, Honourable Lord, that if you wish to look the part, and have people say, 'Now there's a pilot who really knows what he's doing!' − "

"O I do wish, I do wish!"

" − then you would be wise to wear one."

"You are a most sensible person," said Toad, "to see how things ought to be done. I will commend you when the time comes, you may be sure of that, just so long as whilst I am still learning you keep your head very low, and ensure that I am placed very high."

Placated, persuaded and pleased, Toad was now willing to be taken up as a pupil once more, but the pilot, having already given him some stationary lessons on the ground, made sure that Toad was still allowed

nowhere near the real controls and was confined solely
to those in the passenger seat – the now greatly raised
and be-cushioned passenger seat – which did not
function unless the pilot wished it.

The fact that taking off in snow might be a problem
had not worried Toad one bit. Winter, after all, had
given him the protection he needed from the prying
eyes of those who might seek to spoil his fun. So when
the pilot finally conceded that Toad might be ready for
his first flight with the new machine and there was still
snow on the ground, the fledgling aeronaut cried out,
"Clear it, whatever it costs!"

So they had, dozens of them, teams of them, cleared
the lawn right down to the river bank. This had proved
no easy task, but Toad was not daunted by such trifles.
He had the money to order about who he liked, and
even if it took a whole day – it took three in the end –
to get the runway open and his bright red Blériot
started, he would see it was done.

The snow clearing proved an unnecessary expense, though one typical of Toad, for the delay in starting coincided with the thaw, and by the time the great day came, which all unknown to Toad was that same sad day when the Badger and the others had begun their search for poor Mole, much of the snow had gone.

Then, at last, he was off, and it was so exciting that the past delays and difficulties receded behind Toad at the same ever increasing speed with which the flying machine accelerated the length of his lawn. Faster and faster, bumpier and bumpier, with Toad letting out little whoops of delight which ended in one long blissful sigh as, with a final lurch upwards, he was airborne in his own machine for the first time, and the ground was falling away beneath him.

"Yes, I'll go along the river!" he had cried as they rose, as if he was in command and had a say in the matter, though in fact the pilot had long since decided what route they would take.

They rose, they banked, they turned and then they skimmed down-river just above the willows, with the swans and herons, the moorhens, the mallards and the over-wintering geese fleeing in all directions.

Then suddenly, and so much the better for being so unexpected, Toad had experienced the very special thrill of seeing beneath him the Badger, the Water Rat and all the rest – all static as he moved, all staring as he triumphed.

"Faster!" cried Toad.

"Higher!" commanded Toad.

"Steeper!" whooped Toad.

Now, his trials and tribulations seeming all behind him, in a trice Toad brought himself back to the present and thought in his conceited way, "There's no doubt what they're saying! No doubt at all!"

He laughed once more and watched the distant horizon fall away as they rose ever higher into the sky.

"They are saying," he told himself, " 'There's Toad, the great Toad, the *real* Toad! The Toad we are honoured and privileged to know. The Toad who has deigned to talk to us in the past, deigned even to entertain us in his home, but who has recently not been quite himself. Yet now it seems that Toad has found himself once more! He has triumphed again and will bring honour to us all!' "

With such vain thoughts as these, and further thoughts to do with national interest, service to the nation, and some imminent honour that would put all the shadows of the past to flight, Toad revelled in the half-hour that followed. The speed was one thing, the noise another, the power a third, and the aerobatics a fourth – all so much greater than he had dared hope that he was left in a state of giddy, dizzy, breathlessness as, finally, the pilot turned the machine homewards and they retraced their route, till they came to the weir and the river above it, with the Wild Wood now to their left, and to the right, that sorry, scrubby patch of ground where the Mole lived.

"How impressed *he* will be by my flight," chortled Toad to himself as the flying machine banked into a final turn and the pilot lined it up ready to land triumphantly upon the lawn before Toad Hall.

"The others – well, no doubt *they* will scoff and sneer and seek to belittle this great achievement of mine," Toad told himself, for by now he had utterly convinced himself that it was he who had flown the machine; and he who was landing it. Indeed, he held the useless passenger joystick in front of him as if he was, and strained to reach the useless pedals, which were in any case out of reach of his legs, since he was raised so high on his velveteen cushions.

"But Mole is a good fellow and will share my triumph! Yes he will! I shall offer to take him up myself, which will make the others positively green with envy!" laughed Toad.

But as the flying machine came lower, and the ground ever nearer, the smile fled from his face at what he saw waiting for him at the far end of his lawn – waiting at the very place where the machine must soon come to rest and where he had hoped to leap down triumphantly and open some waiting champagne.

"No!" cried Toad with sudden desperation, reaching forward over the fuselage to the pilot in front and digging his fingers into his shoulders. "*Do not land!* Up we go once more!"

The pilot obeyed, suspecting some danger he had not seen, no doubt all the more convinced that something was awry because all the exultant triumph that had been in Toad's voice earlier was now replaced by trepidation and concern.

"What's wrong?" shouted the pilot over his shoulder.

"We cannot land! We must not land!" was all the panicking Toad could say.

81

"Can't stay up for more than a few minutes," cried the pilot, "for the fuel's running out. What's the problem?"

"Them!" responded Toad most dolefully, pointing a wind-lashed finger towards two stolid and stern figures who stood waiting on the ground below.

"It's just a couple of fellows come to –"

"They're not 'just' anything," said Toad, now rather wishing that he did not have quite so many cushions beneath him so that he could make himself a little less conspicuous: "They're troublemakers, spoilers, and they will cause us difficulties!"

"Well, we must go down all the same," said the pilot, who refused thereafter to listen to Toad's wails and pleas and began the landing once more.

Just as Toad had feared, they pulled up to a standstill right where the Badger and the Water Rat waited so ominously, their brows furrowed, their looks disappointed but determined. Toad's heart sank and he wondered how he might best effect an escape and hide till they, and the unpleasantness they were so unnecessarily bringing with them, went away. Out of sight would be out of mind as far as he was concerned, and then his pleasures and excitements in the contemplation of the solo flights yet to come might be unalloyed by accusation and admonition.

But as he pulled the flying goggles from his eyes, and looked about, he could see there was no easy way to leap clear of the machine and make a dash for cover. There was nothing for it but to face them out and send them packing if they tried to cause trouble.

"Well, well!" he cried, as he clambered in an ungainly way to the ground. "Welcome to Toad Hall, my good friends!"

"Toad —" began the Badger in the severest of voices.

"No, no," continued Toad, "do not embarrass me with praise concerning today's extraordinary flight. Tomorrow's will –"

"Toad!" essayed the Rat this time, his voice dark in its warning tone, and his eyes narrowing.

"My dear fellow," said Toad hastily, as a clever ruse came to him, one that would surely make both of them forget whatever it was they had come about and lose themselves in the excitement of what he was offering them, "my dear friends – I am delighted that you are here, and edified, and it saves me the trouble, though it would have been no trouble at all, of sending you the invitation that I had intended to send this very evening, an invitation to have a flight in my marvellous flying machine, with myself as your pilot and guide!"

"Toad," said the Badger very quietly, coming closer, so that he looked down at Toad, and Toad was forced to look up at him, "we shall leave to one side your secret acquisition of this – this thing, and say only that it is possible, just possible, that you may redeem yourself before further damage is done by making it available for one more flight before it is returned forever to wherever you stole it from."

"Returned?" faltered Toad. *"Returned?"*

"Returned!" agreed the Rat.

"But it is not stolen!" protested the grief-stricken Toad.

"That it is not stolen is the only good thing I have heard today," said the Badger, "though why you should waste your money – but enough of that. Would you like to know *why* we need it?"

"Well I would, of course I would, though I daresay

you wanted to try it out yourselves, and of course you *can* and you *must* but – but not then to return it, to banish it, to –"

"Mole is lost," said the Rat.

"Which mole?" repeated Toad, not understanding him at all.

"Your *friend* Mole," said the Badger. "The same Mole who has helped you, listened to you, risked his life for you in the past."

"O, Mole!" said Toad somewhat dismissively, his desire to get aloft overwhelming his better nature. "The one who lives in Mole End. Lost is he? Well he shouldn't get into scrapes he can't get out of, should he? Me? Why, I fly down the river and far over the Wide World and back again and *I* don't get lost, do I?"

"It may already be too late," said the Rat, ignoring Toad's splutterings, "but in case it is not, we intend to requisition your flying machine and search for him while we still can – before darkness comes, and before the river rises further."

Toad fell silent and listened to their quickly told tale, beginning to wish he had not spoken so soon, but seeing a chance that *if* Mole was found he might be allowed to keep his flying machine after all.

"You should have explained sooner," said Toad, bursting into sudden tears. "*Of course* you can use my flying machine to save Mole's life." Then, wiping his eyes and sniffing somewhat, he added in a low obsequious voice, "I shall fly it myself –"

"I think that might be unwise, sir," said the pilot quietly behind him.

"Yes, yes it would," agreed Toad hastily, "for you will need someone who knows these parts and has some common sense as a lookout, to spot Mole wherever he may be sending signals of distress up from the flooding ground."

"Quite so," said the Badger. "The Water Rat has volunteered. Pilot, prepare the machine. Refuel it or whatever you must do!"

"I will, sir, and without delay!" said the pilot, jumping to at this impressive command.

"Toad!" boomed the Badger. "Off with those ill-fitting garments at once! Give them to Rat so that he can at least keep warm."

Out-numbered and surrounded, Toad reluctantly did as he was told, and watched the Rat quickly put on the splendid sheepskin jacket, the modish leather headgear, the raffish goggles and finally the manly parachute. But when he saw Rat heading for what had been his seat in the flying machine, a look of grave alarm came over Toad's face, quickly hidden by feigned concern.

For as Toad had been displaced by the Water Rat he had had a glimpsed vision, a nightmare vision, of the national fame and celebrity that would be gained by Rat instead of him. Rat the Hero! Rat the One Who Cared! Rat the Bold and Brave! Worse still, Rat the Honoured One – a Baron possibly, a Baronet probably, a knighthood certainly! O yes, there could be no doubt of something of the sort for whoever rescued Mole so bravely, and Toad could see it all in every dreadful detail.

"And it *is* at my expense!" he fumed to himself. "It is

my machine, even if it is only on approval, so to speak. It is my lawn. It is *my* opportunity!"

So, ever the schemer, not reformed at all, no sooner had he seen this unpleasant vision than Toad had hatched a plot to thwart it, and gain all the glory for himself. He suddenly seemed positively filled with interest and concern about the coming search, and as the others busied themselves getting ready, and discussing where they might look, he began muttering such things as: "Poor Mole!" and "It shouldn't have happened to him of all animals" and "We must do all we can".

Then, with a cry of "I should have thought of it sooner!", he dashed up the steps of Toad Hall, summoned a servant, gave him some orders and dashed down again.

Toad filled with generosity and care? Toad meek and mild and biddable? Could this really be the true Toad?

It could not, and Badger and Rat would have known better had they not been so engrossed in making plans for the coming flight, and they might have guessed that something was wrong, very wrong indeed.

"My dear friends," said Toad, his face now the very picture of generosity and care – though had the Badger been less busy, and the Rat not concerned with putting on the parachute, they might even then have noticed that his eyes betrayed a certain resolute cunning. "I may have been slow to respond to your call for help, but now I hope I may make recompense. We must not delay, but flying is cold and tiring work and it would surely be wise if our pilot-mechanic here had a quick hot drink before he bravely takes to the skies again. Therefore I have had prepared for him — no, no, don't refuse, it is my pleasure — yes, just at the top of the steps, all ready and waiting, yes —"

Before the pilot knew what was happening, Toad led him up the steps and into the Hall.

"They're taking an awfully long time," said the Rat impatiently after a while.

Almost as if he had heard this, Toad thrust his head out of the French windows, and cried, "He's nearly done, Ratty, and says that to save time you're to get in."

"Well, if it will hurry things along," growled the Rat. "You go and get them moving, Badger, there's a good fellow. Toad's probably gassing away and telling that poor pilot what a glorious fellow he is, or showing him the family portraits!"

"Leave it to me," said the Badger.

"Ah, Badger," cried Toad, again from just inside the door, "I was just about to suggest that you — yes, you're cold too, no doubt? No? The pilot? He's just down there — yes, yes —"

Badger had mounted the steps and disappeared inside at Toad's siren call when the Rat, left alone, climbed grumpily into the passenger seat of the flying machine, which was not easy with a parachute attached to his front, and then looked impatiently up at the Hall.

"Come on!" he called out.

"He's coming!" he heard Toad's voice shout. "He's almost ready!"

Then Toad's voice again —

"Good luck, sir! And bless you for your courage!"

If only the Rat had not been adjusting the cushions just then and strapping himself in, and instead had been looking up towards Toad Hall. If only he had seen Toad, now sporting the pilot's leather headgear, peering shiftily outside towards the machine as he panted with the exertion of overpowering and disrobing the pilot.

If only he had been watching more carefully as Toad, with the sheepskin jacket and goggles completing his disguise and a parachute attached to his front once more, lumbered down the steps, accompanied by his own cries of, "Good luck, old fellow! Good luck! Badger and I will be cheering you brave fellows on, won't we, Badger?"

Badger might indeed have done so, had Toad not locked him in the smoking room after he had tied up the pilot, whence his cries of rage and thumping at the oaken door issued forth in a muffled kind of way.

"Ha! Ha!" chortled Toad to himself as he approached the machine, and before the Rat had a real chance to look at him, or thought to ask himself why the pilot looked somewhat different − shorter, fatter, much less nimble − it was too late! For without more ado Toad climbed aboard and pressed the starter switch.

"Ho! Ho!" he chuckled as the engine started and the machine jumped forward at his command.

"Hee! Hee!" guffawed Toad as the little machine raced down the lawn. "This is easy, this is fun, this is what it's all about!"

If only, even then, Rat had put two and two together he might still have had time to unstrap himself and leap clear as the flying machine, roaring and racing now, swerved this way and that under Toad's uncertain command, and finally lurched towards the river.

But the Rat did not, feeling only some surprise at the roughness of their passage, and then alarm and doubt as the machine tore down towards the river and threatened to crash straight into it till, with a last despairing shudder, it pulled itself up into the air, more of its own volition than by Toad's skill.

Then they were up and away, tearing once more into the sky, with Toad so exultant that he half rose in his seat to wave one hand and turn to the horrified Rat and laugh in his face.

"I've done it! I can fly! I can fly!"

· V ·

Terra Firma

Any thought of actually looking for Mole that might originally have been in Toad's head went right out of it the moment he took off. Even then, he would have had to be able to keep the machine steady, low and flying slowly enough for the Water Rat to have any chance of looking over its side at the ground below. But Toad could do none of those things. The machine had a will of its own, rushing forward and up through the air as Toad clung on to the joystick with one hand and his seat with the other, disregarding utterly his own safety and that of the Rat, and most of all the reason they were there in the first place.

But so fast was their ascent, and so steep, that far from looking over the side the Rat was forced down into his seat and would have disappeared from sight altogether had he not clutched resolutely to the varnished wood of the fuselage that surrounded it.

"Toad, you terrible and wicked Toad!" he struggled to call out, though recriminations now were too late to be of use, too late perhaps to save either of them from the dire consequences of Toad's selfish action. Which was all made worse for Rat by Toad's wild cries of triumph and delight as the machine wobbled this way and that as it flew upwards ever faster, and then, just as the Rat was at last finding strength to pull himself sufficiently high to see what was going on, plunged downwards, almost hurling him out into the sky.

"Toad!" he shouted, grasping Toad's leather-clad shoulders and pulling the wretched animal as near to him as he could – though this had the effect of sending the machine into a banking turn so that the whole spectacle of the river, the meadows, the Wild Wood and then Toad Hall came into view not quite beneath them so much as sliding by at an angle to them. "Toad, take us down immediately!"

"I shan't and I won't and I – can't!" cried Toad exultantly, oblivious it seemed to the dreadful implications of what he was saying.

"Well, at least –"

The Water Rat was going to tell Toad to attach his

parachute strap to the fuselage, for it was flapping uselessly in space, when he realized that his own was doing the same. Always sensible and practical in a crisis, the Rat attached Toad's strap to a hook that he found, and then his own. Not that Toad was interested to be told such things, for he ignored the Rat's further cries and warnings and turned to face the tilting, racing, wonderful world of ground and sky.

The machine ducked and dived ever lower; it circled Toad Hall; it soared again, whether at Toad's command or of its own volition none could say. Any hope of seeing the ground below for more than a few moments was gone, and the only hope that remained was that they might by some miracle get down onto terra firma once more and –

But that was as far as the Rat's thoughts got before something happened that took him over completely. They had soared high once more when, quite suddenly, the engine stopped. One moment everything was all noise and confusion, and the next, with a splutter and a grumble, the world was silent but for the most ominous sound the Rat had ever heard in all his life: the sinister squeal and whine of wind in the wires, and through the motionless propeller in front.

Then, before the Rat could say a thing, or even think what he *might* say in so hopeless a circumstance, the world turned slowly upside down before him, quite unaccountably, it seemed, and he felt himself falling out of his seat into cold air.

"O!" was all he had time to say as the machine, with Toad hanging upside down inside it and looking as ridiculous as the Rat had ever seen him look, appeared to shoot away above him and was gone.

Then, with the roaring of wind in his ears, the Rat, as if in a dream, felt himself turning in the air and found he was gazing down at the ground far below, and at the River, his beloved River, and the very stretch he knew best of all.

He knew it at once: the bridge, Toad's estate beyond it, which looked large to the Rat even from so high above the ground, the dark trees of the Wild Wood, and softer woods and meadows where Mole End was, and the river, shining below him in the winter light. And –

"That's my boat loose on the water!" he said crossly to himself, as if it was the most natural thing to make such an observation as he plummeted towards the ground. But it *was* loose; the little rowing boat he loved so much, which he remembered in a flash he had failed to moor properly because the sound of Toad's machine had distracted him and had now been floated off the bank by the flooding river and was drifting rapidly downstream.

"Drat!" said the Rat to himself. For his boat was turning and turning about on itself, and from where he saw it now it was as plain as could be that once it had passed one side or the other of the island it would be sucked down over the weir and smashed to bits.

Then, another surprise. Above him a by now all too familiar roaring came to him through the steadier sound of the wind in his ears as he fell, and he looked up in time to see Toad's machine righting itself as it turned back his way and, though he could not quite see properly, the engine once more coming to life.

Toad, he presumed – he did not exactly hope – was still inside it. The machine wobbled a couple of times above him and then was gone off eastwards and lost in the bright light of the sky.

All this seemed to take a very long time indeed, and the Rat was beginning to think that falling through air was not unlike swimming underwater. He reached out his arms and legs, much as he did sometimes on a hot day when a little dive in the river served to cool him off, and turned to face the ground once more. As he did so, and tried to fix his gaze once more on the river below him, he saw to his surprise that it had moved a little away from directly below him, or appeared to have done, and that he was now above the Wild Wood. The adjustment was slight, but enough to make him shift his gaze from what he knew to what he did not, which was a place that was not part of the Wide World, but which he instinctively knew was that other place – Beyond.

He looked first downstream, past the weir towards which his boat was drifting so rapidly, and he saw all the great panoply of life – roads, towns, and railway lines, smoke, and people.

Then he looked upstream, past the island, past his own home, past the bridge and Toad Hall, on and on to a place he had only ever imagined might exist. Pale winter sun shone upon it, and it alone, so that in a dull grey roaring world that uncharted part which he felt must be Beyond, the bit he had only ever imagined before, seemed special and separate.

What he saw quite took his breath away. The river wound its way into it, its meanders growing smaller one by one, and where they went was all green and hazy blue, and in parts still white with snow. In some parts too there was a golden sheen where the sun shone down and reflected in his eyes. And there were what seemed mountain heights.

"O!" he whispered, for in all his life he had never seen anything so beautiful. "O!"

Then, as if he had glimpsed a world he should not have seen, and that too long, there was a violent jerk at his shoulders, and that secret lost forbidden place, that ethereal place, was snatched from him and he saw it no more.

Above him, with a great *Whoosh!* and *Crack!* the parachute opened and the roaring in his ears fell away to silence once more."O dear!" he said aloud, for suddenly there seemed no time to think.

The trees came nearer and nearer as he was carried across them, right over the Wild Wood towards its farthest edge.

"Must keep an eye on the river so I know in which direction to go back," said the ever resourceful Rat as the trees came nearer still and the river disappeared rapidly behind him – over – round – and then with a scrape and a bump, a rise once more into the air, and then a final branchy, scratchy, tangly descent, he landed somewhere on the far side of the Wild Wood.

* * *

Meanwhile, distant calls — shouts would be far too strong a word — finally brought the Mole out of the strange beshadowed world he had been in, and he opened his eyes onto a cold and dusky sky.

He had some notion that within the long dream in which he had been lost there had been a great fierce bird flying in the sky, rumbling and roaring, and this had been what had finally urged him towards consciousness. But it was the calling of his name that truly caused him to wake.

Where he was he had no idea, and that he was in the real world of earth and river, tree and weather he rather doubted. Where he had been, well now, that was a different thing again.

He closed his eyes and pondered the question. But he soon gave it up because the strange and comforting images of gentle hands that had caught him and pulled him from the icy silent world of the river into which he had fallen, and strong arms that held him as he was carried and placed him in a soft, warm sweet-smelling bed of reeds and grass, were very hard to retain for long, and they slipped away into the shadows of his mind as those calls summoned him back once more into the waking world.

"Mole! Mo — ole!" they came, drifting out of the dusk, from far far away, yet he did not want to listen to them; he wanted only to slip away into the place he had been and never leave it more.

"I remember —" he whispered to himself, "it was so warm and He —"

Mole felt tears well up in his eyes, and he sniffed, and

97

he cried, for he was waking up despite himself, and he knew that wherever he had been, and Whoever had been with him there, was leaving him now and he could not return.

"I don't want –"

"Mole!" cried the strange sharp voices, further off now, and moving further away.

Mole tried to wiggle his toes, and they *did* wiggle. Then he tried to move his paws, and they *did* move, and he said to himself, "These toes must be mine, and these paws too. I am alive!"

He whiffled his snout and opened his eyes once more and saw the sky was growing darker by the moment, and felt the air growing colder.

"Mole!"

Now their voices were further off still and the Mole was suddenly wide awake. He sat up with a jolt and promptly sank back again into –

"Grass. Reeds. Water nearby. My, I do not feel well. But they – they are calling my name – they –"

Mole sat up again, shook his head, and looked about him. Definitely grass, and beyond it reeds.

"Mo –"

But now their voices were the barest whisper.

"It's me!" called the Mole, his voice so weak and hoarse that it was not even a whisper.

"It's me, Mole! I'm here!"

He got up, feeling very weak indeed, and poked about amongst the vegetation and saw he was near the river and that he could just see across it. It seemed wide and flowed fast and he did not like the look of it at all.

"Over here!" a voice cried. "This way back, lads!"

The Mole peered across-river, saw some shapes flitting through the dark – thin, narrow weaselly shapes, stoaty shapes, the kind of shapes the Mole did not like, and yet it seemed it had been they who had been calling him.

Badger! He had got them out and searching! That was it. Why else would weasels and stoats stray so far from their miserable lairs in the Wild Wood?

The Mole broke through the reeds, teetered on the very edge of the fast-flowing water and tried to attract their attention.

"It's me! I'm here! *Mole is here!*"

But he seemed to have no voice at all, for they did

not hear what little he had, but faded away into shadows, into darkness, and then were gone.

"I'm here!" said the Mole finally, only then realizing that he seemed unable to speak at all. Or rather, he spoke but no real sound came forth.

He had never felt so ill, so thirsty, so woozy, so strange, and so lonely and forlorn in his whole life. That world he had come out of felt gone forever, and he missed it already; and the real world into which he had come did not seem to want him at all.

"Where am I?" he wondered, and began to flounder about, splashing in the well-puddled ground, unable even to find that warm dry place where he had been before.

"O dear! O dear! I am lost and lonely, and miserable and – and I shall make a hole, and hide away into it til day returns."

He snuffled about, scented at the gloaming, turned back the way he had just come, saw to his alarm that the water was nearer to him than before and was rising, and finally, completely awake now, made his way to slightly higher ground. There he found some willows and beyond them drier ground, and then some ash trees Beyond them the ground dropped away towards the rising river again.

"I'm on an island, and on it I shall have to stay!" he said aloud. "For tonight at least."

The Mole went back to the highest point he could find, made a serviceable scrape and, covering himself with what old leaf-litter and dried grass he could find settled down to sleep.

If he saw that Being who had saved him beckon him once more, if he journeyed back to that place wherein he had almost melded and become part of something far greater than himself or anything he knew, and if now he was only able to observe it as if he was but a temporary visitor whose time had not yet come to be a resident – he did not quite remember it when he awoke the following dawn to the soft chucking of mallard ducks, and the rustle and chirp of coots down by the river, whose flow he could hear nearby as a sure and purposeful rippling, but further off as a torrential roar.

"That must be the weir," he said to himself, "and I must be on the island. O dear! O my! How *will* I ever get off?"

He did not move, indeed he did not open his eyes for more than a moment, but lay where he was, snug yet apprehensive, hungry yet just a little bit excited. It was the excitement of the survivor for whom the worst is over, who though he feels his life is no longer threatened knows he still has some way to go.

He knew he had fallen through the ice, and that he had somehow managed to get – or be helped – onto the island. Now, alone but safe, he must somehow get back to his friends and his home. He had not forgotten that his original intention had been to try to find Rat and Otter, who were in trouble.

"Some help I have been to them!" he scolded himself. "I am a foolish mole to have tried to do so much alone. Now they may well still be in trouble – or worse! worse! – and I myself seem to be the subject of a search — or a hunt! not a hunt! — by the weasels and the stoats. I must up and away from here!"

With such purposeful thoughts as these the Mole rose to his feet and set off to explore his new domain. It was many years since he had been there, and that only when Portly was very young and had got lost and found his way here just as he had now done. The island was a place animals tended not to go, not that they were afraid so much that they felt a certain awe and respect when near it, sensing that if ever help and succour were truly needed, it was here that He who could provide them might surely be found.

Mole soon saw that the island seemed somewhat smaller compared to his last visit, for the river had flooded and broken its banks, and made incursions into the little reedy inlets all around it which were, Mole remembered, secret placid places in the summer and autumn, where bees buzzed, and flies hovered, and the blue and violet dragonflies flew, settled, and flew on again.

Now all seemed to be submerged beneath a flood of muddy water beyond which, where the river raced, dangerous waves and rapids showed, and no creature, not even the Water Rat, would risk venturing. The sky was blue in parts, cloudy in others, so that once in a while sun shone down fleetingly on the island, or over the racing river and across the willows and meadows beyond. Mole looked for signs of life, or someone to wave to, to show that he was alive and safe, but all in vain. Nobody was about at all, and he could only wander about from one side of the island to the other, from top to bottom, to the water's edge and back to where he had made his base, in the hope that he might eventually attract someone's attention.

He found a little food, just enough to give him sustenance, though not enough or of quality sufficient to satisfy the gnawing pangs in his stomach and prevent him suffering all kinds of unwelcome remembrances of happy fulsome repasts that he had enjoyed at Mole End. Every time he settled down for a snooze he found himself thinking of plum pudding, or sizzling sausages, or leek and potato soup laced with a little –

"O, but I mustn't!" groaned the poor Mole, opening his eyes once more and restlessly setting off again on his little round to see what, if any, signs of life and help there were.

Later in the afternoon, with the river showing no inclination to rise further and Mole, returning from his latest tour, beginning to feel decidedly better, that the errant sun shone briefly once more across the island and he caught a glimpse of something through the crowding sedges beyond one of the inlets.

It was no more than a flash of blue – but of a colour and at a height that seemed somehow familiar, somehow comforting. He stopped, peered, negotiated the flooded ground, pulled aside the tall sedge grasses and there he saw it, plain as could be: the Water Rat's rowing boat.

"It cannot be!" Mole exclaimed, for none knew better than he how very careful Rat was with his boat, and how he never ever left it without mooring it fast, not Rat! Why even when it had once been sunk while

103

under Toad's command the Rat had gone to the pain of salvaging it and then making it as good as new again.

But there it now was, its bows thrust in among the sedges, its painter trailing out into the water towards the open river, rocking gently to and fro. It swung a little, then heaved forward as a wave pushed it, and then back, back towards the river's flow as the wave retreated.

The weir's roar assailed the Mole's ears, and even as the dreadful thought occurred to him that the Rat might recently have been *in* the boat but was no longer so, the more immediate danger of the boat drifting off forever out of his reach, and anyone else's if it reached the weir, spurred him to action.

Mole splashed forward through the reeds, grasped the bows with the same assurance as if he was the Rat himself, and heaved it a little way onto firmer ground.

"It is Rat's boat, that's for sure. O dear! I hope he did not lose it in search of me! I trust there is some better explanation of how it comes to be here than the one I fear!"

The Mole peered downstream in the direction of the weir, whose fall of water he could not see, though a steady rise of spray and watery haze showed all too clearly how especially dangerous the weir was when the river was in such spate.

"Well, I shall just have to wait till the water subsides a little, as it surely will, and then consider what to do. At least the sculls are still in the boat, which I take as a good sign. Providence may have sent this boat to me – indeed, I shall consider that it has till I learn otherwise. Meanwhile –"

Mole's "meanwhile" lasted three days more, during which the only mercy was that no rain fell, though the sun shone no more after the day of Mole's awakening as grey and dreary weather set in. They were miserable days in which the grumbling of the Mole's stomach grew worse, and the dreams of food and drink he might be having, instead of the plain dull fare which was all the island offered him, tormented him continually.

He had no idea how long he had been on the island, and his sense of isolation and timelessness was increased by the complete lack of life on the banks of the river, along which, in spring, summer and autumn he might have expected to see a great deal of the coming and going of life.

All now was cold and dull and flooded, and the only life that showed, and that briefly one morning, was a flock of grey geese passing through, and a ragged heron, which settled for a time in the meadow beyond the trees opposite, looking as lost and forlorn as he felt.

The Mole was much concerned about his friends, for either they were in trouble and needed him, or they were fretting on his account – and both possibilities sorely troubled him.

"Even Toad!" Mole told himself. "Even he will be worried for me, I should think!"

So the sooner he got off the island and was able to show them that he was alive and well the better.

"But I shall try nothing till the river has subsided and I have regained the strength I shall undoubtedly need if I am to scull the boat against the river's current and onto proper land once more. I have made one mistake — I shall not make another! Then, when I am able to reach home again, and trusting that my friends are safe and well, I shall invite them to a feast, the greatest feast I have ever given! There will be —"

Once more the Mole suffered himself to enumerate the many things he would like to eat as he contemplated the miserable berry or two which was all his latest foraging had thrown up.

"Hmmph!" he declared finally, making his way to Rat's boat, the same boat in which he had so often in summers past sat with a wicker luncheon-basket overflowing with good things as his friend rowed them to some quiet and shady nook. "Hmmph!"

Almost without thinking the Mole climbed into the boat and sat in the little seat he knew so well, as if, thereby, he might get just a little closer to those fond memories of better days. Closer, even, to a full stomach, despite the darkening afternoon and the chill winter wind. But sitting thus gave him cold comfort for a time.

Three more long days, with longer nights to accompany them, passed by before the water began to recede and the river began to look and sound like itself once more. Mole had long hoped for that moment, and remembering some of the boating lore the Water Rat had taught him, had pushed the boat back towards the river as the water receded, lest it was left high and dry and he unable to shift it, and therefore to use it.

Practical matters such as these, and a routine tour of the island every hour or so to see if any animal was about to whom he could signal his existence, kept him preoccupied through those days, though the ache in his stomach grew no better, and the dreams of food had long since turned into hallucinations of great feasts just out of reach over the water.

But sleep and time are healers, and somehow the Mole got through his long wait, regaining his strength, and gaining in confidence so that when the time came, and if help had not come already, he would venture forth in Rat's boat and try to scull upstream and deliver himself home once more.

But it was not till a full week had passed, and the water was almost back to normal, the river nearly placid again though discoloured by the mud and rubbish that a flooding brings, that a day came when it looked as if he might try to get the boat afloat. The sky had dawned clear and bright, and the day frosty, so that the leafless willows on the island and across on the bank hung still and white with rime, and the meadows beyond were all covered in white as well.

"I could *try*," Mole told himself many times to give himself courage, "I could have a go at least!"

But dawn had passed to morning, morning to midday, midday to a dulling afternoon, and still he did not quite dare, though he eased the boat into the water, and readied the sculls for himself several times, till each time his nerve failed him. Then the sky clouded strangely, and the air grew still and heavy.

The Mole might easily have let the moment pass, and stayed where he was for another night, had not a few tiny flecks drifted down and told him that snow might soon be on the way once more. The threat of which put a greater fear in him than venturing onto the river, for the snow might turn heavy, and it might settle, and it might continue and then, eventually, it would melt.

"And that could mean – no, it *would* mean – that the river would rise once more and then –" And then the poor Mole had visions of more days and nights, more weeks even, stranded on the island, his whereabouts unknown, missed by his friends for a little longer and then forgotten.

"O Ratty, I wish you were here to advise me! I wish I knew what to do for the best. The weir seems so near, though it *is* much quieter than it was. But supposing I drop a scull into the water, or lose my strength, or – or –"

There seemed then to come a scent with the evening breeze that was beginning to stir the willow boughs, a scent which was of many things, but most particularly of the cheerful burning of a fire in his hearth, of rice pudding in a bowl held in his own hand, and of some warm and potent brew set down on the little table close by his armchair.

"O my!" he sighed.

More than that, that scent contained something of the Rat's very best tobacco, and, magical scent that it was, seemed almost to conjure up the Rat's voice, telling him some tale or other of his doings on the river.

"I shall!" he declared. "I shall push this boat out, so! I shall ready the sculls, just so! And I shall turn the bows to the current exactly, so! And finally I shall leap aboard as Ratty would, with confidence and style – so!"

Then, Mole was aboard, and the boat drifting out

into the river, and before he knew what he was doing he had grasped the sculls as if he were the Rat himself grasping them, and was sculling up-river against the current, slowly but steadily.

"And not a moment too soon!" he declared with satisfaction as the weir receded downstream, and the island as well, and as the little flecks of snow turned into bigger flakes, and the sky turned stranger and heavier still, and the snow settled in the boat, and upon his black fur.

"This is all right!" said the Mole, panting with effort. "Imagining that I am Ratty, I shall conserve my strength by staying close to the bank; I shall press on upstream! I shall not give up! And when I feel my strength sapping, or my purpose failing, I shall think of all the food that Ratty and I shall have when we are together once again! I shall! Mole End, here I come!"

With this most heartening cry – which would certainly have been heard had there been anybody along the banks nearby – the Mole pressed on against the current, determined not to give up till he reached his destination.

·VI·

In Memoriam

The one and only light that Badger could discern in the dark tunnel into which he had been plunged by Toad's abduction of the flying machine and Rat, and his wild ascent into the heavens, was that Rat might still be alive.

Whether or not Toad was alive seemed to matter not one whit to the Badger now. If Toad was alive and well – and it would not surprise Badger one bit if he were – then he, Badger, would personally make sure that the wretched animal was never allowed to darken the portals of Toad Hall again, or sully the banks of the river.

"He shall be banished! He shall be persona non grata! He shall –" Thus the Badger had fumed for a very long time.

But far more important was the possibility that the tiny dark object that he and several others had seen falling from the flying machine over the Wild Wood, whose rapid downward descent had been arrested by the opening of a parachute (after what had seemed a period of several lifetimes to those watching it), might be the Water Rat.

"It *must* be Water Rat!" declared the Badger as that distant black object drifted beyond the Wild Wood and then out of sight.

"As for that – that animal, that disgrace to us all, that Toad," he growled, watching as the flying machine disappeared in the opposite direction, its engine re-started and purring high in the sky once more, "beware the wrath of Badger!"

But the Badger was not the only one who had watched Toad's flight in mounting alarm and dismay, for the Otter had also witnessed events. He had seen and heard the first flight, just as the others had, and as his searches for Mole had thus far been in vain he had come to much the same conclusion as the Badger and the Rat, and headed for Toad Hall.

His passage there across the fields was much slower, however, and he still had some distance to go when he saw the flying machine careering towards him, and spotting Toad himself at the helm deduced in a trice all that had happened. Then, watching open-mouthed, he followed the fatal flight, and observed that same black dot falling through the sky, and the machine's revival into life in mid-air before its disappearance eastwards.

Full of wonder and dismay, the Otter wearily made his way to Toad Hall, where he joined the Badger and Mole's Nephew. Together they re-organised the search, one party under the Otter's leadership to continue the hunt for the Mole, the other led by the Badger himself, to see if they could find the Rat and discover whether, as seemed likely, he needed help.

The Badger's mood was bleak as he pressed on through the wilderness of the south-west reaches of the Wild Wood, beyond which Rat (as they hoped it would prove to be) had been seen to disappear. In the space of half a day the Badger had been torn from the comfort and security of his home, and had then proceeded to lose his closest friends in Mole and Rat; and Toad was gone as well.

"Toad!" fulminated the Badger again, as he crashed on through the undergrowth, thrusting aside a huge raft of unkempt bramble, with the terrified weasels and stoats in his wake.

"And Toad again!" he growled, kicking a rotting log out of the way.

"Toad one more time!" he snarled, tearing aside a holly bush and marching on, as behind him his helpers muttered "That terrible Toad!" and "Most shocking Toad!" and "Very insufferable Toad!"

The Badger heard all this, and it did not improve his temper at all, for he could detect in their "terrible's", and their "shocking's" and most definitely in their "insufferable's" a vein that ran counter to what they seemed to mean. A vein, in short, of respect, admiration and downright awe for a creature whose rebellious and radical spirit they had long since concluded was gone forever, but which they had now seen resurrected Phoenix-like with the flight – the terrible flight – of the flying machine.

To add still more to the Badger's ill-humour, and the ferocity with which he attacked any obstacle in his way as he sought out the Rat, was the reluctant acceptance that in his heart there was a morsel, perhaps only a mite, of liking and respect for Toad. Without Toad, after all, what would he and his more reasonable and sober friends have had to talk about all these years, and vent their occasional irritation on?

Without Toad there would indeed have been a lot less colour about the place, as that most worthy and reasonable of animals, the Mole himself, had quietly said on more than one occasion.

Now, it seemed, Toad was gone forever, or if he was not, and it was Toad they were now searching for and not the Rat, then Toad *might as well* be gone forever as far as the Badger was concerned. Which left a little sadness in the Badger's heart, for terrible, shocking and insufferable as Toad indubitably was, he meant no harm by what he did. It was not all his fault, for what hope could there be for an animal as irredeemably self-centred as he was?

"That Toad!" declared the Badger, thrusting his way through the last swathes of undergrowth of the Wild

Wood and emerging into the daylight that illuminated the frosty ploughed fields before him, and the canal beyond. "That inconvenient Toad!"

But even in that moment all thoughts of Toad were banished, and all fears and dreads not just for the Rat but for life itself.

For there, wrapped about the base of an old gnarled oak that formed part of the distant boundary of the fields, and not far from the canal itself, were the billowing white folds of a parachute; and standing on the canal's edge was the Water Rat, plain as could be, and alive!

It seemed that the Water Rat was too far off to hear the Badger's happy call immediately, for he did not respond to it, but stood stock-still, staring off across the canal as if he had seen something there from which he could not tear his eyes, not even to turn and greet his rescuers.

"My dear fellow!" cried the Badger, coming up to him at last and beginning to think Rat had turned deaf, for he had not responded to their joyful cries. "It is I and some helpers and we have been searching for you. I cannot say how glad I am to see you safe and in one piece. Water Rat, dear chap! It is Badger!"

Only then did the Rat turn to look at his friend, and at the weasels and stoats accompanying him, but he stared at them so vaguely, from so strange a distance, that they all stumbled to a halt, and the Badger said, "Dear fellow, you don't seem yourself at all."

"Badger," said the Rat, shaking his head, "you have come then?"

"Of course I have come!" cried the Badger. "When I saw what happened, and your passage through the air, and its arrest to a safer speed by means of that newfangled thing over there, that —"

"Parachute," said the Rat quietly, "a wonderful invention."

"Yes, well, the parachute," went on the Badger, "I naturally hoped it was you, and so we came as soon as we could, not at all sure what we would find. You seem a little shaken, I must say, and perhaps —"

"I am shaken," said the Rat quietly, "very shaken."

"It can be no pleasant thing to be hurled out of a flying machine so high above the ground," said the Badger.

"I didn't notice that at all," said the Rat. "And falling through the air was not unlike swimming through water, which as you know, Badger, I am well equipped to do."

"Well then, all is well, all is well," said the puzzled Badger.

"I saw Beyond," said the Rat very quietly.

"Now we had better get back," said the Badger, ignoring him. "I fear Mole has not yet been found and Toad —"

"I saw — Toad? *He* was safe enough," said the Rat. "Badger, you just don't seem to understand, I *saw* Beyond —"

But again the Badger did not hear the plea, or the wonder, or even the loss in his voice but interrupted him busily, saying, "Now, it would be better if we did not rest here but back at my home, to where, by the time we return, I am sure Otter will have sent a report. Is that all right, Rat? Will you come along now?"

"Come along?" repeated the Rat, looking back across the canal in a distracted way once more. "Come with you now? Yes, yes, I suppose I shall. Has Mole not been found then?"

He said this with what seemed almost indifference, at which the Badger, much perplexed, said with some asperity, "No, he *isn't* found, Rat; he is very much unfound. He is lost and gone."

"But the river flows on, I daresay," observed the Rat moonily.

At which the Badger finally decided that the poor animal was worse affected by the accident that had befallen him than he had at first thought, and the best thing was to abandon conversation and get him back somewhere familiar, safe and warm without more ado.

"You are to come to my home, Rat," said the Badger gently but firmly, "and there you will be fed and looked after till you fully recover, which may take weeks, months even. You must sleep and take things very easily and –"

"Badger –" said the Rat, trying to interrupt him.

"Now, old chap, it's really best if you don't try to talk or even think –"

"But, Badger –"

" – because," continued the Badger overbearingly, "you are not quite well, you see –"

"But –"

" – so now we will set off and discuss things later."

"Yes, Badger," said the Water Rat meekly, for he had

117

given up trying to talk sensibly to his normally sensible friend. "For now!" he muttered to himself as he obligingly settled in behind Badger on the long journey home.

The Badger was now quite convinced that the Rat was unstable, or at least in a bad state of shock, that the Mole was lost for good, and that Toad was unlikely to return; accordingly he began to behave in what he no doubt felt was a firm and resolute manner. Decisions must be made, orders given, and although nothing would now ever be the same, at least things could be returned to some order and stability if a purposeful course were followed. This became his dominant and overriding principle, and it rode roughshod over all else, and appeared quite out of character for the animal all River-bankers had always thought to be the wisest, the kindest and the most trustworthy they knew.

"Otter," declared the Badger after a week of brooding, during which the Rat showed no signs of recovery, but persisted in speaking of having seen Beyond and the wonders that were there, "we shall have a memorial service for Mole the day after tomorrow."

"You really think that's for the best, Badger?" said the Otter doubtfully. "Isn't it perhaps a little forward? I mean Mole could still be alive for all we know."

"Could be, could be!" snapped the Badger. "We must be realistic and face the facts. He has gone from us. He is no more. He may very well be better off for it, for all I know. Meanwhile we are left behind and must recognise that if Rat is not to go completely out of his

118

mind – and I have seen similar cases to his where the delusions increase till irreversible dementia sets in – we must gather together and say goodbye to Mole in a fitting manner. This may settle Rat back into reality."

"But –"

"O, not you as *well*, Otter," cried out the Badger, in a voice of such irritation that the Otter almost backed away in surprise. The truth was that the Otter was beginning to think that *he* was the only normal animal left along the river, now that Toad and Mole had disappeared, or whatever they had done, and poor old Rat could only mutter about Beyond, and now the Badger had become quite impossible to talk to, and determined to do anything rather than do nothing, when nothing, thought Otter, might very well be the most sensible thing to do.

"We'll hold the service tomorrow at dusk," said the Badger. "We shall gather and celebrate the memory of Mole at the spot where he gave up his life, that others might live."

"Yes," concurred the Otter in a low voice.

"Don't forget to tell Portly. We must look our best. I shall instruct the weasels and the stoats in how to comport themselves."

"They need to be there, do they?" said the Otter. "Mole was not especially fond of them, nor they of him. They only helped with the search because you offered them the prospect of high tea."

"Tea? At a time like this? O wretched animals that they are," responded the Badger passionately. "No – they do not deserve to be there! Let them skulk in the

Wild Wood! The rabbits can come instead. They will swell the numbers. Now, I must consider all that needs to be done."

"Yes, Badger," said the Otter once more, catching a sudden glimpse of the Rat who was peering round the guest bedroom door, for he had been confined to bed and told to rest and sleep. As the Badger hurried off busily to make his plans the Otter sidled over to the Rat and said, "I wish you'd come back to us, Rat, and be normal once more. Badger's gone off his head. I mean, do you really think Mole's – er – gone for good?"

"Mole's no more passed away than you have, Otter," said the Rat softly. "At least I don't think so. Why, without Mole nothing would be the same, would it, nothing at all? But it *is* the same, isn't it? It's just that he's not here. But, Otter –"

"Yes, Ratty," said Otter gently, for his friend sounded a little frail.

"Did you look really hard for him?"

"Right up past Toad Hall and right down to the weir and over its dreadful edge," said the Otter, "and there was neither sight nor sound of him. Not a thing. We called and called, in case he was trapped, but – nothing. And I myself, without Badger's knowing, made the stoats and weasels help me with one last search, but it was no good."

"He *was* alive," said the Rat, his voice dropping to a whisper, as it sounded as if the Badger was coming back, "for the River told me so. And I do not feel – I do not think – No, Otter! I'm sure he's all right and this is just a dreadful dream. But we had better go

120

through with Badger's plan — if only for his sake! He's the one who needs to say goodbye!"

There was a sudden twinkle in the Rat's eye, brief but comforting to the Otter, for it suggested that shaken though the Rat was he was on the road to recovery, rather than heading for dementia as the Badger seemed to think.

"Tomorrow it is then!" said the Badger, returning. "At dusk. Assemble Portly, assemble the rabbits, assemble Mole's Nephew and let us say goodbye to our good friend Mole in a splendid and fitting manner and with due decorum!"

"Yes, Badger," said the Otter, before sliding away back down to the river, thinking that he would get a few helpers together and have one last final look and then, if that did not produce anything, he supposed he could say goodbye to Mole feeling he had done all he could.

The night passed; dawn came; the morning was bright and cold. Then as the afternoon wore on a strange discoloured sky appeared which portended the return of snow — the same sky that Mole had also seen, and which made him think that perhaps he ought to venture onto the water and try to return home — and it cast its pall all along the river.

The animals assembled at the very tree where the Mole had written his generous last will and testament, and the Badger, looking very serious and wearing a black armband, led the Water Rat, the Otter, Portly and Mole's Nephew through the throng of rabbits

121

who had long since gathered, more out of curiosity than anything else.

There was a certain solemnity about the scene, despite the fact that at least two of those present – Rat and Mole's Nephew – were utterly unconvinced that the Mole had passed away. Nothing *felt* as if he had, nothing at all. Rather the contrary, in fact. Yet now they had gathered in the late afternoon, with the river flowing heavily and mournfully by, and the threatening sky finally swirling and changing as the first snow began to fall.

"My friends," said the Badger, "we are gathered here today to celebrate the memory of one who –"

As the Badger spoke, even those who had had doubts – even the Rat himself – began to think that Mole had indeed gone from them and would not walk their way again. Indeed, the more the Badger's voice intoned on the sadness of passing, and the bleak comfort of memory, and the darker and more cold and snowy it got, with flakes of snow swirling about them and adhering to their heads and coats, and to the trees about, the sadder and more mournful the group became.

The rabbits, always much affected by such things, were beset by sniffles and tears. Mole's Nephew stood ever more sombre, ever more still, while the Rat seemed to age with each new rolling, funereal phrase the Badger uttered – his voice deepening, and sometimes shaking a little to betray the depth of his emotions.

But it was poor Portly who was affected most of all.

Mole's Nephew had had to support him all the way from Mole End, from where the party had set out. He felt (not without reason) that it had all been his fault and began by sobbing to himself, at first quietly and with decorum. As the Badger droned on, however, and the snow fell, Portly grew wilder in his distress, crying out, "O, it was all my fault, all mine!" and "I shall never forgive myself!" and "How can I live after this!"

Which did not improve the Badger's temper or composure one bit, for he was forced to stop in mid-sentence and order Otter to quieten Portly down a little. Which he did with soft words and persuasion and by telling him to sit down on the tree roots and watch the proceedings from there.

"Also I'm hungry," said Portly in a whisper loud enough for others to hear. "Maybe I should go back to Mole End and leave you to it?"

"Sssh!" said the Badger sternly. "Wretched animal. You will stay and mourn, and show respect for this great and much loved Mole who –"

Badger was off again, and with each word he spoke Mole – ordinary Mole, humble and familiar Mole – was elevated inexorably into Great and Noble Mole, certainly the greatest and noblest Mole *they* were likely ever to meet, whose like would never –

As the Badger went on, Portly, sitting down out of the breeze and so more comfortable, began to feel himself grow drowsy. It was, of course, a pity about Mole but, well, there was Mole's Nephew to fill his place and perhaps it had been Mole's own fault for going out onto the ice …

"Yes!" Portly told himself comfortingly as his eyes began to close, "if Mole hadn't been foolish and – and –"

His sleepy gaze went past the sombre upright forms of the Badger and the others to the grey flow of the river.

" – and I think it was *definitely* his fault!"

Even as Portly said these uncharitable words to himself, and eased into a position in which he hoped none would see his eyes close, he saw, or thought he saw through the falling snow, something strange upon the river.

Something that moved slowly and smoothly. Something pale and odd.

He leaned forward, peered and woke up with a sudden jolt.

"It looks like – it – it is coming –"

These were not words that Portly was actually able to speak aloud as he struggled to make sense of the dreadful apparition that had undoubtedly come into view on the river a little way downstream and was making its slow way up it; these were the mute appeals of an animal who had quite lost his voice.

He half rose as that apparition, all white and unearthly, became clearer and ever clearer and, even as he watched, turned across the great river and came towards *him*.

"*Badger!*" Portly tried to call, though no sound came out. "*Rat!*"

Then, finally, he turned to Otter and looked at him, mouthing silent words of terror and anguish, his eyes nearly

124

popping from his head in alarm as he raised his right hand and pointed at the Thing that came ever nearer.

It was Mole's Spirit that came, for it had the shape of Mole, of that there was no doubt, and it –

"Sit down, Portly, and stop being such a nuisance," said the Otter, placing a firm paw on his miscreant son's shoulder.

"But –"

He saw that Mole's Spirit rode in an ancient craft, also pale and ghostly, and this now carried him – no, It – to the bank in full view of the others, if only they would turn round. But they did not, and would not hear Portly's silent cries of warning, or understand his wild gesticulations, which grew ever more desperate as the form approached.

It was undoubtedly in the shape of Mole, but ghastly white and slow-moving.

"Look out!" cried Portly, finding his voice at last. "It's Mole returned to punish me!"

"Sssh!" hissed the Badger and the Otter together.

"Not long now," said the Rat, patting him in a friendly way.

"Nobody's blaming you, Portly," said Mole's Nephew kindly.

"But –" whispered Portly, for the Thing, having tied up the ghostly boat with a ghostly painter, was turning now towards them and beginning to ascend the bank.

It was then that the rabbits saw it too, and with one accord, turned tail and were off into the night. Which made the Otter look towards where his son was pointing in time to see for himself the ghostly shape of Mole,

his ascent completed, standing there staring at them, without a word.

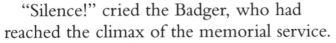

"Badger —" growled the Otter, for though he was a sturdy creature and not easily frightened, this was very much beyond his experience.

"Silence!" cried the Badger, who had reached the climax of the memorial service. "For we are nearly done. We must pay homage in silence to one who —"

Otter reached out to Rat and he to Mole's Nephew, and pointed wordlessly at where the apparition stood.

Then all the animals but the Badger himself, who would not be stopped, backed away as the ghastly form began its determined advance towards them.

"Badger, I really think you had better come with us," said the Rat quietly, the only one among them who seemed to have retained some presence of mind. "You had better come now!"

"Now?" cried the Badger. "Not now!"

"Now might well be better than later," said the Rat, backing away with the others.

Then panic overtook them all; just as a whirlwind among trees sets first one and then others falling, fear set Portly, Otter, Rat and all but Badger scampering away behind the great tree on which Mole's will and testament had been written, and to which he had now returned in spirit form, no doubt in judgement of them all.

"Better get clear, Badger. It's nearly upon you!" cried the Rat from his place of vantage.

"Unworthy animals!" cried the Badger after them, shaking his fist. "Does a little snow cause you to run and hide? What could be nearly upon me, as you put it, but grief and sorrow and heavy thoughts of —"

He was about to launch off yet again when some sense must have told him that there really was something creeping up behind him. He turned, and saw, and stared, open-mouthed.

For there it stood staring up at the Badger, pale and awesome in the twilight, Mole's Spirit. No doubt about it at all.

"Badger!" it whispered terribly with a strange chattering voice. "Badger, I am alive!"

The Badger's response was extraordinary and unforgettable, perhaps aided and abetted by the many irritations he had suffered in the past days.

He stared, he wondered, he thought, and he was not afraid.

Raising his great paw most impressively, he cried out, "Whatever you are, whatever you want, go back whence you came! Leave us in peace! Leave us, I say."

"But, Badger ..." it whispered.

"No but's, no if's!" thundered the Badger. "Wherever you came from you shall return to and we shall lay thy restless soul in peace. This is hallowed ground now and thou shalt not sully it!"

Then the Badger advanced upon the Mole, utterly unafraid, astonishing in his courage, and as the others watched in awe from where they half hid themselves,

128

the ghost began to retreat back down the bank up which it had come, protesting as it went.

"Yes, Spirit," cried Badger, undaunted by its plaints, "leave us in peace to mourn the loss of Mole."

"I *am* Mole!" said the Thing very irritably indeed, finally standing its ground. "And I am cold and hungry, and I –"

"O lost creature, do not –"

While the others shivered and stared in alarm, dawning recognition came at last to the Rat, and hope as well. He climbed over the roots and came to the Badger's side.

"Why, I think it *may* be Mole," he said, peering through the gloom.

"Of course I'm Mole; who else would I be?" said Mole.

"But you're pale and white –"

"O yes, that!" said the Mole. "Snow and ice upon my coat, and in my eyes as well."

"But, Mole, how did you – ?"

"By boat," said the Mole shortly; "how else would I come upstream from the island – swim? Really, you are all being very exasperating. What are you doing here anyway?"

"By boat –" whispered the Rat, beginning to make sense of things, "and from the island. You were there all this time, and my boat –"

"Yes, yes, Ratty, but must we talk about it here? You are all, if I may say so, behaving most strangely."

"You *are* Mole!" cried the Water Rat with sudden conviction, pushing past the bemused Badger and

129

grasping his friend in a warm and delighted embrace.

Then all the others came forward to peer at the Thing that was Mole, and helped him scrape the snow and ice from his fur before they led him away from the river and towards his own home, to warmth, and rest, and food.

While behind them, muttering as darkly as ever, came the Badger.

"Toad," he was saying, "that Toad. He's mixed up with this in some way, bound to be. Certain to be."

Then the Badger stopped and cried up towards the snowy night sky so loudly that the others turned and stared. "If you're up there, you reprehensible and dreadful Toad, you had better never come down, for I, Badger, have a great deal to say to you!"

"Badger doesn't seem quite himself," said Mole quietly.

"He isn't," said the Water Rat matter-of-factly. "Hasn't been for days. And nor will Toad be, if he ever dares return."

· VII ·

How the Mighty Fall

It is a sad reflection upon Toad's moral character that no sooner had the Water Rat fallen from the flying machine and his parachute opened than he said to himself, "That's all right then! Rat'll be all right, for the parachute will save him, so now I can enjoy myself!"

But the truth was that Toad had behaved even more infamously than the Rat would have given him credit for. The machine had not stopped of its own accord at all. Toad had turned the engine off himself, hoping

131

thereby to get the Rat to bail out first on the false promise that he, Toad, would follow, which he had no intention of doing at all. Voluntary parachuting was not Toad's style.

But it had not quite worked out that way – when the engine was turned off the flying machine had turned over and the Rat had fallen out, while Toad had managed to cling on for dear life till the machine righted itself. With trembling hands, Toad had managed to re-start the engine. Only then, when he was safe and sound once more and flying merrily about, did the cowardly Toad think of his erstwhile friend again, who for all he knew had already crashed onto the ground far below. No doubt it was with a sigh of relief that he saw the Rat floating downwards in relative safety, though the sigh would have been less at seeing the Rat safe, than at knowing that others might not have reason to blame him for the Rat's demise.

All this took but seconds, after which, with the engine roaring before him in a fruity and agreeable manner, and the spoilsport Rat out of the way, Toad could get down to what really mattered – his own enjoyment.

"Aha!" he cried, grasping the joystick with a "Wheeee!" and a "Whoops!", as the cold air drove excitingly into his face and he began to experiment with flight. Up he went, and down, down so that his stomach felt as if it was falling through the seat; then up once more, towards the clouds above and right into them!

"O yes!" he cried, for there was a brightness above,

"O my goodness me, we are heading for somewhere wonderful now!"

Then on up through the clouds he went, and out into bright sunshine, to a prospect so vast, so awe-inspiring that even Toad, who liked things to excess, was forced to mutter, "Well! Did you ever see such a thing as – as –" and he delighted in banking the machine to examine and explore the great and glorious domain which suddenly he had taken for his own.

How long Toad gloried in this wonderful world of bright light and endless space none could say, least of all himself. He was absorbed by the views, and the freedom, and to one who had been chained and fettered by the likes of Badger for so very long (as it seemed to him) time was of no account before such limitless wonders.

"I am," he began to say to himself as he banked one way and then another and hummed to himself at the same time, "I am a Toad extraordinaire, a magnificent Toad! None is my equal. What Toad, what creature, has ever showed such capacity, such expertise, such brilliance with so powerful a machine as I have today?

"Alone I did it and alone I do it. I, Toad, care not for your Honours and your Sirs and your Lords, for I am sovereign of all I survey!"

With wild words and ever more outrageous ideas such as these – and more, and worse – not to mention various songs of triumph and conquest which he made up by the moment and sang into the sun-filled air that streamed by, while the real world remained cut off by the bright clouds below him and his infernal machine,

133

Toad lost himself utterly in his own selfish pleasures.

> *"Toad is up, high in the sky,*
> *Toad is up and away.*
> *Toad is the monarch of all he surveys,*
> *Toad is not stuck down below!*
>
> *There goes Toad*
> *And Toad goes there,*
> *And they're all down below!*
>
> *Toad is great —"*

It was not long before Toad, having grown tired of singing his own praises, imagined that others must be singing them as well. It was but a short step – and a short flight – to modify his self-centred song in a way that others might sing it if, as he would have wished, they could see him flying his machine so brilliantly

> *"Look at Toad! He's high in the sky;*
> *Look, he's up and away!*
> *He really is monarch of all he surveys,*
> *While we are all stuck down below!*
>
> *He's a wonder is Toad,*
> *A wonder to see,*
> *But us? We're stuck down below!*

"Yes you are!" cried Toad over the edge of his craft to

his imaginary admirers. "But I'm not! Nor ever will be again, tra la la —

> *"Toad is up, high in the sky,*
> *Toad is up and away*
> *Toad is . . . "*

— and he was off again into his song, chortling, laughing, almost weeping with the pleasure of it all.

That all could change and be lost in a moment did not occur to him — not even when the machine's engine spluttered and stopped briefly for a moment or two, before starting up once more.

"Ha!" cried Toad. "Nothing can defeat me, nothing!"

Not even when the machine seemed to slow a little, and not pull out of his latest loop the loop as fast as it had before, so that it skimmed briefly through the clouds below and plunged him into misty gloom before heaving and shuddering its way at his heavy touch up into light once more.

"Not me, not us!" he cried, as if the machine was now alive and had become his friend.

No, not even when, as the machine spluttered some more, the sky ahead darkened quite suddenly, the sun was gone and the prospect before him was no longer glorious nor fine, but heavy with the swirl of cloud-laden winds.

"We'll turn from all that — that *nuisance*," said Toad, pointing a mocking figure at what even he could tell were stormy winds, "and return once more to that — that —"

He was going to say, "That light and wondrous place where I was but moments ago and which is surely still there somewhere behind me", and he was going to bank the obedient machine again to go back where he had been and so forget about the "nuisance" into which he was flying.

But bank and turn he could not, nor could he speak. The engine's spluttering grew worse, and the darkness of the skies seemed to surround him and take him and his machine upwards with a power far greater and more dreadful than any he might have imagined for himself. Then, as suddenly as he had been taken up, he was plunged unerringly down, down, down into darkness, far faster than he had gone down before. As this nastiness began something else happened, and right in front of his very eyes: the propeller stuttered, stopped briefly, started for a few laboured revolutions and then stopped utterly, as finally and inevitably the fuel ran out.

No amount of frantic pushing and pulling at the controls, or twisting of the joystick, or looking about for something else, *anything* else, to make the propeller start again, had any effect at all. And still the machine plunged down. The terrified Toad, realising that his game was up, or rather on the way down, could see little, for his goggles were covered by what seemed mist, then black stinging rain, and the exposed part of his face was assaulted by a wind no longer bright and clear, but one dark, and cold, and savage.

"Help!" bleated Toad, turning back to see if by some miracle the Rat, having fallen out of the machine earlier when he no longer needed him, might perhaps have fallen back in again when he did. But no Rat was there to rescue him now.

A little later Toad re-opened his eyes – for he had closed them some time before – saw that the clouds were shooting vertically upwards and he and the machine therefore shooting downwards, and he huddled down into his seat and covered his head with his hands in the hope that his problem might go away.

He dared open his eyes again only when the world about him lightened, and he found he was through the clouds and hurtling towards the ground, though not quite as vertically as he had thought. The propeller was just as motionless as before.

Then the machine jolted, banked, shuddered and, slowly and inexorably, turned over and went along upside down, rocking from side to side in a very confusing way.

Toad gulped, for somewhere above him – or was it to his side? – he could see what looked suspiciously like ground, very solid ground, with trees, and rivers and fields, and not far off, houses.

"The Town," he said aghast, "we're going towards the Town."

Now while this was generally true, the route became a somewhat errant and chaotic one, for Toad and his machine were caught up in the very centre of a storm of wind and rain and cloud. This caused him to loop the loop in ways unimaginably horrible, and to fly upside down at speeds quite intolerable, and to shoot off at angles quite incalculable before, unerringly, the storm winds brought him back to the one place he had no wish to go, or to be seen near, which was, as he had rightly told himself, the Town.

It spread unavoidably wider as he got nearer to it, and he saw all its terrible detail: the Cathedral, for example, with all the suggestion of sinfulness and retribution it implied; the Police Station, large and square and unmistakable, which loomed towards him from below, and towards which the machine seemed to twist and twirl and throw out embarrassing signals of contempt and disdain; while nearby, even more imposing, dark and sombre in its crenellations, the Court House reached up towards Toad threateningly as his machine helter-skeltered down towards it.

"No!" cried Toad rather desperately. "O no!" he whimpered, beating the wooden dashboard of the machine and then in his panic looking down past his seat at its flimsy floor as if he half hoped there might be a back stairs there down which he could scramble to safety, and escape.

But all this seemed as nothing when – the Cathedral, the Police Station and the Court House successfully flown over, and Toad beginning to think that perhaps the winds might let him down gently in some quiet and private field from where he could slip away and return to Toad Hall, never to go astray again – when he saw (and though he was upside down again, and going sideways he knew it instantly) something he had never ever, not once, wished to see again.

It had walls dark and dolorous, it had a keep huge and impregnable, it had great stout gates of wood and horrid rusting nails, and it had a dungeon, deep and dank, where once, a lifetime before as it seemed, he had been confined: it was the Castle.

Towards this place, which was the highest, thickest, darkest castle in all England, with the lowest, dampest, most dungeony dungeon imaginable, his machine now rushed through the air.

"Out is surely better than in!" Toad now cried terribly, gripping the side of the machine and heaving himself up against the forces that held him down. "They shall not confine me again! Death is better than such a life as that! I, Toad, aviator and explorer, shall go gloriously to my final liberty, saying farewell to everybody now!"

With that, and the prospect of crashing into the Castle too much for him to bear, Toad leapt clear, his fear of death infinitely less than his fear of the fate that lay in store for him if he were recaptured by the forces of justice.

And indeed, had not the very thoughtful and resourceful Rat tied the cord of his parachute to the fuselage Toad might well have fallen to his doom — a doom, some might say, which he partly deserved. But Rat *had* secured the cord, and Toad had not tumbled far when with a sudden and unexpected jolt, and a loud report above him as the air filled his parachute, he found himself floating towards the ground.

As he did so his machine, which had seemed set on a course destined to bring it somewhere near the top of the impressive Castle keep, leapt in the air as it was lightened of its load, skimmed over the top of the castel-

lations, and went slowly on to crash harmlessly somewhere in the empty meadows beyond.

Meanwhile, Toad discovered that the winds had not
yet quite finished with him. It was not, it seemed,
parachuting weather, and his passage down was accompanied by several return journeys upwards as, quite
helpless, and nearly suffocated by the strapping around
his middle and chest, and with his goggles all steamed
up, and his body bitterly cold, he made a slow and
erratic descent towards the earth.

It was not in Toad's nature to count his blessings,
remarkable though they were, but rather to assume
them, as spoilt animals usually do.

"I am, then, alive," he was saying to himself as he
made his erratic descent, "and I therefore remain the
clever and insuperable Toad I was before – before my
attempted self-sacrifice. Clearly, I was not meant to be
caught and confined, and I shall not be. I shall land in
that verdant field of which I dreamed only a short time
before, and from there I shall decide what route to take,
and what my future holds.

"Flying was fine while it lasted, but now I am
returning to earth I declare I feel a certain happiness and
contentment. Let none say I have not lived, nor seek to
guess what the future may hold for one as full of genius
as I!"

The ground was now coming uncomfortably close,
except that it was not mere common ground towards
which he was floating, even Toad could see that: it
was some vast estate – a good bit vaster than his own –
with a huge house, and outbuildings, and all the

accoutrements and more that such estates generally have.

Unfortunately it was towards a particular part of it that Toad now found himself helplessly drifting, and the nearer he got to it the less he liked what he saw. He tried tugging at the strings of his parachute in a vain attempt to change direction somewhat.

"Only a little bit, that's all I need!" he muttered to himself with increasingly alarm.

Since that produced no change, and if anything seemed to bring him ever more swiftly and inexorably towards the object of his fear, he tried waving his arms about, and wiggling his legs and feet in a most ridiculous way. But it was all to no avail. Destiny may have saved his life (so far) but destiny seemed intent on punishing him all the same.

For what Toad found himself floating so rapidly towards was a great and shining tropical hothouse, which looked quite as big as Toad Hall itself, and which was filled, as he could all too plainly see, with tropical trees and jungle blooms. It was true that these might at least cushion his landing, but it was what he must first crash through to reach them that concerned him.

Nor could there be an easy getaway if he made so spectacular a landing. The noise alone would surely bring forth the whole estate – though one thing, at least, seemed in his favour: by some happy chance there was not a single worker or person about who might be witness to his descent.

The shining glass and white metal structure of the hothouse was rushing up at him. One moment it was there, all neat, perfect, elegant beneath him, the fronds of greenery just beyond, and the next there was a *crash!* and a *thump!* and Toad was –

Toad was –

– coming dizzily to his senses to discover that he was neither in nor out, but rather betwixt and between. The top half of his body, his head, shoulders and arms, was stuck outside the superstructure into which he had fallen, with bits of wood and metal, and nasty shards of broken glass, poking at him from all sides or lodged irredeemably in his thick jacket, whose lambskin and thick inner lining had undoubtedly saved him from anything worse than heavy bruising, and a few cuts here and there.

His lower half, from his middle down, seemed to dangle a very long way below him and felt – and here he could count a single blessing at least – pleasantly warm. His parachute was spread to one side across the unbroken curves and elevations of the hothouse, where its silky folds swayed and fluttered in the light breeze.

Toad tried to heave himself up, hoping perhaps to clamber onto the roof and then slither down its shallower angles and so to the ground. No good. He could not raise himself.

Toad tried to lower himself, by drawing in his stomach and chest and so slide down into the branches and foliage of whatever rough tree it was in which he now felt his legs dangling. But that was no good either. Neither up nor down could he go.

"Help!" he shouted, though rather half-heartedly, for he still entertained the hope that he might free himself and be off before he was discovered.

142

"There ought to be some common worker about," he thought to himself: "some fellow who for a small consideration – though it will have to be the promise of one since I have no actual money on my person – will release me, and ask no questions."

He peered from his ungainly, if superior, position about the extensive and well-kept lawns and vegetable gardens, and towards the impressive walls and windows of the House itself – for help, and with an expedient eye to future advantage if he was detained. But his reflections were interrupted by a rapidly growing sense of discomfort down below, equalled only by a conflicting sense of discomfort up above.

For in his lower half, where his legs and feet were dangling and unable to get any purchase or hold on the foliage, the agreeable warmth he had felt earlier was rapidly building beyond warmth into a hothouse heat. Indeed, the lower half of him felt very much as if it had been immersed in a bath that is a shade too hot, and for which there is no conveniently placed jug of cold water to cool it down a little.

While above, where his head and shoulders were, the air was cold, very cold indeed. And getting steadily colder, as it seemed to Toad.

"I am –" he began.

But he could find no word adequate for what he was, since one vital part of him was bitterly cold, and the other vital half was fearfully hot.

"I must escape," Toad told himself, his vocabulary failing him and beginning to struggle once more, "for if I do not I shall die of – of pneumonia."

Toad now began to panic, beating at the tough glass about him, which though it had been so easy to fall through now proved quite impossible to dislodge. He wiggled his feet and toes downwards, only to find that mounting, terrible, humid heat below was now being aided and abetted by the tickling, and the scratching, and the malevolent rasping, of the spiny leaves, and prickly fruits, of the upper branches of the exotic tree into the top of which he had fallen.

It was not long before Toad began to imagine the worst of outcomes: the pneumonia – he already had a headache, and could feel a sore throat coming on very fast – would overtake his frail body; and while his lower half suffered heatstroke his upper part would freeze. It would be a dreadful fate.

"Help!" he cried again. "Let me down! Money is no object!"

These cries went unheard, and despite the fact that so vast and rich an estate must surely have a vast staff, not a single person was to be seen, or appeared to have seen him. He might as well have landed on the moon, or on a deserted island, for all the signs of life there were.

Then, in the distance, he heard the bark of a dog.

"Help!" he cried. But no help came.

Then Toad heard, again out of sight and in the distance, a door opening, a snatch of male laughter, and then the scrunch of feet on gravel.

"Help, you heartless fools!" cried Toad, whose teeth were by now chattering, but whose lower half was being braised in that tropical hell beneath him.

"Help! Help! Help!" he cried again. "Surely you can

see me up here, can't you? I'm —" He was about to say he was Toad of Toad Hall, for he assumed that those below would be common staff who would be impressed by who he was. Yet he was still sufficiently composed to remember that beyond the river, beyond his own estate, Toad of Toad of Hall was not merely persona non grata, but, in some eyes, a common felon and escaped prisoner, and it might be better if he did not reveal his identity.

"I'm — an aviator in distress!" he bleated, which was the best he could offer.

Then the opening of another door, a metal one, and a vibration in the superstructure around him, followed by the clank of feet upon the kind of cast–iron grille that often lines the floors of hothouses, caused him to fall silent and still. He would wait and see who they were, these fools and dunderheads, and if they seemed friendly and sensible, and likely to yield to a small consideration in return for freeing him and saying nothing, then he would call down to them.

He could have wished that the foliage that tormented him would fall as still as he now tried to, but it did not. It continued to tickle at him, to scratch him, and to make him want to scratch and itch his legs, which he could not, unless he raised one foot and scratched the other leg with it, which surreptitiously he did.

The clanking of the visitors' feet grew steadily louder below, and though the humid air muffled their voices somewhat, he could hear their talk getting louder and clearer. Fear stilled his legs and feet, which he hoped might look, from below, like a part of the foliage, or

145

perhaps some extra fruit or two, or even, if he was lucky, new growth.

He hoped too that those below – and there seemed to be three of them from the vague images he could make out through the fogged-up glass – would not pause too long in the general area where he hung, for the longer they did so the more likely it surely was that they would notice any debris that his crash had caused, and so look upwards rather more carefully than they might otherwise have done. He wished to identify them before calling on them for help.

Then he could see the top of their heads – bald heads in two cases, grey hair in the third – and they did stop. Right below him.

"Very interesting indeed," he heard one of them say.

"My Lord –" the other began.

"'My Lord'!" repeated Toad to himself desperately. This was not good, not good at all. He quieted himself and listened to what else they said.

"My Lord Bishop," the speaker continued.

Toad relaxed somewhat, for a Bishop, whatever the colour of his cloth, might be expected to be charitable in a case like his. This was most promising, and Toad was almost inclined to call out right away and reveal himself, for a Bishop would take care of him. But some instinct kept him silent.

"My Lord Bishop, this particular species is the only one of its kind in all of England, and we guard it carefully, as the Commissioner here knows."

"That's right," said a cruel, harsh voice.

"'Commissioner'!" muttered Toad. "That sounds to

me ominously like an elevated police officer down below, a Commissioner of Police no less. From such a one I can expect no justice, no quarter."

But then Toad heard something else, something worse, something dreadful.

For the Police Commissioner continued, with a joviality that almost froze Toad's heart, "Well, all I can say is that if so splendid a specimen as this tree were stolen, or vandalised in any way, then I would not give the perpetrator a dog's chance in *your* High Court, Judge!"

"'Judge'?!" gasped Toad, his legs beginning to feel itchy again. "And 'High Court'! That is more than an ordinary Judge – that is a Very Honourable and Senior Judge. That might almost be the Lord Chancellor himself!"

The three below showed no signs of moving, but talked on in an amiable way till Toad, peering down to see what he could, saw one of them peering up, and then stepping forward and to one side to get a better view.

"My Lord!" the inquisitive and unpleasant Judge called out – for the other two seemed about to move on. "Tell me, do you keep tropical beasts in here as well, perhaps for purposes of fertilizing the blooms, or the natural elimination of pests?"

"You mean tropical insects, spiders, that sort of thing?"

Insects! Spiders!

How dreadful were the creepings and the crawlings and the itchings about Toad's lower half now. How near

147

he was to crying out for mercy. A life sentence in that drear dungeon from which he had escaped so long before − and so cleverly − seemed a holiday compared to the sufferings he was now being forced to endure.

"I was thinking of something rather larger, as a matter of fact."

"You mean fruit-eating bats, or the larger sort of snake or −"

Bats! Snakes!

"No no, something larger like, well, I am not quite sure − like *that*!"

It was no good, Toad could endure it no more. They had seen him, and if they had not then how long might he be left here after they had gone, to be frozen above, while below, something worse: basted by the humid heat, and then nibbled, and eaten and stung by spiders and insects, horrible snakes and fruit bats!

"Help!" cried Toad. "I am stuck! Free me and I shall go quietly!"

"Goodness me!" exclaimed My Lord Bishop.

"A thief!" cried the Commissioner of Police.

"We had best not judge till we have heard all the evidence," said His Honour, Justice of the High Court.

"Help!" cried Toad. "I am an unfortunate aviator, who has fallen on hard times!"

As his muffled cries came down to them, others came running and there was great consternation down below, though Toad was too terrified, too panicked, too eager to escape the purgatory of his position to listen to what was said. If only his top half might be comforted by hot water bottles, and his lower half packed with ice so that his body might recover something of its equilibrium, then he might be able to think clearly once more, and plan his escape.

But as they came to his help he did at least hear the declarations below that a flying machine had been seen to go over, that an aviator had plunged to the ground and that this poor fellow stuck above might be he. For the moment – and for Toad's continuing liberty this was the most important thing – for the moment, at least, none guessed that Toad was Toad.

In one respect, at least, Toad's presence of mind did not desert him. He guessed that once his flying gear was removed the game might be up. So when the glasshouse men ascended their ladders, and carefully came to free him, he said in a pathetic voice, "Do not take off my jacket or headgear, please do not, for I am nearly perishing with cold!"

Then, remembering something about the perils of deep-sea diving, he added knowledgeably, "It has to do with oxygen in the blood, you know. Remove my headgear and I die!"

This appeal was heard and obeyed, and Toad at last felt himself being lowered onto the hothouse floor, there to be ministered to by the many people now milling about, as his mind swam away into fevered and humid unconsciousness.

· VIII ·

Back from Beyond

When Toad drifted back to consciousness he felt his eyelids gently touched by a subdued light, and he seemed to be wallowing in a caressing atmosphere filled with the healing scents of lavender and rosemary.

He slowly opened his eyes to find his head supported by the softest of down pillows, encased in the finest of linen pillowcases, and his hands resting upon the crispest and whitest of turned-down sheets, beyond which, ruffled only by his now blissfully cool legs and feet, was a quilted eiderdown overlaid with a silken bedspread.

He was gratified to find himself still attired just as he had been, complete with goggles, his identity as aviator thus far seemingly intact.

He peered about suspiciously before taking the goggles off so that he might take a better look at where he was, and found himself in a large and spacious bedchamber, about as large as the refectory in Toad Hall itself.

He lay, like a well-framed picture, in the largest, highest and grandest of mahogany four-poster beds. Toad sighed with contentment and lazily examined his surroundings from his supine position. Across the room, though not quite opposite his bed, was a splendid coal fire, its flames warm and merry. Off to his left was an exterior wall, with two tall windows, reaching nearly as high as the lofty ceiling, and nearly as low as the floor, and curtained with the folds and drapes and hangings of the softest, palest of pale pink and mauve materials.

The curtains were not fully drawn, and from what he could see the windows offered a view of the very extensive grounds above which he had flown, and down onto which fate had decreed he fall. Shifting his gaze further about the room, Toad saw with pleasure that, as if to match the room's general magnificence, its wardrobes were of the finest and shiniest, and its dressing table of the most elegant, and there, on its fluted washstand, a Worcester bowl awaited his leisured use, and within it, steaming amiably, a huge jug containing hot rose–scented water.

Toad sighed once more and wiggled his feet, easing himself first to one side and then the other to feel how extensive and lasting his wounds and injuries might be. Certainly he ached, though not as much as he might have done, yet sufficiently to moan and groan a little to himself.

"Nothing broken," he whispered feebly, "I think." Then, raising first one arm and then the other, he pulled the sheets down a little for a moment, and added, "And no sign of blood or mortal wound. I shall survive! I shall live!"

He swallowed, and then felt his forehead, to test perhaps the advance of the pneumonia he had earlier feared would take hold of him.

"I have fought it off! I am still strong! I have been to the extremes of endurance without too much harm!"

Thus reassured, he glanced towards the windows once again and, wishing to see something of the world beyond, he leapt nimbly out of bed, went to the door to see that no person was outside it, turned the key in its lock and strode over to the nearest window.

It was now nearly evening, though not yet dark enough outside to prevent him seeing that the view did not so much take in all the grounds, but rather offered him what was surely the most elegant part, the most striking turn and vista of lawn, of balustrade, of choice rose-beds and most ancient and established of trees.

"Splendid," he said, "and just what I would expect of a House honoured by a visiting aviator such as myself. However, we must be careful: this place appears riddled with Judges, Commissioners of Police and malevolent Lords, and as I saw on my descent, the Castle with its dungeon is not far off. Therefore, I must escape as soon as —"

But he was interrupted in his thoughts by a discreet turning of the door handle, and then an even more discreet knock, followed by the concerned voice of an elderly male saying, "Sir! Are you quite all right?"

Toad hastily closed the curtains, leapt back into bed with alacrity and in a tremulous voice called back, "I am ill, gravely ill I think. I should not have got up."

"The door is locked, sir; I cannot come in to give you the food and drink which His Lordship has sent up. Shall I leave it outside, perhaps?"

All this was spoken in an agreeably servile way by one whose only task in life, as it seemed to Toad, was to serve Toad, and it seemed a pity not to oblige him. The more so if food and drink was at hand, the mention of which caused Toad to feel immediately hungry and thirsty.

"Wait, while I struggle to the door," called out Toad pathetically, which he did, very quickly.

He opened it a mite and peering out saw a butler standing there, tray in hand.

"I am not well at all, and the light disturbs my eyes," whispered Toad. "I pray you let me get back into bed before you come in, and do not bring light into the room when you do — or, if you must, for though I can

154

drink little and eat less it would be a shame not to at least try, place the light far from my bed."

This was a pretty speech, but one which Toad sensed might appear a little too robust, so he sighed and moaned and groaned a little more, provoking the kindly butler to make soft sounds of concern.

"No, no, I am – well enough," whispered Toad hoarsely, as he retreated back to the bed, skipped quickly into it and pulled the sheet up to his nose, before ordering the butler in.

He watched the butler potter about and eyed the tray he carried very greedily, for its contents gave off mouth-watering odours. The butler then placed a candle on the far mantel and retreated to the door.

From there he said, "His Lordship and his guests wish you a speedy recovery, sir. They are greatly honoured to have you here and will no doubt wonder if perhaps you need any medical attention? I believe that Nurse felt the best remedy was sleep in the first instance."

"Sleep and time," concurred Toad, "are what I need. Please thank His Lordship and ask for his patience for a day or so, that I might be allowed to recover in peace –"

The butler nodded and slipped silently away.

Toad waited for no more than an instant before throwing his covers off and leaping up to examine the contents of the tray. There were scrambled eggs, and thinly sliced toast with the crust cut off, and tea, and a compote of fruits, and a small decanter of dry white wine of undeniable vintage.

"It would be perfect if there were more of it," said Toad, scoffing the lot in an instant. "But adventurers must take things as they find them. Make do, that's what I say!"

Toad sank back with a contented sigh onto the soft bed and pondered what to do.

His leather flying gear was now getting somewhat hot, so he must see to that. It was dark outside so there was no use in trying to escape quite yet. Apart from the lack of immediate further sustenance he seemed well placed.

"I shall stay awhile," he decided, "and have a bath and a sleep. I shall leave an instruction for that butler in the hope of ordering up more food. In the morning I shall decide when and how to depart!"

The instruction was duly given through a crack in the door to some passing chambermaid or other, in an even paler and frailer voice than before, to the effect that though ill and much fatigued his appetite was somewhat restored and he would essay a little more food, including, perhaps, some meat, potatoes, vegetables, sweets, sweetmeats, wine (red and white) followed (a little later in the evening) by some port and sweet biscuits – enough to last the long night through.

At the same time, and to save the servants trouble later, he asked that some hot water be sent in, sufficient to allow him to soak his body right up to his chin. If this, along with a portable bathtub, might be brought as soon as possible it would aid his recovery wonderfully, he said.

"No need to tire yourself coming to the door," the maid explained. "Ring the bell by the fireside and Mr Prendergast the butler will come. That's 'is job. The bath and that'll be up straightways – ring after that and supper'll be there in no time!"

The tub and water duly came, and Toad took a leisurely bath, humming to himself as he did so. Then, duly coiffed, perfumed, dusted and betowelled, he rang the bell as he had been advised and clambered up onto the bed to await the delivery of his second supper. The feast was duly delivered, and spread upon a large mahogany table near the fire (which was re-fuelled, stoked and pokered for him) all ready and, as it were, willing.

"Ho!" cried Toad once he was alone, and the door locked again, sitting himself down at the carver provided, and beginning to eat whatever took his fancy, and to drink whatever he could reach. "This is the life! This is the natural order of things. I do not regret that Badger and Rat and Mole cannot see me now, for if they could they would feel envious. They are lowly animals, I fear, without ambition and therefore without hope. But I, Toad, make things happen! This is my life as it was meant to be!"

He ate rather more than he should, and certainly drank more than was good for him, so that as the evening wore on and the fire grew dimmer Toad began to slip into a slumber that was dangerously like a stupor. Then he crawled back into bed.

So Toad's first night in luxury passed by, and it was the beginning of three days of utter self-indulgence at the expense of someone else, during which he took the greatest advantage of his situation, putting from his mind the thought that his good fortune could not last forever.

Nor did it, for on the fourth morning the butler Prendergast, now his friend, called upon him. Toad hastily put on his headgear and goggles once more and allowed him in.

"Sir," said he, "as I intimated the day before yesterday, and again more strongly yesterday, His Lordship is now anxious that you should descend."

"Descend?" said Toad, muttering the miserable word most reluctantly, for he knew what it meant — that he must descend the stairs into reality, and the certainty of discovery. He vaguely remembered explaining a good many times that he was still ill, and must still wear his aeronaut's outfit, and thinking that his excuses and prevarications were wearing thin.

"Yes, sir. The time has come to go downstairs. His Lordship awaits you, as he has these days past, and others too."

"Others?" whispered Toad, with the gravest of forebodings.

"Certainly, sir. There is the Royal Commissioner of Police, His Honour the Right Eminent Justice of the Very Highest Court Imperial, and several gentlemen of the Press."

"All wishing to see me?"

"Yes, sir," said the butler.

"To speak to me?"

"To interview you, sir, I should say. In the absence of your person they have been striving to interview me, sir, but my lips are sealed."

Interview! He was right then. He was suspected, despite his disguise, and even he could not easily fool a Commissioner of the Police and an eminent Justice.

"I am in a desperate situation," said Toad sombrely.

"You are too modest, sir."

"Ah!" thought Toad. "It is even worse than I thought! If being 'desperate' is merely 'modest', in what position must I really be!"

"I am not a rich man," began Toad in his most unctuous voice, "but if you would help me escape, unseen, then I could perhaps slip you a – a florin."

"A florin, sir?" said the respectable Prendergast, puzzled.

"Two then, though that is generous."

"Two, sir?"

"You are a hard fellow, and a heartless one!" cried Toad. "A gold guinea is the highest I can go —"

The butler smiled and shook his head.

"I think I understand, sir, but regretfully I must decline. Though we all applaud your modesty after so extraordinary an achievement, yet England must be allowed to give credit where credit is due and you must get your just reward, if I may say so, sir, without being presumptuous."

"Out of here, you crawling fellow!" cried Toad, incensed. If the butler would not help him — indeed, was inclined to throw his difficulties into his face with sarcasm — then he, Toad, would find another way.

"Out!" said Toad.

And out the butler went, though not without saying as he did so, "His Lordship *will* insist on seeing you later today, I fear, to prepare for your reception tomorrow."

Toad set to work thinking about his escape, and it was not easy. He had long since discovered that he was quite unable to open the huge window, so that way out was barred to him. The corridors outside were patrolled by tall lithe footmen and chambermaids with loud voices, and he saw that he would not easily get past them. So that as the morning wore on he could only shake his head and reflect that his period of freedom was nearly over and that if he could manage another splendid lunch, and port to follow, and coffee, and a sleep, then he would at least have another happy memory to take to gaol with him.

It was as he was mournfully pondering on this, and staring out of the window at the gardens and outhouses below, that he saw somebody and something that made him sit up, clap his hand to his brow and say, "That's it! Not only a means of speedy escape, but of disguise as well! But wait! He's leaving! I must act!"

Without more ado Toad took up that morning's copy of *The Times*, screwed it into a ball and stuffed it up the chimney, which immediately began to smoke and send forth choking fumes.

Coughing and spluttering, Toad staggered to the bedroom door and called for help, which soon came.

He needed do no more than point mutely at the smoking chimney before there was a shout down the corridors of, "Sweep! Stop the sweep! Send him to the Most Honoured Guest's bedroom."

"Cunning and brilliant," said Toad to himself, retreating to the bed and hiding beneath the sheets, coughing and spluttering for show.

Moments later the chimney sweep, the same he had just seen leaving the grounds and who no doubt had been at work in some other part of the House, appeared, broom-laden and sooty. Others appeared with him, but Toad ordered them out.

"Leave him to help me alone," he croaked. "Too many people distress me."

The sweep took a slow look at Toad, then at the chimney, and then at Toad again. "Bad, very bad," said he, "and dirty too. Be an extra sixpence on the job as was, Yer Ludship."

"The silly fellow thinks I am His Lordship," said Toad

gleefully to himself, "or one of them. I can see he's not just a sweep, but a foolish sweep. All the better for me then!"

Without another glance at the bed where Toad lay malingering and letting out an occasional cough or wheeze for good measure, the chimney sweep quickly set to work. Toad watched covertly as he produced from the voluminous sack he had carried, some very pliable canes, and a number of pieces of cloth. With a "beggin' yer pardon, sir" he took the water jug from the closet and doused the fire. Then, bending the canes into the awkward corners of the huge fireplace, he used them to fix the cloths in place so that anything falling down the chimney would be caught in their folds.

"Won't be so much as a speck of dust inside or out when I've finished," he said, largely to himself, "for I am renowned throughout the shire for my cleanliness."

Toad marvelled that this was so, seeing as the sweep was as grubby and sooty a person as he had ever seen.

"Do you mind if I watch?" said Toad. "For I rarely see such a master craftsman as yourself at work."

"Why, sir," said the sweep, who was just in the act of screwing on the first length of cane to the head and thrusting it up the chimney through a fold in the cloths, "I should be honoured."

Toad crept nearer.

"It must," he said in a sympathetic way, "be a thirsty job."

"It is, sir," said the sweep, screwing another length onto the bottom of that already going up the chimney, "and though I'm not a drinking man by nature I will say it is my habit to end the day with a small drink."

Toad eyed the bottle of wine left from the night before.

"I daresay you can afford only common beer," said he, grasping the vintage wine and jiggling the bottle a little, and then clinking it against the glass.

"Beer's enough for the common man," said the sweep.

"And wine for the Lord, eh?" said Toad laughing loudly. "Here my good man, have a glass on me."

"Well, sir, seeing as you insist, sir, and trusting you won't tell –"

"Tell!" said Toad. "Not me!"

It was a sorry and despicable sight, the way that Toad tempted the sweep and led him astray, and all the more despicable for the ease with which it was done. One moment the sweep was a master craftsman and the next he was a slumped and sorry mess incapable of completing the job in hand and with strength only to drink another glass of the wine that Toad pressed on him.

"My dear fellow," said Toad eventually, "you seem a little tired. Pray, put your feet up on this bed, so!"

The sweep was asleep in an instant. From then it was a matter of moments for Toad to exchange his own aeronaut's garments for the filthy shirt and sooty red neckerchief of the sweep. That done, he carefully took down the canes and cloths and, using what little soot there was to dirty his own face, neck and hands, Toad put back into the bag what the sweep had taken out of it. Then, eager now to be gone, he heaved the sack over his shoulder, went to the bedroom door and opened it.

"Finished, sweep?" came a discreet call from down the corridor.

"All done, Yer Honribble Ludship," said Toad, thinking himself very clever to adopt the sweep's voice and vulgar accent, "and very blocked up it was. As for 'im, 'e says to leave 'im for a bit."

"Follow me then and I'll show you the way out down the servants' stairs," said the footman.

Toad eyed the splendid curve of gilded stairs up which he presumed he must originally have come and down which he would quite like to leave and said, "Beggin' yer pardon, Ludship, but I ought to see the flues on the way out."

This seemed to impress the footman, who turned

back and led the delighted Toad down the Great Stairs, past portraits in oil and great wall hangings, ancient swords and cutlasses, along with some impressive stag heads.

To his alarm, however, as the stairs curved round and down, he found himself descending towards a huge hall in which a number of important people stood about and stared up whence he came. His heart was suddenly in his mouth, for there, unmistakable, his nostrils beaky, his eyes cold as flint, his brows bushy and imposing, his face long and his forehead huge, was the very Chairman of the Court of Magistrates, now a Judge, who had once sentenced him to twenty years' hard. There too was the policeman who had arrested him, now an exalted Commissioner. And there –

Toad pulled himself together and with a humble and apologetic air, but chortling to himself all the time, he scampered past these unsuspecting persons in the wake of the footman, and then through some dark arched way into the back recesses of the great House.

Here, to his alarm, he found himself face to face with Prendergast the Butler.

"O Yer Royal Honour," said Toad, "I am obliged to you for deigning to let me clean the chimney of that great and important gentleman so troubled by the smoke."

"Take this extra shilling," said the butler, apparently completely taken in.

"Why thank you kindly, sir," said Toad, doffing his cap. "I –"

But here he was interrupted by a commotion from

the front of the House, and bells ringing in the servants'
quarters as a footman came hurrying and a great to-do
began.

"'E's up and coming down!" cried the footman.
"'E's out and on 'is way!"

"Who is?" asked Toad, puzzled, and quite forgetting
to drop his aitch.

"Why the great airernought, of course!" said a
scullery maid rushing by, adding over her shoulder,

quite taken up by the excitement of it all, "'E's the bravest and most 'onrable man what ever was, isn't 'e! Risked 'is life ter save the Town from being crashed upon. I'm going to take a peek at 'im if I can!"

Toad saw that he was immediately forgotten in the rush and with dark suspicions beginning to form in his bosom – suspicions which carried most dreadful implications that he might have quite misunderstood the situation and have failed utterly therefore to capitalise on it – he decided to follow in the wake of the maid.

So it was that he found himself among a cluster of whispering and excitable servants at the door to the back of the House through which he had hurried moments before, in time to see a sight that was most horrid and most painful to him.

For at the grand curve of the stairs, with the butler supporting one arm, and a tall footman the other, tottered and staggered the drunken sweep, dressed in the headgear, the goggles and the jacket that but a short time before had been Toad's own.

"Don't 'e look 'andsome!" said the scullery maid.

"But –" began Toad.

"O," said the second under-cook, "I think I'm going to faint at just seein' 'im, and to think I 'ave the 'onour of knowing 'e's eaten the 'taters I 'elped peel!"

"But –" protested Toad.

"If 'e looks my way I'll faint, I'm sure I shall!" declared a fifth deputy housemaid, clutching Toad's arm in readiness.

"But I was the –" cried out Toad in his agony, for it was all too much to bear. To think that the honour and the glory that should have been his were being stolen by this — this wretched impostor of a sweep who was staggering and swaggering down the stairs to where the Highest in the Land were awaiting, and clapping, and cheering.

"It is I you should be —" he cried again, his voice barely heard above the hubbub of adulation for the triumphant figure that now reached the bottom of the stairs.

Toad was about to thrust himself forward, to claim the honours as his own when, perhaps by chance, perhaps because his strangled cries had been heard, His Honour the Judge looked his way. Those cold eyes and that beaky nose quite withered Toad's soul.

Then the Commissioner cast him a glance, as it seemed to the self-obsessed Toad, and those gaoler's eyes, the vindictive brows, caused Toad to retreat back into the scrum of servants from which he had tried to emerge.

Yet still he might have tried to reclaim his proper place had not My Lord the Bishop glanced his way. What judgement was in that gaze! What formidable reminder of a Greater Day than This! It caused Toad to shrink back a third time, and withdraw.

So that as servants pressed forward about him, and the false airman was quite swallowed up by the crowd of admirers, his hands shaken and his back slapped, and his drunken babblings mistaken by the crowds as the excitement and confusion of a modest and reluctant hero recovering from his injuries, Toad slipped back through the kitchen, thence through the scullery, and then across the cobbles by the stables where, with a sigh of profound regret, he arranged his sweep's bag and brooms upon the crossbar of the sweep's bicycle, mounted it with difficulty, and wobbled his way unseen and unnoticed down the long lonely carriageway of the House, and out towards the wintry world beyond.

* * *

The miraculous return of the Mole, alive and well, had proved but a two-day wonder, and soon the River once more exerted her calming influence on the Rat and the Mole and all their friends and acquaintances.

"Of course, *I* knew he would be all right!" was the general opinion of nearly everyone. "I never doubted for one moment that Mr Mole would turn up safe and sound!"

But for those forty-eight hours at least there was a great deal of celebratory coming and going around Mole End, despite the snow and the inclement, unsettled weather. So what should have been a wake was happily turned into a celebration – till in the end the food and drink ran out, as did the animals' capacity to continue eating and drinking and being of cheer, and one by one they left Mole End to go back to their own homes, leaving only the Badger, the Rat, Mole's Nephew and the Mole himself.

"Well then," said the Badger, "you can see how glad we are to have you returned home, Mole, and none gladder than us three. But now the time has come to rest a little, and reflect perhaps on what might have been and what is.

169

"I would be much obliged if your Nephew would accompany me back to the Wild Wood, Mole, for there's a promise I must keep before long, which is to entertain to high tea a number of weasels and stoats. Your Nephew can help me prepare for that, and his sharp young eyes can help me watch out for any difficulty or trouble that might arise from the fulfilment of my rash offer.

"Rat, too, may well wish to return to his home," added the Badger, hinting in this thoughtful way that Mole might like to be left alone for a little, for few understood so well as he the need for a time of solitude and reflection, especially after such excitement, and even more especially in the dark wintertime.

"If my Nephew is willing to go," said the Mole with some relief, "then who am I to stop him! I hope he will help you in the days ahead, Badger. But Ratty might like to stay a while longer, today at least, to help me get sorted out once more and, well –"

The Mole looked a little mournfully about his now nearly empty rooms, and beyond to the darkening winter evening sky. Leafless branches fretted and tapped at his window, and spring still felt a long way off.

"Of course," declared the Badger, quite understanding that the Mole might want to talk a little with his friend before he turned in for some well-earned sleep.

When the Badger and Mole's Nephew had gone, the Mole said little, and the understanding Water Rat stayed silent as well. Together they cleared up what untidiness remained – though the Rat had long since organised the rabbits to tidy and clean and put away before *they* left, so there was not too much to do. Then the Rat cleared out the grate in no time at all, laid a new fire and set it merrily ablaze just as the sky darkened into twilight outside Mole End.

Mole felt sombre and tired, and, sensing this, Rat bade him sit down once more in his favourite armchair and declared that at such a moment, and in such a case, there was nothing better than a bowl of light soup, and new-made bread.

"But Ratty," said the Mole, who felt not only tired, but just a little inclined to tears for no good reason that he could think of, "I haven't any soup or –"

"It's all done, all ready," said the Rat, taking his friend's arm and leading him to his chair. "I gave orders for it to be made this morning. Now, Moly, be a good and obedient fellow and sit down and let me serve you what you deserve."

"I really – I don't think – I mean –" said the Mole, sniffing and wiping away the untoward tears that began to course down his cheeks. The Rat saw them, of course, and he heard the Mole's sniffles, but chose to say nothing and let things be.

So the two animals sat on either side of the fire, eating their soup, having second helpings, and cleaning the bowls out with crusts of buttered bread, neither saying a thing for a very long time. Finally, when the Mole had taken a little nap and the Rat was already on his second pipe of the evening, and both their noses were red with the firelight, they talked at last.

"My dear chap," said Rat sympathetically, for Mole still sniffled to himself from time to time, "if you have the inclination, would you like to tell me what really happened down there in the river?"

"I would," said the Mole fervently, saying nothing more.

"I confess," said the Rat at length, "that I was gravely worried for you. The river is a dangerous thing and few animals, not even myself, would survive if they fell through the ice as you did."

"No," said the Mole, "I don't suppose they would."

"Yet you did, Mole, and here you are back home again, and no one more glad, more happy, more *pleased* than myself."

"Yes," said the Mole, staring at the fire.

"So —" began the Rat again, puffing at his pipe.

"I don't know *how* I survived, Ratty, really I don't. I remember so little about it, you see, except how my concern to get across to your house got the better of my prudence, and how I felt foolish to have tried so dangerous a thing, even as the ice threatened to break. Then it *did* break and I could do nothing to save myself, nothing at all except grasp a floe and hang on! Then I felt that — in that dreadful dark icy water — and I couldn't think or breathe — I really couldn't — I mean I knew, I believed, I was sure I was going —"

Poor Mole was quite overcome by the memory of those terrible moments, and the Water Rat sensed that the best thing was still to do no more than make murmured noises of support. Then, when the Mole's sobs and tears threatened to quite overwhelm him, the Rat put down his pipe, got up, and put a comforting arm round his friend's shaking shoulders, and still said nothing.

"But – but – but –"

"You take your time, Mole, for there's plenty of it now. Don't try and hurry yourself because I'm not going away till you send me away."

"No, don't go!" cried the Mole, who in his distress did not quite understand, and then: "I'd rather you stayed, *much* rather."

The Mole was silent a good while longer, but then seemed a little more settled, and the Rat felt it safe to go back to his own armchair and take up his pipe.

"When all's said and done," said the Mole at last, "I *don't* know how I did survive. It's all rather vague, really, rather strange."

"But you remember something, even if it is vague and strange?" murmured the Rat.

"I remember –"

The Water Rat was surprised to see the Mole suddenly sit forward in his chair as if he had seen something in the fire, which perhaps he had, for he stared at the flickering of the flames, and into the deepest reds and mauves of the embers, his eyes open, his face alert, and he continued quietly thus: "I remember that I was sinking into a darkness deeper and darker than any I had ever known or imagined before. More than just towards the river's depths, of that I'm sure. It was cold, fearfully cold, and there was a peace in the oblivion towards which I was going, and an endless sleep, and I wanted to go there, Ratty, I really did. I felt I could go on no longer, not fighting the cold and the swirling current and the ice."

"Yes, I remember that. Then – and then –"

Now the Mole leaned forward even more, and the Rat put down his pipe and leaned forward himself to stare into the fire, as if there, together, they might somehow summon forth once more the memory that was eluding Mole.

"Ratty," continued the Mole, casting a glance at his friend as if to be sure he was still there and attentive, "we have said from time to time that we know there is Beyond, have we not, but have never been there, and cannot imagine it?"

"Yes," said the Rat softly, very surprised and a little awed.

"Well, as I slipped towards what I had thought was eternal sleep, I had the strangest feeling, almost a vision really, that there was a Before, just as we have said there may be a Beyond. And no sooner had I remembered some dim memory of Before, and something that had happened, than I felt, or thought I felt, Him there."

The Rat remained very still and quiet when the Mole spoke these words, as did the Mole himself, so that the only sound in his parlour was the soft crackling and shifting of the fire.

"I felt I was taken up in His arms out of the dark flow of the river, up into the night, and then placed down somewhere warm and dry where I could go to sleep knowing that when I was ready I would wake once more in a place where the river meanders up into a blue distance, and where there are mountains shining with the sun, and – O Ratty, do you understand?"

The Rat nodded slowly, his eyes never straying from the fire.

"As I was thinking that, knowing that, I said, 'Stay with me' and He said – He said – O, I wish I could be sure of this, or remember it better, but it flows and ebbs in my mind, it shifts and swirls, like the dark currents of the river itself, coming from who knows where, and going to somewhere else. Yet I am sure that He replied, 'They're still there, your friends, and they will be waiting for you, Mole. Your time is not yet, nor theirs.' "

Mole was quiet again and slowly sat back, tears on his face.

"Ratty, I don't know quite what He meant by that, but when those words were spoken I thought of Badger, and of Toad, and of my Nephew, and of *you*, Ratty, of you – and all the animals of the River Bank, and the Wild Wood. I thought of all the places, and the things, and the people that I know and love – and I let myself slip into a different kind of sleep then, for I knew they would be there, waiting for me, when I came back. Just as I knew that the place I thought I saw –"

"Beyond," murmured the Rat.

"Yes, Beyond – just as I knew then as I know now that it will be there for us, waiting for when we're finally ready to go to it –"

The Mole said little more, for it seemed he was exhausted by striving to regain these memories. He slept awhile, and the Water Rat watched over him, building up the fire when it began to die, and placing a warm plaid about his friend, for the wind was getting up outside, and there was a draught from beneath the door.

The Mole had not wanted him to leave, nor would

he, for he knew he was needed for a time and might yet be needed more, for his friend's sleep was restless and sometimes he muttered to himself, and seemed to push out his arms and legs as if to ward off the waters of the river, and to struggle away once more from that endless darkness that had so nearly taken him.

"No!" he cried out more than once, and "I cannot –" and then finally, before he slipped into a more peaceful sleep, saying, "Yes –" and "O yes –"

All of which made the Rat feel surprised, even disturbed, when rather later it was *he* who found himself coming out of sleep, and the Mole who was tending to *him* in a most concerned way.

"Are you all right, Ratty? You were quite distressed and your cries woke me up!"

"My cries? I – I must have dozed," said the Rat a little grumpily.

"A long enough doze to call it a sleep!" said the Mole, who sounded very much more like his normal self. "Look, I have made some peppermint tea and toasted a little of the bread that was left."

The two animals tucked in and when they had done so to their satisfaction, the Mole said, "We've talked quite enough of what happened to me and now it's your turn. What's been happening since I had my mishap? Nothing unusual, I hope?"

"Ah!" said the Rat cautiously. "Not unusual if you have been expecting, as I have for a very long time, that Toad would show some of his old form again."

"Toad!" exclaimed the ever tolerant and trusting Mole, "but is he not altered and reformed? He has been for so long that I would be very surprised if he had slipped back."

"Then be surprised, Mole; allow surprise to overtake you: Toad has done something even more dreadful than anything he has done before. Something I hardly dare to mention on so happy an occasion as your safe return."

"But what?" cried the Mole. "Surely, whatever it is it cannot be so bad that it cannot soon be forgiven and forgotten!"

"Forgiveness! Forgetting! You would be wise not to mention such things to Badger when next you see him. No, Toad has gone far beyond the limits of our endurance, so far indeed that I think I may safely say that we shall never see Toad in these parts again. If he is still alive, which I very much doubt, we may hazard that he is lost to the River forever!"

These were final words indeed, and despite the Rat's reluctance to say anything at that moment the Mole would not let the matter rest till he heard it all, and more. For despite everything, Toad was surely as much a part of river-bank life as they themselves were. "Anyway," added the Mole finally, "he may be exasperating, and the things he does vexatious, but he is, in the end, always fun!"

"Fun?" repeated the Water Rat with some heat. "Fun! Do you call being dragged up into the air fun? Do you call being hurled across the skies *fun*? Do you dare suggest that being thrown at an ever increasing velocity back towards the ground is *fun*?"

The Rat glared at the surprised Mole and clenched his pipe between his teeth so hard that it cracked.

"Fun!" he exclaimed finally, falling into a brooding silence.

"I think, perhaps, you had better begin at the beginning," said the Mole in a quiet and conciliatory way, so as not to provoke the Rat into another outburst.

The Rat duly began his tale with the discovery that Mole was missing, continuing with the first searches for him, and thence to the monstrous appearance of the airborne Toad, and all that it was to lead to.

"And all for me!" exclaimed the Mole more than once during this recital. "All for me!"

Of Toad's trickery regarding the Badger and the pilot-mechanic, and the Rat's subsequent abduction, the truth had to be told, and the Rat did not stint in telling it.

But the more dramatic his account became, the more terrifying his developing ordeal, the more difficult it was for the impressionable Mole not to feel a little of the excitement and adventure that his friend Toad must have experienced.

"I trust, Mole, you are not enjoying this at my expense," growled the Rat, interrupting himself.

"No, no, of course not!" declared the Mole, though without much conviction. "What you say Toad did was wrong, I'm sure, quite wrong, but –"

"*But?* But *what?*" said the Rat warningly.

"Well ..." faltered the Mole, "I mean that – you see – I have never *seen* a flying machine and though I imagine they are quite dangerous things, nevertheless they do seem quite exciting and it's no good me pretending otherwise."

"Hmmph!" said the Rat, frowning. "Be that as it may, having stolen the flying machine, for we may be sure he had not paid for it despite his claims, Toad then abducted me and up into the air we went. Needless to say he forgot all about looking for *you*, so excited and absorbed did he become in flying the thing."

"So he didn't actually crash it, then?" said the Mole. "I mean he did succeed in flying it?"

"Mole, you are trying my patience too far. Of course he flew it – if he crashed it I wouldn't be here, would I? Or if he *did* crash it, and some of us might think that is the very least he deserved, he did not do so till the machine and I had parted company at altitude."

Mole's eyes widened in astonishment, and his mouth silently opened and closed, words utterly failing him.

"Yes," continued the Rat rather more slowly, glad to see that his report was finally having a properly sobering effect on the Mole, "I fell out of the machine, high above the ground, *very* high."

"But Ratty!" exclaimed the bewildered Mole. "Are you all right? You *look* all right. Have you broken bones, perhaps, or bruises I cannot see?"

"Broken bones! Bruises. My dear Mole, if I had fallen to the ground from that height without being slowed down I would have a lot of broken bones, and a great many bruises. Too many, in fact."

"Yes," said the Mole weakly, "I suppose you would have."

"I had a parachute."

"Ah!" said the Mole with relief, not quite sure what a parachute was. "That was just as well then. You think of everything, Ratty!"

Patiently the Water Rat explained the workings of a parachute, and how he came to have one, and how he now rather regretted securing Toad's parachute, for it might mean that he too survived that dreadful flight!

The Rat described how he had come out of the machine, dropped like a stone for what seemed a very long time, and then had his descent suddenly arrested when the parachute opened.

"And then – and then, Mole –"

Mole saw immediately that a change had come over his friend. Till that moment his account had been straightforward enough, if occasionally rather inclined to irritation and annoyance, but now it became something else. There was a curious distance in his voice, and a far-off gaze in his eyes which settled, as the Mole's had earlier, into the ever moving and mysterious depths of the fire.

"Why, what is it, Ratty?!" exclaimed the Mole. "What happened to you up there?"

"It was not what happened to me," said the Rat quietly, "it was what I saw on the way down."

"A very long way, I should think," said the Mole matter-of-factly, not yet quite understanding the extent of the Rat's wonderment.

"Mole," said the Rat, turning his gaze slowly to the eyes of his friend, who saw a look of awe, and a touch of loss, on his face, "I saw more than a long way. I saw Beyond."

"Beyond!" whispered the Mole.

The Water Rat slowly nodded his head, his eyes very serious, and then turned his gaze back to the fire.

"I tell you, Mole, I saw Beyond."

"But what was it like?" asked the Mole.

"It was not unlike a description you gave earlier — there was the river, stretching on and on, curving one way and then another, first between the fields beyond Toad Hall, and then beyond the Wild Wood, and then ever further, on and on till the landscape was strange greens and blues, reds and pinks, and there were hills that were more than hills, Mole —"

"More than hills!" echoed the Mole.

" — and mountains that were far more than mountains, where the river seemed to reach up into the sky to the place which was Beyond —"

181

" – up into the sky!" said the Mole breathlessly.

"And I knew, Mole, I *knew*, that it was there waiting, as it always was and always will be, waiting for –"

" – waiting for us all –" said the Mole very quietly and dreamily.

"I'm not sure, but I think so," said the Rat in a very subdued way. "But from the moment I saw it I knew, or I felt, all sorts of things, strange, vague things that *seemed* unconnected and yet are not at all. One thing I knew was that you would be all right. I *knew* it. And I was very surprised when Badger, who has always been so wise, did not know it, or want to believe it. Then, for another – for another –"

"What is it, Ratty?" asked the Mole, for his friend seemed almost as moved now as he himself had been much earlier.

"For another," said the Rat, "I knew I would one day go there. Since then I have thought of almost nothing else. Indeed, were it not for you being lost, and the winter upon us and travelling foolish and dangerous, I would have long since left to go up-river to find Beyond."

"Well then," said the Mole firmly, "I'm glad I was lost! And I'm very glad it is winter!"

"But I've got this hankering, this restlessness –"

"Ratty, you've always been like that, you know you have. Don't you remember once how after you met a relative of yours, the Sea Rat, it was all I could do to get you to stay here with us? I had to be quite firm about it, and that's not something I'm good at."

"I remember very well indeed," said the Water Rat,

"but this was different. You see, Mole, though you and I have talked of Beyond from time to time, Badger has often warned against even thinking about it. That's why I couldn't tell him what I had seen. But you — I knew you'd understand."

"'Beyond'," repeated the Mole slowly, finding as he did so that all kinds of curious half-memories came into his mind, of summer days when he and the Rat had talked and mused, of that time long ago when they had gone in search of Portly and somehow they had found him on the island, but quite where, or how or — and his own recent experience with the river and the memory of He that saved him. Was that Beyond as well?

"Yes," said the Mole at last, "I think I understand. Well, we'll just have to wait and see what happens, Rat. Perhaps you did see something, and perhaps it will ache in your heart for a time, and perhaps it's as well that such sights and memories fade with time, and become less irksome. Why, the spring will be with us soon, and the sooner the better with the severe winter we're having. When it comes we'll forget all those dreams again in the excitement of going out and about once more."

"I'll never forget!" declared the Rat. "And nor will you!"

"Perhaps not," agreed the Mole finally; "now tell me what happened *after* that!"

But the Rat had lost interest in the rest of his tale, and finished it in no time at all, ending with how the Badger had found him, and how the Badger had behaved most peculiarly and had seemed in a great hurry to bury

Mole into memory and be done with it all.

"Then you appeared from the river, and you know the rest —"

"Not all of the rest," said the Mole, "for there's Toad to worry about."

"You mean there's Toad *not* to worry about any more."

Mole laughed.

"Old Toad will come back, just as I did," said the Mole. "I was saying to my Nephew only the other day that life wouldn't be the same without Toad. I'm sure Badger will forgive him, as he always does – as you yourself have surely begun to do already."

"If he does return then I pity him, for Badger will be ready and waiting, and so will I. And so should you be. Badger may forgive him as you say, but not *too* easily, I hope!"

"He'll still come back, and we'll be glad when he does," said the Mole finally.

"Hmmph!" said the Water Rat, and that was the last thing either of them said before sleep finally overtook both right where they were, and the candles guttered about them, and the fire died, and they fell into the deepest, kindest, most blissful of slumberings, which lasted all the longer that they had both been through so much, and needed time to rest and recuperate, just as wise Badger had guessed they would.

· IX ·

Rack and Ruin

The Mole was right to warn his Nephew about that winter. It was a hard and savage one, so much so that the high tca the Badger had promised to hold for the weasels and stoats was first delayed for a few days, and then postponed "till the weather grew more clement".

The Water Rat spent a few more days at Mole End before he sensed that the time had come for the Mole to be left alone again, while he himself wished to get back to his own house and make any repairs necessary following the flooding of the river.

Such matters, so tiresome and difficult to the Mole, were as nothing to the Water Rat, for he enjoyed the vicissitudes that living so near the river brought him, and without them so restless an animal might easily have grown bored.

A good many days passed, and finally became some weeks, during which the winter storms raged, bringing rain and hail, and wind and sleet of a kind and variety that made Mole and Badger and Rat, in their different homes, feel grateful that they were as safe and snug as they wished to be.

The Rat was the most active of them all, and once in a while he would cross the river, if it was safe to do so, and make his way up to Mole End to make sure his friend was all right. He had been more troubled than he cared to admit by the Mole's misadventure and now, with a new relish, he was glad to have him as a friend and neighbour to call upon, and looked forward more than ever to sharing the coming busy days of spring, and the lazy days of summer.

Then too, when the weather looked settled and a little less cold and wet for a time, if only for a few hours, the Rat would stroll along the bank by way of Otter's home, casting an expert eye on the river's flow, and the clarity or otherwise of the water, before going on into the Wild Wood to see if the Badger had decided on a date for the tea he had so rashly agreed to host.

"Can't keep putting it off forever, Badger," he observed during one such visit, "and the sooner you get it over the better. Some of the weasels are beginning to complain, and as for the stoats, well, you know how awkward they can be if they get irritated."

"I'll decide about it tomorrow, or the next day," grumbled the Badger, who rarely had guests in his home, which was what had made his invitation so appealing in the first place.

"After all, they did help as they said they would," prompted the Rat.

"They did, they did," continued the Badger, fixing Mole's Nephew with a frowning stare as if it was all *his* fault, though in fact he was enjoying the youngster's company, "but it's not easy, what with the weather being unpredictable, and me being not quite ready to mount a feast, the winter being a poor time for such affairs —"

"Just a cup of tea will do, I'm sure," said the Rat.

"And some scones," added Mole's Nephew who, like his uncle, was fond of his food.

"And clotted cream, no doubt, and strawberry jam!" exclaimed the exasperated Badger. "Where am I to find such things, as *well* as plates and saucers and teaspoons? My dear Rat, you are a very unreasonable fellow if you think my larder and cupboards are packed ready and waiting for such an occasion!"

The Rat looked about the Badger's modest quarters amiably, and without feeling in the least put out by the Badger's plaints. He looked at the worn elbows of the Badger's old dressing gown, which he habitually wore all day at that time of year to keep himself warm. He glanced at the threadbare armchairs ranged about the

Badger's fireplace, reflecting that they would look a lot more threadbare had not Nephew taken it upon himself to cover the worn parts with some lace doilies he had found in the recesses of the dresser; and yet more forlorn, perhaps, had not Nephew also taken it upon himself to keep the Badger's fire ablaze, for that was something he was inclined to forget about from time to time.

The Rat looked too at the kitchen table, upon which were spread some of the learned Badger's books and papers, which it might be difficult, even unkind, to disturb and tidy away for something so uncharacteristic of his home as a tea party.

But the Rat reflected also on the happy celebration when the Mole returned, and how the unsociable Badger, drawn out of his lair by all the excitements and to-do of the Mole's disappearance, had by the end seemed to rather enjoy the company and companion-ship of a celebration.

Perhaps, after all, it *was* unreasonable to expect the Badger to organise a tea party all by himself, and that he needed an animal with rather more experience than the Mole's young Nephew who was willing enough, no doubt – and was certainly right to mention scones as a starting point for the edibles – but who lacked the authority and tact to be firm with Badger.

Then, too, a promise *was* a promise, and the Water Rat saw well that unless something was done, or at least some invitations sent out and a date fixed, the weasels and stoats might get restless and cause difficulties that might lead to a resumption of the hostilities that had plagued the Wild Wood, and many along the river as well, in times not so long past.

It was plain, then, that the Badger would need some tactful help; and it was plain too, thought the Rat, that the Badger was worried by something else entirely, which explained his strange irritability and distraction of recent weeks. Perhaps –

It is often at moments such as these that something is said impulsively which hits the mark and leads on to better things, almost without anybody realising it, and that is what happened on this occasion.

"We could," said the Rat, "borrow some crockery from Toad Hall! It wouldn't be for long, and Toad is hardly going to miss it, and in all the circumstances even if he hears of it when he gets back he can't complain."

"No," growled the Badger, but so inaudibly that the Rat barely noticed it and carried on with his suggestion.

"The crockery and cutlery and all such things can come from Toad Hall, then, and as for food, well, there will be plenty of willing helpers, I'm sure of that! I mean to say, Badger, if we widened the scope of the tea somewhat, inviting a whole lot of animals and not just those two or three weasels and stoats who have pushed themselves forward, then you might find it all much more palatable."

"Cups and saucers from Toad Hall?" muttered the Badger with distaste, shaking his head. "No, I'll have nothing of Toad's here. That place is doomed to rack and ruin as it is, and I'll not be labelled a pillager."

"Rack and ruin! Pillager!" exclaimed the Rat, rather taken aback by this response. Everyone knew that the one grand place along the bank *was* Toad Hall, so rack and ruin did not come into it. As for pillaging, well!

"We'll return them straight afterwards, Badger. All *you* have to do is to make yourself scarce for half a day by going over to Otter's for the morning, or down to Mole End if the weather gets better, and we'll do the rest. Eh, Nephew?"

"Of course we will."

"Toad Hall!" muttered the Badger once more, slumping into his armchair and looking gloomily at the fire. "O Toad!"

For the first time in the Rat's hearing the Badger uttered Toad's name without anger, or rancour, but rather with a kind of dreadful finality, as one might mention the name of a close relative just passed away. Which realization rather touched the Rat's good heart, and made him see the Badger's anger and rage about all that Toad had done in a somewhat different light.

"Badger," said the Rat carefully, for he guessed that he might be treading on sensitive ground, "I really am quite sure that Toad will come ba —"

"I don't want him coming back!" roared the Badger, rising impressively to his full height and fixing the Rat with an awful glare. "I don't want his name mentioned in my hearing! And I certainly don't want to rely upon his crockery and silver, his table linen and his napkin rings, his cake stands and his cake knives, and any of that wretched paraphernalia with which he surrounds himself — or used to — being brought here into my Toad-free home!"

With that the Badger sat down again, glowering, and

Nephew signalled to the Rat that it would be better if he left.

"He's been like this for days and I don't know what to do," whispered Nephew helplessly, as he saw the Rat off at Badger's front door. "I think he's tired."

"Tired!" said the Rat, grinning. "He's not tired, my dear fellow, he's missing Toad! I should have seen it before. Why, it was staring us all in the face and we never guessed. Badger's always liked having Toad to complain about, always – and Toad has generally given him plenty *to* complain about. You've not been here with us for long enough to remember the days when Toad was truly bad, as bad as bad could be in fact. Why, in *those* days Badger was much more cheerful than he is *these* days. But when he leapt out of his armchair just now –"

"I was dreadfully afraid he was going to attack you, Water Rat!"

"Attack me!" cried the Rat, laughing aloud. "Far from it! I haven't seen him looking better in years! Badger may look fierce a lot of the time, he may even *sound* fierce some of the time, but he's got a warm heart and a gentle disposition. No, I see it all plainly now – this brown study into which Badger has fallen has been a long time coming – ever since, in fact, Toad turned over a new leaf after that business with the motor-car and his near life-imprisonment. Since then we've all made the mistake of thinking that Badger's been pleased to have an altered Toad, and so he may have been on the surface. But deep down, in that kind, wise heart of his, perhaps he knew he had no right to be quite so hard on Toad, and to sit upon him, and crush him.

"Perhaps, after all, he's rather missed the Toad of old. Now, with Toad's disappearance and possible loss, preceded as it was by your uncle's mishap, perhaps Badger may be thinking that he's realized these things a little too late. So though he may seem to be angry, very angry indeed, and *say* he doesn't want Toad's name mentioned, I suspect he thinks of nothing else but Toad."

"What should I do?" wondered Nephew, much perplexed.

"Tell him from me," said the Rat with firm purpose, "that whatever the weather, Mole and I will be setting off from Otter's at nine o'clock tomorrow morning. On second thoughts, make it the day after tomorrow morning, just to give him time to come to his senses."

"Setting off for where?" faltered Mole's Nephew.

"Toad Hall, of course!" called the Rat over his shoulder, as he went cheerfully out into the dusk towards the Otter's house and the river bank once more.

The Rat was as good as his word, and two days later, at nine o'clock sharp, he stood with the Mole and the Otter outside the latter's front door, all of them rubbing their hands and stamping their feet against the frosty cold.

Rutted icy snow lay in the northern-facing nooks and crannies of the river bank, and also amongst the roots of trees along the edge of the Wood, where the occasional winter sun of recent days had been unable to reach it. But on more open ground the snow was mostly gone, replaced now by a heavy hoarfrost which marked and darkened the moment anyone stepped on it.

The Rat had seemed eager to set off exactly on time, and so the other two were surprised when he said, "You two go off now, but don't go fast. I've got something to do here for a few minutes more."

"But, Rat," said the Otter, not understanding at all, "we can wait for you."

The Mole grasped the Otter's arm and led him off.

"It's no good asking him what he's up to, or to try to change his mind," he said. "Ratty's up to something and you may rely on it that the best thing to do is to go along with him. You say we're not to hurry?" he called back as they left.

"That's right, take your time like Otter does when he's after a great big fish!"

They heard the Water Rat chuckling cheerfully to himself as they set off along the bank, but could not quite guess what he was up to. Meanwhile there was much to see, for they warmed up once they got moving and a little winter sun obligingly broke through the pale sky and softened the frosty reeds to their right, and grey river beyond. Somewhere to their left, amongst the trees along the edge of the Wild Wood, a rook scuttered irritably about, and a wood pigeon briefly billed and cooed high in the leafless branches of an oak.

"Not too fast," the Mole reminded the Otter, and the two slowed their pace, and dug their paws deep into their coat pockets to keep warm.

Meanwhile, the Water Rat had slipped back inside Otter's house, and was lurking near the window, watching the dark path that went into the Wild Wood, and led eventually to Badger's house.

He was humming to himself, and after a few moments more of watching he patted his jacket pocket, found his tobacco and set about filling his pipe. But he had only half done so when he stopped, peered out of the window once more, and then went to the front door which he had left ajar.

"Ha!" he said to himself with a certain satisfaction. "I thought so!"

Out of the gloom of the Wild Wood, and moving with a reluctant slowness as if this was not a journey he wished to make and at the slightest excuse he would abandon it and return home again, came the Badger with Mole's Nephew trotting along at his side.

Catching sight of the Otter's front door, which the Rat had by now quietly closed, the Badger said, "There! What did I say! No one in sight. It was all talk after all. All talk! Come on, we're going back!"

"Maybe they're inside Otter's house waiting for you," said Mole's Nephew, not unreasonably.

"Waiting? You mean still a-bed, more like. And here *I* am right on time —"

"Almost on time, Mr Badger, for it is some minutes after nine o'clock."

"Near enough on time, then!" said the Badger with a markedly more cheerful spirit than he had displayed earlier on the journey. "Here I am and nobody else about —"

Mole's Nephew had gone forward and had seen the footprints on the frosty ground left by the others, and the clear evidence that they had already gone off along the river bank.

"Why look!" he said excitedly. "They've waited here for us and now they've gone, but probably only just. If we hurry —"

"Hurry?" growled Badger, turning back once more towards the Wild Wood. "Hurry after animals who do not even have the good grace to wait a few moments for a colleague who was reasonably delayed and who made every effort to make up the lost time!"

"But you *dawdled* along," said Mole's Nephew with some spirit, and much to the admiration of the Rat who was listening to their conversation through the Otter's letter box, "and I told you that the Water Rat said he would leave at nine o'clock *sharp*."

"Well, be that as it may, they've gone now and we have no idea where they are going, or quite why."

"But – but –" protested Mole's Nephew, as the Badger, duty done it seemed, turned back towards the Wild Wood.

"Come along!" said he, with considerable relish. "There's nothing for us to do here now. If they wanted *me* to come with them they should have had the courtesy to wait!"

"Why, Badger!" cried the Water Rat, emerging suddenly from Otter's house and feigning astonishment to see the two of them there. "This is a pleasant surprise, a delightful surprise."

"But I thought you had gone," said the Badger in a very disgruntled way. "There are your bootmarks on the ground and –"

"So I had, so I had," said the Rat, "but I did so most reluctantly and against my better judgement for I knew you would not be long. But 'Come on,' Otter said, 'let's be off!' And even Mole, why what an impatient, untrusting fellow *he* can be! But I said, 'Wait! Badger has always been the most patient and wisest animal I have known, and perhaps we were wrong to leave so promptly. It's not like him to be late, or to give no support to such an enterprise and undertaking as we are embarking upon, not like him at all!' "

"Did you?" said the Badger dubiously.

"I did, but though I hate to say it, such has your dislike and distrust of Toad been these weeks and days past that first Otter and then Mole declared, 'Bother Badger! We can't rely on him any more! Let's be off!'"

"O!" said Badger, considerably deflated.

"But not I, Badger, my friend, not I," said the Rat magnanimously. "I said, 'My instincts tell me he'll be there in good time and so I shall retrace my steps and satisfy myself that I am right. I must confess I was disappointed not to see you here when I got back, so I went inside Otter's house to fill my pipe and, coming out, what do I find? My confidence proved absolutely right. You have come to lead us upon Toad Hall, Badger, and have thus confirmed my own hopes, and I am sure it will restore the confidence of Mole and Otter in you too. Also, you have set an example of probity and tolerance to Mole's Nephew here, the like of which he is never likely to forget."

"I have?" said the Badger slowly, not resisting when the Rat took his arm and led him onto the path which the Mole and the Otter had taken.

"But —" said the Badger, the last vestiges of his resistance melting away before the Rat's ingenious flattery, "well, I suppose we *should* try and let bygones be bygones when it comes to it. Hard though that is in the case of Toad, and in this *particular* case of Toad. The truth is, Rat —"

"Yes, Badger?" murmured his doughty companion.

"Well, of course, Toad must be punished, and perhaps he already has been but, well, I wouldn't want that punishment to be too extreme, too — final as it were."

He spoke very sombrely indeed, and with furrowed brow cast a grim gaze skywards as if there to see some terrible vision of Toad's final struggle at the controls of his flying machine, of his desperate efforts to get clear of the thing in which his own pride and vanity had trapped him, of a final realization of his many sins and omissions and his own moral worthlessness, till, thus spiritually condemned, Toad and his machine plunged to their inexorable doom on the cold indifferent wintry ground far far below.

The Rat and Mole's Nephew shuddered at the terrible vision which the Badger's mute gaze alone had power to put before them, whilst Badger himself shook his head sadly and slowed his pace till he had quite stopped.

"No," he whispered, "even Toad, even he, does not deserve so grim a fate."

Thus beset by sober thoughts of their erstwhile friend, and treading that easy path along the bank which summer and autumn, spring and now winter, led to his unnecessarily vast and inflated domain, into any minute corner of which their own abodes could have fitted comfortably ten times over or more, the Water Rat led Badger on.

Perhaps to brighten things up a little, for the Rat was not an animal inclined to gloom and despondency, he said, "Don't worry, we'll catch them up soon enough —" And but a short while later they did so, which was not surprising because the Mole had finally half-guessed the Rat's scheme, and had persuaded the Otter to pause and sit upon the bank despite the cold, and wait.

So it was that Badger found himself, as often before, at the head of a file of animals heading resolutely for Toad Hall.

"Now, Badger," said the Water Rat, "tell us as we go

along exactly what you meant a day or two ago by describing Toad Hall as 'doomed to rack and ruin'."

"You'll see soon enough," said the Badger shortly, hunching his shoulders purposefully and thrusting his head forward as if to get there all the sooner and show them exactly what he meant.

"My word!" declared the Water Rat as they paced about the rooms and corridors of Toad Hall a short while later. "I really had no idea!"

"Dear me," added the Mole, eyeing the scene with something akin to shock, "I never imagined things could have got so bad so fast!"

"O yes," said the Badger, "they can and they have and that's what comes of spending all your money on splendour and trumpery and not spending a little more on maintaining it. It happened with Toad's father, and now it's happening with Toad!"

The three animals were alone, for Mole's Nephew and the Otter, not enjoying one bit the chilly interior of the Hall, and seeing the glorious winter sunshine that was shining warmly outside it, had gone to sit on the steps that led from the ballroom down towards the main lawn.

The scene inside was grim indeed. Whether from neglect, as the Badger implied, or oversight, or some mischance which might have happened to any structure as vast as Toad Hall, somewhere in the floors above the water pipes had frozen in the weeks past, and had burst.

Had such a misfortune been promptly dealt with the damage might have been kept to a minimum and quickly rectified. But with most of Toad's aides and

199

servants already gone off for the festive break some time before his own less planned departure, and those that were to have stayed behind having left of their own accord following the disappearance and seeming demise of Toad himself, there was nobody about to deal with the burst pipes.

It might well be that some had come back, seen the extent of the damage, raised their hands in helpless horror and departed once more. Whatever the truth, the results were all too plain to see: water damage everywhere. Great stains in the ceilings, the mouldings all ruined, and wallpaper discoloured and in many places hanging half off.

Carpets were covered in fallen plaster, as were some of Toad's most expensive armchairs and sofas, including even the chaise-longue in his summer room, upon which, in better days, he had been wont to hold court to such acquaintances as he could persuade to fawn and admire him. The Badger, of course, had never accepted invitations to such occasions, though the Rat and the Mole were both perfectly willing to eat cucumber sandwiches and drink iced Indian tea with Toad from time to time, and thoroughly enjoyed doing so.

But now, even that chaise-longue, upholstered as it had been in the finest scarlet silk to set off Toad's legs to the best advantage, was ruined by water and the filth it had brought down with it. In place after place the water had run down the walls, or dripped through the ceiling roses and thence onto the floor beneath, there to ruin the carpet, or the polished oak boards.

"O dear!" was all the Mole or any of them could

bring themselves to say when they pushed open the door in the great banqueting hall. Here the floor had not been carpet or oak boards, but beautifully laid and much polished parquet flooring which seemed to stretch its shining reflective way forever till, by great gilded double doors at the far end, which led on towards the kitchens, it reached its end in a huge moulded skirting board, with a wainscot above.

But the floor shone no longer! The water had come down here as well, had flooded the floor, soaked into it, and then on one of those dark and bitter nights past had frozen once more, and in the ensuing expansion had lifted the floor all over. It looked now like the ruts and hollows of a fallow field, ploughed up and left to fend for itself the seasons through.

As if to heighten this effect, and showing the great power of something as innocent-seeming as water, chairs and dining tables, stools and card tables, had been lifted up as well, and were crazily tilted this way and that.

"To think that we had that great banquet here to celebrate the re-capture of Toad Hall from the weasels and stoats those years ago!" said the Mole, while the Badger and the Rat could only sigh and shake their heads, their gaze shifting from one distressing scene to another.

With foreboding the three animals decided to embark upon a thorough exploration of the Hall to see if they might find the source of the trouble, and set in train some temporary repairs. In this, the Rat was glad to note, the Badger took the lead, though less from a desire to please Toad (should he ever return) than from a desire for order and propriety, for it distressed his austere and simple heart to see such ruin and disorder.

Of the journey into the upper floors of the now deserted Toad Hall none of the three was ever prepared to say much, so distressing and terrible did they find it. The flood of water seemed to have come down in two places rather than one, affecting the central part of the Hall, and its right wing. But many of the bed-rooms had fared no better than the reception rooms below, and one of the finest was in much disarray because the great velvet curtains had become water-logged, and dragged down their fittings and half the ceiling with them.

They finally climbed one of the narrow staircases that led into the attic rooms in something like despair, their way lit only by the flickering candle which the Rat, ever the resourceful planner for such ventures, had thought to provide.

As they reached the last few steps there was a sudden blast of cold wind from above and the candle went out.

"Hmmph!" said the Rat, pushing on upwards and thrusting open an attic door.

Cold white light flooded down on them, and wintry draughts, and they immediately saw the reason why: there was a huge hole in the roof with many tiles missing or fallen on the attic floor, and everything was open to wind and rain and snow.

The attic room stretched a long way, leading to others, and that hole in the roof was not the only one, though it was by far the biggest. Nor was it hard to find the burst pipe, or one of them, for the more they explored the more frost damage they found. Here and there, where the water had spread out across the floors and collected in pools, sheets of slippery ice had formed, and both the Mole and the Rat took tumbles before they learnt that it was best to grasp the rafters above for support.

"There's nothing we can do here," said the Badger finally, "and precious little we can do in the rooms below."

"We can cover some of Toad's valuables, and some of the furniture against any further damage," said the Mole thoughtfully.

"Yes, we can, and perhaps put some of the more valuable things and his papers and suchlike into a room which we'll lock, to protect them from thieves," said the Rat.

It was with heavy hearts that they returned to the ground floor and got the Otter and Nephew to help them with these tasks – work which seemed to add up to very little indeed when set against the extensive damage and ruin they had discovered.

"Toad will be heart-broken," said the kindly Mole, who had never for one moment doubted that Toad would return.

"Well, it may seem a hard thing to say," said the Badger, "but I fear that wealth and extravagance does bring this kind of disaster in its wake. What Toad wants with all this space and all these things I cannot imagine. But I cannot deny that I feel sorry for what we have seen today. And –"

But he paused and then stopped, unwilling for the moment to say more.

Their tasks complete, they gathered those few modest wants they had for their tea party into boxes, feeling, sadly, that these few objects – a tea service, a hot water urn, some silver – were likely to be better protected with them than if they left them where they were.

Then, closing the great doors behind them, they went outside once more, breathing the clean air of winter and taking in the ordered scene of the river and the trees beyond with considerable relief after the dank ruin they had left inside.

"What was it you were going to say, Badger, but which you didn't quite finish?" asked the Water Rat.

Badger sighed.

"I was going to say, I was going to suggest rather, that perhaps, after all, it might be kinder upon Mr Toad, for all his folly and his faults and his selfishness, if he never came back to Toad Hall to witness what we have seen today. As Mole has rightly said, it would surely break his heart."

They all nodded sadly, sharing Badger's sentiment, and with heavy hearts and slow steps set off across Toad's great lawn with their few burdens, and thence along the bank towards the peace and harmony, the order and the warmth of their own much humbler homes.

· X ·

Toad's Luck Runs Out

Toad's self-congratulation upon his escape from His Lordship's House was short-lived, for he soon discovered that stealing a chimney sweep's bicycle is a very different thing from riding one.

For one thing, at their greatest extension, its pedals were rather further off than his toes could comfortably reach; for another the hard leather saddle seemed to have all sorts of bumps, knots and protuberances that made Toad sore in places where he preferred not to be sore; and for a third, the handlebars and frame were made of crude wrought iron and therefore very heavy indeed, rather than the fine, strong, light tubular steel he might have hoped for – and for which he would have been only too happy to pay had he had the chance.

As it was this was not a bicycle made for Toad, and his progress down the long – to him almost endless – carriageway was sporadic and wearisome. So that by the time he reached the metalled road beyond, and turned thankfully southwards in what he hoped would be the general direction of home, he was already tired.

Yet flawed though Toad's character was in so many ways, it had certain strengths and resources upon which he could draw if the occasion demanded, and no occasion was more demanding of him than a threat to his life, to his limbs and to his liberty.

It will be no surprise, therefore, that weary and saddle-sore though he already was, and very ready to abandon the bicycle altogether, when soon after leaving the private road and joining the public one he heard the unwelcome baying and barking of a pack of hounds heading in his direction, vigour returned to his thin spent legs. More than vigour indeed, for the baying grew more fearsome, and the barking closer and more vicious.

Toad's legs veritably pumped like pistons at the awkward pedals, and what had been slow progress soon became very rapid indeed as, gasping with that most stimulating of combinations, fear laced with terror, he sought desperately to escape the blood-thirsty beasts that seemed now to be upon his trail.

To add to his alarm there came the dread sounds of a hunting horn, sharp and terrifying, and worse still, the thunder of approaching hooves, and the sickening yodels and cries of huntsmen and women. Then, the final remorseless horror, along the road behind him, and near enough for him to hear, the soft pant pant pant of their mouths, and the gentle pad pad pad of their paws as the hounds came ever closer. Ahead, appallingly, the road steepened and his pace began to slow, and it suddenly dawned on Toad that somewhere along this anonymous, wintry, miserable stretch of road he might finally meet his end.

It was not a pleasant thought, for on those occasions in the past when he had imagined what his end might be – and there had been a good few such occasions, some quite recent – he had always believed that his demise would be a glorious one, a great one, heroic to the last.

A calm came upon him which (though it made the panting and the slavering of the hounds just behind seem all the more inexorable) gave him pause to say to himself what he imagined might be his last words: "I shall stop and turn and face them! I shall confront them! I shall be a terrifying Toad and they shall flee before my courage and ferocity."

In the madness of his desperation – for the calm he felt was entirely illusory – Toad convinced himself that the chimney sweep's broom, if wielded with sufficient confidence and power, would serve as cutlass and blunderbuss combined, and he readied himself for his last stand.

A moment more, indeed, and he might have leapt from his metal mount, broom in hand, climbed the adjacent verge to gain height, and turned to rout the baying hordes – but it was not to be.

Even as he loosened his grip on the handlebars and reached down to take the brush, there was an ear-splitting blast on the hunting horn, a surge of canine paws and snarling yelps just behind his rear wheel, a clatter of horses' hooves onto the road behind him, and in his abject fear and fright Toad's front wheel wobbled and mounted the verge that was to have been his bulwark and front line.

Toad shot forward over the handlebars, turned head over heels through the air, and plunged deep into the leafless and prickly hedge.

He had some final sense of slobbering tongues about his face, and scenting snouts upon his clothes, and a fleeting image of the bellies of flying horses, and the flapping of hunting red, before all was darkness, and all a growing silence made the deeper for the gradual retreat of those sounds and persons and animals that had brought him so very near his end.

Painfully, achingly, Toad pulled himself from the blackthorn hedge and looked about. Not a person, nor a horse, nor a solitary hound in sight: only his sweep's brush and bag, and the bicycle, buckled now and useless.

"I fooled them!" cried the panting, bruised and bloodied Toad. "I put them off the scent! So near death, and yet I have escaped! Who would dare not agree that I am the greatest, cleverest Toad alive! Were the hounds of hell itself after me I would escape them! Ha! Ha!"

Thus Toad, sitting on the verge, dressed and sooted as a chimney sweep, satisfied himself that his luck was the product of his own cleverness. Then, triumphant once more, he rose unsteadily to his feet and eyed the bicycle.

"O metal steed," said he, "it grieves me to leave you here, for you were faithful, like no other, and you gave your life for me! I shall give you an honourable burial, and ever remember you in my prayers!"

With some difficulty, for it was heavy and every muscle and bone of his body ached, Toad took up the bicycle and portered it across the road to the ditch, into which he unceremoniously threw it, lest some busybody or other passing by should see it, and use it as evidence that he had passed that way.

As for the hunt, and what its quarry might have been, which had been of such life and death importance to Toad moments before, it mattered not one whit to him now. He had lived to tell the tale, and tell it he certainly would in the most heroic terms at the earliest opportunity. Meanwhile, he must away!

He picked up his bag and brushes, liberally dusted his face and clothes with soot again to maintain his disguise, and with a resigned and weary sigh, as of the hero who has survived another crisis but expects to face many more ere his return home, he set off down the road once more, this time by foot.

It must be said that by that same evening Toad's hero-ic view of himself had declined somewhat, for already saddle-sore, he was now footsore as well, and hungry, and thirsty. He had hoped that some opportunity for respite might have come from a passer-by, but there had been none at all. His escape from the hunt had convinced him that his disguise was a good one, and so far from having any fear of meeting people he now positively yearned to, and was coming to the conclusion that the road he was on was as minor and as unimportant as could be.

But just as passers-by were absent, so were crossroads, and, therefore, any hope of changing direction towards somewhere busier, which might offer him greater opportunity. He had no inclination at all to try crossing country, not only because he had little idea where he was, but also because a chimney sweep upon a road might pass muster, but one perambulating the fallow fields and jumping the dykes was sure to arouse suspicion in a hostile world. So Toad plodded on, hopeful if not fully confident that his persistence would finally be rewarded.

The glimmer of a chance did not come till dusk began to settle in, by when in addition to various aches and pains, hunger and thirst, there came upon Toad the first painful tinglings of the bitter cold which would only get worse as the winter's night drew in.

It was indeed a glimmer that he saw, in the gathering gloom, to the right of the road ahead. Coming nearer he saw it was the light at the windows of a delightful roadside cottage which even in the near-dark Toad could see was of the kind whose simple garden borders would burgeon forth with snowdrops and daffodils the moment winter was past, and whose elevations would be bedecked with honeysuckle once summer had come.

For now, he told himself that he could surely expect a warm if simple welcome from whatever common peasant or labourer lived there, and perhaps the overnight use of the barn he espied nearby. Surely all the more so, he mused as he went confidently up the garden path, seeing that he himself would appear a common fellow from a similar station in life to those in this humble house and thus worthy of their sympathy and temporary support.

"On my return to Toad Hall," Toad vowed silently as he rat-tat-tatted at the door, "I shall send these poor folk some provisions to see them through the winter, out of gratitude for what they are about to do for me."

But any further good intentions Toad may have had were nipped in the bud when he heard a rough and assertive female voice on the far side of the door say, "Is that you, ducks?" followed by something even more odd as far as Toad was concerned: "Look lively, you lot, Pa's home!"

The door was quickly opened, and Toad got a much warmer welcome than even his normal over-confidence gave him any right to expect.

For there she was, vast in a lateral sense, huge in her greeting, monumental in her embrace.

"Lord's me!" said she, grasping the surprised Toad with a brace of arms as rotund as plump pheasants, "it's my beloved come home at last!"

Nor did this mistake in identity falter one bit when thrusting him from her, but holding him up-right with a passion that was almost savage, she said

"Ducks!" again, and kissed him first on one sooty cheek and then the other.

This greeting so astonished Toad that for some moments he was quite incapable of speech, let alone rational thought, and all he could do (as she held him up and eyed her Adonis adoringly) was to stare dumbfounded, first at her, and then beyond the threshold of her – no, *their* – home.

The children – *his* children, as she seemed to accept – stood by the bright hearth, all five of them, all boys of descending size, all rotund, and all sooty replicas of something between her and, well, himself. On the mantel, quite unmistakable, was a daguerreotype of a bewhiskered sweep complete with brushes, beneath whose sooty form were inscribed in an uneducated hand the words, "Our Gramp".

Above this, attached to the walls as if it might be a hunter's trophy from the good years gone by, or a weapon brought home from the crusades, was the final evidence Toad needed to tell him to where Fate, so malign, so unjust, so malevolent, had brought him: an ancient sweep's brush of polished hickory, its brass screws and ferrules as bright as a sergeant major's buttons.

"Welcome home, Pa!" chorused the quintet of youths, their smiles bright as the brass above their heads.

It must be said that for a moment Toad actually weakened. He was perhaps over-tired from the long day, and over-strained from his close shave with the pack of hounds. So that, though he realised that he had arrived at the very cottage where the sweep he had earlier duped actually made his home, and that due to the brilliance of his disguise the sweep's wife had mistaken him for the sweep himself, Toad was tempted not to disabuse her of her mistake.

In this moment of weakness Toad saw the advantages of his plan in a rosy light. For one thing there was the hot meal that was undoubtedly his for the asking, for he could smell it, and see and hear something like a thick stew with dumplings simmering away upon the range. For another, drink was certainly to hand as well, for there hanging above the hob, ready and willing, was a large pewter tankard all ready to be filled with beer or cider or some other rustic brew.

But the temptations were not purely gluttonous. There was a large and comfortable armchair in full view of where Toad stood, upon which, had he had the chance to examine it more closely, he would not have been surprised if in such a warmly domestic establishment as this, there might have been a plaque upon which was inscribed, "Pa's Own".

Lastly, and in some ways the most tempting of all, was a little door that stood ajar and through which Toad could see a simple staircase leading to the rooms above, in one of which, he had no doubt at all, was a large, comfortable, soft bed awaiting his hard-used body.

These, then, were mighty temptations, but Toad was not so far gone as to yield to them without some vestigial thought of the consequences, nor to delay matters for a few moments by saying, in what he imagined was a rude and rustic way, "An't yer going to ask me what I bin delallied fer?"

Out of what repository of his former lives these extraordinary words and sounds came from Toad dreaded to think, but out they came, and they served.

"Bless you, Duckie, but yer not even out the cold yet."

"It's that bone-shaker of a bicycle," said Toad, procrastinating.

"Felled off again?"

"Did," said Toad.

"Now I looks at yer face, I can see it's swolled."

"Swolled bad," said Toad.

Those temptations which had loomed so large a moment before now rapidly receded before the dreadful dangers that began to loom in their place.

These were, first of all, the quintet of youths, his sons and heirs it seemed, all scruffy, all sooty, all about to launch themselves upon his person.

"Beware!" a warning voice in Toad cried out.

Then there was the galvanised bath tub he had spied, already steaming, and surrounded by any number of bars of carbolic soap, flannels, towels, brushes, and even – and this surprised Toad in so humble a home – a long and scratchy-looking loofah.

"Take heed!" cried that voice once more.

But lastly, worst of all, worse in many ways than a pack of slavering hounds, was the sweep's eager, potent, gargantuan wife. If she who seemed to love her partner so well knew him so ill that she could mistake him for Toad, to what bounds beyond dreadful imagining might such a woman's passions lead when – there was no "if" about it, not with the bathtub at the ready – she realized that what she had within her grasp was not her husband, but someone *new*?

"Escape this fate while you can," Toad's inner voice wisely commanded.

With a wild and dramatic gesture Toad cried, "Came ter say I got ter work late tonight, my love! Be back afore the dawn!" and without more ado he turned, and ran out into the wintry night, never looking back, despite the heart-rending calls and cries of "Pa! Pa! O Pa!"

But finally these grew faint, as did the glimmering and once welcome light, and for the first time in his life Toad came to see how it could be that the shelter of a hedgerow might be as good and safe a place as any to spend the night.

* * *

Of the days that followed, which were some of the darkest and the bitterest of Toad's eventful life, even he rarely spoke. Whatever he might like to think he was, whatever he might once have known himself to be, the fact was that through those wandering winter days Toad was no more than a common tramp.

His disguise seemed to serve him well enough, but if he fancied himself a Tradesman Chimney Sweep, trained, skilled, and experienced, the world saw him as one who had fallen on hard times, and could no longer find employment.

He found charity enough along the way, and when the weather worsened and the hedge was too cold a shelter, kindly folk would let him sleep in their barn, if they had one, or the pig sty, if it was not already occupied. As for food, well, a bowl of gruel and dry bread was enough to keep him going, and he accepted it with a word of thanks, and a humble doffing of his cap. If words of complaint came to his mouth, or a sense of misery and despair, he had only to remember that pack of hounds, or ponder for a moment the chimney sweep's wife's unwelcome embrace and where it might have led him to, to know that he was lucky to be alive, free, and unencumbered.

Winter, he told himself, would not last forever, and anyway, if only he could get his bearings he might find his way back to the river, and thence to Toad Hall and all the home comforts that awaited him there.

It may seem strange that he found getting home so difficult, but his flying machine had taken him to pastures strange and new, far afield from anywhere he had ever been before, and nothing seemed quite the same on this far side of the Town to which his destiny had brought him. In any case, and this was perhaps rather more to the point, he had a certain reluctance to return to Toad Hall, for that would mean he must face something as unpalatable as those many trials and dangers from which he had only barely escaped. For the Badger and the Rat and the Mole would be awaiting him, always assuming, of course, that the last two were still alive.

How could he *ever* face them? Mole, whom he had deserted in his hour of need! Rat, whom he had to all intents and purposes hurled from his flying machine! And Badger, who had trusted him but whom he had fooled so easily, and left locked up in his smoking room (where, for all Toad knew, he might still be).

So Toad's wanderings, avoiding the Town as he now had to, and the river out of cowardice, were roundabout and aimless. Perhaps he hoped that when spring came he might be allowed to turn over a new leaf, which done, he might slip quietly back into his own domain, reoccupy Toad Hall, and live a modest, charitable life from which all thought of machines and escapades would (this time) be permanently banished.

These cheerless ruminations preoccupied Toad during those lost and wretched days when the world, which owed him nothing, gave him rather more charity than he deserved. Perhaps such thoughts sustained Toad then, and kept him moving on, hopeful in some way of eventual rather than immediate change.

The weather improved, and though it was not true

that spring was in the air, at least winter seemed a little more out of it than before. Here and there a snowdrop showed; and sometimes when he woke and found himself lying on the dank and chilly ground, the bright yellow petals of winter aconite had burst forth with the dawn to cheer him on his way.

It was on such a morning, with the sun shining brighter than had been its wont, that Toad saw that he was approaching a village. He saw its church tower from afar, and was passed more than once along the way by carriages both horseless and horse-drawn, filled with people dressed in what seemed their Sunday best, though it was not Sunday.

"They can't be going to pray," thought Toad, "for they're all too merry for that. There must be a wedding on. Here, surely, I may find sympathetic folk who in the happiness of the moment will give a poor Toad – I mean, a poor chimney sweep – a shilling or two, or perhaps something more. Ah, what would I do to have enough to stay a night in some friendly hostelry!"

Thus Toad spun simple hopes and pleasures as he went along, waving almost cheerfully to the wedding guests as they passed him by upon the road.

"This is certainly a big wedding," thought Toad as he came nearer, and his eyes grew a little more keen. For a sizeable occasion might swell that shilling to a florin, or even a half guinea!

The nearer he got, the greater and more impressive the assembly about the little church seemed to be, what with carriages great and small, two or three automobiles of the most modern sort, all colour, brass and wheels.

There were crowds of guests, the men in formal morning wear, the women in their finest finery, and yet bigger crowds of onlookers, some almost as finely dressed as the guests, others of the lower and common orders and even more rudely dressed than Toad.

By the time he reached the church's ancient lych gate and stopped to stare, it seemed that the guests had all arrived and had gone into the church and out of sight. The groom had long disappeared into the interior and though Toad made efforts to find out who the lucky pair might be, no one was much interested in talking to him, for they were all eagerly waiting for the bride to arrive.

This she soon did, and prettily too, for it seemed she lived in the regency manor right opposite the church and from there she was now processed by her father, a tall white-haired gentleman who walked as proudly as if he were about to marry her himself.

Well might he be proud, for if a couple were going to get married on a winter's day, they could not have hoped for better: bright sunshine in a clear blue sky, a churchyard filled with daffodils jewelled with dew, and those same snowdrops and aconites that Toad had seen beginning to appear in days past, now in full bloom, all busy and eager about the verges and stone walls of village, house and church.

Toad should not be blamed if, in the excitement of these charming moments, he failed to notice some last-minute arrivals. There were, for example, a brace of Bishops, all purple and black and with silvery white hair. Along with these, and a fine complement to them, were a quartet of footmen of the tallest, most aquiline and most senior sort. The kind indeed that one might think would only deign to accept service in, at the very least, a Lord's employ.

Yet Toad did get an inkling of the danger he was in, for following this holy twain and haughty four there slipped out of a black shiny vehicle – discreetly tucked away down a nearby lane – no less than an octet of men in blue: the police! Into the church they plodded, senior officers all, their uniforms giving off that sudden flash of iridescent colour such as an idle occupier of a riverboat might briefly catch a glimpse of when a kingfisher flashes by.

This glimpse Toad caught, and though he did not realise its import at the time, it left him feeling vaguely uneasy, as if he knew something was not quite right but could not work out what.

He shook his head, he frowned, he shivered slightly, and then he overrode his instinct (which was to flee, and flee fast) and fought the pressing crowds to keep his vantage point by the church gate from which to enjoy the wedding scene.

The bride and her father crossed the village green to cries of "Good luck!" and "Bless 'er!" and in they went. By order of the manor a hot toddy and mince pies were handed out to the assembled throng as they waited outside during the wedding service, gossiping and chattering cheerfully till, guessing that the service was nearly done, they began to fall silent in expectation of hearing the wedding march from the organ inside and seeing the church door thrust open, and the happy couple emerge.

Toad was carried away by the spirit of it all, and made light-headed by the availability of free food and easy drink, so that he pushed himself forward with the best and worst of them, raised his brushes in the air, and joined in a song or two.

Having missed the warning signs of the arrival of Bishops and footmen, and failed to respond to the dangers implicit in a police presence, Toad might still have realised his mortal danger when one of the crowd said to him, "Here officially are you?"

"Me?" said Toad, not understanding at all.

"On duty, like?"

The fellow grinned and laughed and Toad thought it best to laugh back. If only he had understood!

"'Ere comes the bride!" the shout went up, for the church doors were being flung open, and the vigorous strains of the wedding march came out into the wintry morning.

At first all was well, for what harm can there be in a happy bride and her new-made groom? What possible threat from proud parents? What danger in aunts and uncles, brothers and sisters, friends and —

"Bishops?" whispered Toad to himself, alarm bells ringing as yet only distantly in his mind as the brace of Bishops he had not seen earlier emerged, followed by one whose purple was even purpler, and whose embroidered chest supported a cross that was ominously larger than all the others, and whose shepherd's crook positively glittered with High Holiness.

Toad gulped and his eyes grew a little wider as he stared upon the face of this ethereal person, for he knew

222

him, and his visage struck sudden terror into Toad's heart. For My Lord Bishop was the same one whom Toad had seen from on high, unwillingly perched as he himself had then been in a hothouse roof.

But even as Toad vainly sought to back away (the crowd now being too thick behind him) the footmen emerged, and with them the ghastly sight of that same butler whom Toad had so successfully bamboozled into serving him sweetmeats and nectars in bed: Prendergast.

"Him!" gasped Toad, suddenly realising that the wedding he was witness to involved, on the groom's side, the son and heir of the House where he, Toad, had been for three days a cuckoo in the nest.

He struggled to back off once more, but it was no use, for the crowd grew thicker still behind him. Then, before Toad's shocked eyes, there issued forth from the church porch more police than he had ever set eyes upon even in his nightmares. Perhaps by now his mind was fevered and he saw more than were really there. But out they came, like bees from a hive, and at their head – the bride's godfather, it would seem – was the Police Commissioner himself.

Was the groom's father, then, His Lordship?

"He is," groaned Toad as he too emerged, striving to sink towards the ground, but quite unable to since he was supported by the crowd behind and the church gate in front.

Toad's nightmare now gathered about him apace, and began to overtake him.

A photographer appeared with an apprentice carrying

his paraphernalia, which was set up in front of the church for portraits to be taken. The flashes of the lights were like warning beacons across the heavy seas in which Toad now found himself struggling. Yet still he might escape, he thought, simply by staying still and unnoticed in the great thronging crowd.

"Who would bother with a simple Toad?" thought Toad hopefully, forgetting in whose garb he was disguised.

"The sweep! Bring him out here for luck! The chimney sweep!"

Toad had been espied by the photographer's eager and sharp-eyed assistant. A chimney sweep always brought good luck to a wedding scene, and an extra guinea for the photographer who thought of providing one.

Willing hands reached out to the reluctant and desperately self-effacing Toad.

"No, no!" he cried.

But it was no use, and even as he was hauled out before them all, and placed between the bride and groom — even as that happened, the police and footmen formed a guard of honour, to frame and complete the picture of which (to the shared delight of both the wedding party and the crowd) the chimney sweep, alias Toad, was now the very centre.

Flash! and Flash! again.

"And just one more!" cried the photographer. "Try to smile this time, chimney sweep — you look quite sick!"

O, the merriment! O, the laughter! And O, what a haze of ecstasy Toad was suddenly in. He smiled, he laughed, he guffawed — for he *was* triumphant after all.

He had no need to be afraid. His disguise was perfect and he remained utterly undetected.

"Another!" cried out Toad, exulting in his position, and causing even more merriment.

"My right profile is by far the best!"

O folly! O vanity! O pride! How great and swift its downfall can be.

There was a commotion in the crowd, an accusatory cry, and then a shrieking female voice, all too familiar to Toad, which said, "That's no chimney sweep, that's a toad! It's *the* Toad! The impostor who tried to steal my heart! The –"

And there she stood at the church gate, even more massive in her anger and outrage than she had been in her domestic welcome: the chimney sweep's wife!

"He done away with my old man to take 'is place!" she screeched. "'E's a murderer, I tell yer!"

No charge could ever have been more clearly or more baldly stated, or express so well in its simplicity the heinous crime, the motive, and the victim's suffering as that: "He done away with my old man to take 'is place."

Perhaps Toad spoke, but more than likely he did not.

He remembered a final flash of light – no doubt the photographer's last photograph; he remembered better still eight flashes of blue, and four of black, and two of accusatory purple. Then all was lost forever as Toad was arrested, handcuffed, put into leg irons, manhandled into a shiny windowless automobile and off on his bumpy way towards a dungeon deep within a castle great and grim.

Down long steep stone steps he was escorted, along

rough-hewn corridors and passageways, past bars and impregnable nail-studded doors, till he was held fast and deep and close-confined where hope was gone forever, and bleak despair could surely be his only friend.

Toad was at liberty no more.

· XI ·

Habeas Corpus

The national sensation caused by Toad's arrest – or more accurately his re-capture after his gaol-break some years before – may well be imagined. It is all too rare that so unscrupulous and habitual a confidence trickster and common criminal is arrested in the midst of the Society Wedding of the Year.

The photographer was able to retire immediately upon the proceeds earned from the photographs he had taken of Toad the Terrible, cavorting between the innocent bride and groom, and showing off his right profile. The photographer's assistant needed to be assistant no more, for his career as Photographer to Nobility was established at a stroke.

The arresting officers were immediately commended for their courage and bravery in confronting so desperate a criminal, and promoted Deputy Commissioners to a man. The footmen all found employment as butlers in establishments as widely spread as China, Italy and the United States of America.

The Bishops could not be promoted much higher than they were – though one discovered his ambitions for a different see as a result of the events of that day – but if there were spare cathedrals going they were theirs, and all sorts of ecclesiastical commissions and sinecures came their way.

While the chimney sweep's wife, whose righteous indignation was spread across the front pages of newspapers throughout the land, and in twenty-eight foreign lands and all the colonies as well, received more than fifty offers of marriage by the following weekend.

It was as well she accepted none of them, for bigamy is a serious offence, yet who could have blamed her if she had? For while it was true that her chimney sweep husband was missing presumed dead, the harsh fact was that having so unexpectedly discovered the pleasures of being the heroic aviator who risked his life to save the Town by steering his flying machine so bravely beyond it (all thanks to Toad) he was in no hurry to revert to his humdrum and sooty life – and wife.

But of all this poor Toad knew nothing. Re-captured

and confined as he now was, he had no access to news, or friends, or help. Villains such as he, whose heart seemed stained more than that of any criminal in living memory – must be put away, and utterly forgotten.

"But –" he faltered some weeks later to the only one he might call friend, his gaoler, a talkative but pessimistic man, "won't they at least try me? Won't they give me a chance? I can explain everything."

"They would try you if they could but they can't, for they say there aren't any laws big enough, and wide enough, and terrible enough to try you by," said his cheerful friend. "It's a poor lookout for you, Mr Toad!"

"Is there no hope at all?" whispered Toad.

"None," said the gaoler, "or none that I can see. You're in here for life plus twenty-five years I reckon."

"O dear!" said Toad, slumping.

"But look on the bright side," said the gaoler, who liked to try to cheer his charges up, for he had a kindly heart, "you're getting on a bit so you're not likely to survive more than twenty years or so. It'll go by in a flash!"

But twenty years of prison life did not pass through Toad's imagination in a flash at all, but rather dragged by, long second by second, tick–tock–tick–tock, or as slow as the drips of water from the roof of his dank cell, and as aimless as the cockroaches which trod their heavy way across the granite flags beneath his iron bed.

"What's the charge?" asked Toad, some time later.

"Charges plural, you mean. Charges manifold. They do say they are too many and too great to name."

"Is there no hope?"

"None."

"No news?"

"None."

"No – sign of anything at all?"

"Hardly any."

"*Hardly* any?" repeated the desperate Toad, sensing if not quite a glimmer of hope, then at least a distant chink of light.

"Shouldn't say this, Mr Toad, but they're thinking of having an identity parade."

"For who?" whispered Toad with widening eyes, for far from finding hope in this he saw only further trouble.

"Can't say more, Mr Toad, as I've said quite enough. Now eat your bread and dripping like a good fellow, and would you like a second mug of cold water, seeing as it's Sunday?"

Toad shook his head and sighed.

"I'm not very hungry or thirsty," he said in a very small voice.

"Well, I'll leave it there all the same," said the gaoler, and went on his way.

An identity parade! Could there be doubt about who he was? Of course not! He was Toad, the reprehensible escapee Toad, they knew that. No, the only possibility was very grim indeed, it meant that Toad had been accused of some additional crime, and his accuser was to come and pick him out, just to be certain.

Toad bowed his head, and sighed again.

"I am lost and forgotten forever," he told himself. "I have no friends to care for me, and if I had what could

231

they do for me now? Nothing. Yes, Toad is forgot."

Great tears came to Toad's eyes and rolled down his cheeks and fell with audible plops upon the ungiving stone floor.

"Forgot," he whispered once again, and wept.

Yet Toad was not forgotten at all. His name, for those few days after his capture and before other more salacious news displaced him from the scandal sheets and daily papers, was on every lip and elicited much excitement. More than that, so serious were the implications of his suspected crimes considered to be, so profound the possible threat to society, so very grave the threat to national security if such a trend continued, that questions were asked not only in Parliament and Privy Council, but in the Mansion House and in the Royal Courts of Justice too.

All of which meant that the matter of the infamous Mr Toad attracted the attentions not just of the popular press, but also of *The Times*, in which it was granted a single paragraph of type, somewhere below the Agricultural News.

Now, it was many a year since a newspaper from the Town had found its way anywhere near the inhabitants of bank and river, meadows and Wild Wood. Indeed, the only newspaper most had ever seen, and those were the rare and lucky ones who had at some time in their lives won the confidence of the Badger sufficiently to catch a glimpse of a copy he had framed on his wall, was that which carried the report of the Jubilee, which was back in his great-grandfather's time.

But somehow, some weeks after Toad's incarceration, a copy of *The Times*, or rather that fell paragraph of print concerning Toad, found its way to the Badger, who, having read it, summoned the Mole and the Rat forthwith.

"My friends," he said gravely, "I have bad news."

"It *is* Toad," said the Mole, spontaneous tears coming to his eyes as he saw the Badger raise the newspaper up to read aloud from it, "just as I said on the way here!"

He addressed this to the Water Rat, who sighed and said, "I fear it must be," and they both sat down disconsolately.

"It is indeed," said the Badger, not quite sensitive to his friends' assumptions, and distress. "It certainly is."

"Read it," said the practical Rat.

"I was about to," said the Badger. What he read out was printed under the forbidding headline "TOAD ARRESTED" which was followed by a second headline: "FULL CHARGES TO BE BROUGHT WHEN ALL HIS CRIMES ARE KNOWN".

The paragraph succinctly set out the long list of wretched crimes and felonies which all the circumstantial evidence pointed to Toad having committed, and said much else besides. It spoke of weddings ruined, of brides distraught, of Lords and Bishops, and the police, and it exposed the attempted abduction of an innocent wife, a crime of the lowest and most scurrilous kind. It left no doubt that Toad was guilty, very guilty indeed, and the only question remaining was how exemplary and how savage must his sentencing be.

"What does it mean?" asked the Mole, who did not understand at all.

"It means that Toad's got himself in a mess again," said the Rat reasonably. "But at least he's not — he hasn't passed away as we feared, Mole."

"It means that it is a mess Toad is unlikely to get out of this time," added the Badger.

"Is there nothing we can do?"

"Against such evidence, when Lords and Bishops and police and wronged wives have been invoked?" said the Badger. "I doubt it very much indeed. I suppose that a successful plea might perhaps mean that rather than being quartered, he might be merely hanged."

"O my!" said the Mole softly. "I feel quite unwell."

They sat in silence, ruminating sombrely, for this was so far out of their domain that they saw no way to help their errant friend.

"One thing's rum about it all," said the Rat last. "In fact, I would call it peculiar."

"What's that?" said the Mole almost indifferently, for what was the point of musing on it when nothing could be done?

"There's no mention of the flying machine, is there? That's right, isn't it, Badger?"

Badger sat up, suddenly a little more alert.

"You *are* right," he said, examining the newspaper once more. "That is most observant of you and it is certainly, as you put it, very rum indeed. I must think."

The Badger began to think very hard and went into so profound and impenetrable a silence that the Rat and the Mole eventually left him to it, and set off towards Otter's house.

It was the time of year when winter seemed almost done, but spring had not yet quite shown its face. Snowdrops and the catkins of alder are all very well, and certainly signal the stirring of something or other, but what animals like the Rat and the Mole really want to see and feel is bright warm sunshine on the budding branches, and what they yearn to hear and smell is the rushing song of the smaller birds busy about their broods, and the first balmy scents of the bluebells through the wood, and the violet on the banks.

Then, too, both knew full well that winter was quite capable of asserting itself again, and bringing upon them all its cold and rain, winds and hail, as if to say, "I'm soon going for quite a time, but this is just to remind you that one day I shall be back."

"Ratty," said the Mole, as they drew near the Otter's place, "do you think there's any hope at all for Toad? Or should we try now to forget him, remembering him sometimes only in our wishes and prayers?"

Mole said this so gently, and in so caring a way, that it almost brought tears to the sturdy Water Rat's eyes. Yet, what hope could there be, given the mess Toad had got himself into? Why, not even Badger –

"I think," said the Water Rat cautiously, "that if there's anyone hereabouts who could find a way out for Toad, however slim and slight it might be, it would be Badger. I don't know what he was thinking about when we left him, but that he *was* thinking there can be no doubt. We both know that when Badger thinks like that things tend to happen. So we'll just have to wait and hope. Now, let's see if Otter can cheer us up with a warm drink and better news than we've had so far today."

Badger certainly did think, hard and long, barely moving from the chair that the Rat and the Mole had left him in till nightfall, when he rose slowly and stiffly, stretched and, lighting a candle, went into his study and sat down at his desk.

It was many years since he had been moved to write a letter, and never before had he felt sufficiently moved by the importance and injustice of a matter, that he must address his letter to that most august and revered personage, The Editor of *The Times*.

But so he did, marking the envelope clearly in his bold hand: PRIVATE AND CONFIDENTIAL, NOT FOR PUBLICATION.

Such was the result of his thoughts, and when morning came he summoned to his presence the swiftest and fleetest of the stoats, and began to address him thus:

"We have not always seen eye to eye, you and I. Nor can I say that in the matter of the promised high tea in these modest rooms of mine I have behaved with the speed I should have. That can be rectified, and it will be. But there are some things harder to rectify, before which, when we face them, we must all forget our differences and fight for the common good."

"Yes?" said the stoat dubiously. "What particular thing have you in mind?"

"A grave miscarriage of justice," said the Badger. "Now, listen to me. You will take this letter and, using all your cunning and experience of the Wide World beyond the river, you will deliver it as addressed."

"What's it all about?" asked the unwilling stoat.

"Ask not what it's about, but who it's about," said the Badger. "It is about Toad of Toad Hall."

"Ah, yes – Toad," said the stoat, not without a certain respect and awe in his voice, which Badger did not miss, nor was surprised by. Toad's escapades held a sorry fascination for the stoats and weasels, which one might expect, given their general low character and untrustworthy nature. Like with like. But at a time like this, needs must, and the Badger needed stoats, and this one in particular.

"Will I, too, get an invitation to this tea you're having?" he asked.

The Badger smiled slightly and reached behind him to his mantelpiece, from where he took down a stack of elaborately printed cards on which in the most scrolly and embossed of lettering shone and shimmered the word INVITATION.

"One of these shall be yours," said the Badger, "if you take this letter and deliver it as I ask."

The stoat's eyes glittered and glistened with social greed and expectation.

"Personally inscribed by me with your own name," aded the Badger.

"And shall I be sitting on your right-hand side?" asked the stoat in a soft insinuating voice.

Badger blinked at the boldness of it, bit back the words he might normally have spoken, and said, with some effort, "You shall!"

The stoat did no more than sigh and reach forward to take the letter, before he turned and was off on his mission.

"I can do no more," whispered the Badger to himself, shaking his head sadly, for he cherished little hope that his words would hold much sway in the offices and corridors of the most influential in the land. "We can only hope –"

Hope was very far from Toad's mind some days later when the heavy door of his cell was heaved open, and his gaoler, along with three of his largest colleagues, strode in.

They chained and manacled their dangerous charge once more, leaving him only sufficient movement to shamble and struggle along the ancient passageways of his place of confinement, and then up its endless stone steps and stairways, which he saw now were worn and slippery with the downward passage of so many long-forgotten criminals.

"Not that way!" cried his pessimistic friend, grasping Toad's arm and directing him away from the especially grim and oppressive corridor into which his laboured steps seemed automatically to have led him. At its end was a set of bars beyond which was an archway leading out into the open air, where, caught by the first sunlight Toad had seen since his incarceration, was what was unmistakably a hangman's noose, swaying invitingly in the morning breeze.

Toad let out a gasp of dismay, but his gaoler reassured him. "It's all right, sir, you're not on today's list."

"List?" faltered Toad.

"Of the finally and irrecoverably condemned."

"Where am I being taken?" gasped Toad, sweat breaking out on his brow.

"To your Preliminary and Final Hearing," said the gaoler, urging him on up a last few steps.

"Preliminary and Final! Isn't there a Court of Appeal?" asked Toad.

"That's been and gone in your case, sir. The Court you're going to is as Final as they come. So final, in fact that it's almost pointless to go through its doors, but one never knows, there might be an upset."

"An upset!" cried Toad, desperately grasping at

straws. "There has been an upset before then? When?"

"In 1376, sir, in the case of Saint Simon the Innocent. That was the last time," said the gaoler dolefully.

Each dragging step that Toad now took rang out about him like the tolling centuries and he dared not even raise his eyes when, brought finally to an immense oak door, the gaoler knocked upon it.

There was a long wait, during which Toad could hear his own heart beat, before a thin voice called out from within, "Bring in the prisoner!"

The door opened and Toad was led forward into an immense and echoing chamber, whose ancient arched windows rose before him and sent down such shafts of light into the dusty interior that for a moment he could see nothing more. But as his eyes adjusted to the light he saw that set beneath the windows, lengthways, was a vast oaken council table, on whose far side were ranged seven great high chairs, within whose imposing confines sat seven imposing figures, berobed, bewigged, long of face, cold of eye, aquiline of nostril, and judgemental of general disposition and effect.

"Clerk, help the prisoner to the chair," said the most severe-looking of them all, who sat in the centre, and was the High Judge.

Toad's gaolers had fallen away, to be replaced by a bent and aged man who gesticulated Toad forward with impatience, but not towards some dock or lectern where Toad might have found some physical support, and some cover behind which to hide his shaking form. Instead, his footfalls, chains and manacles all echoing out his obvious guilt, Toad was pushed towards something

more fearsome by far than any dock, even the infamous dock of Court No 1, Old Bailey.

It was a chair, huge and hard – so huge indeed that the Clerk produced from somewhere a small wooden step, that Toad might clamber up and be seated in a seat far too big for him. A seat so immense that his back was not quite supported, nor his knees quite far enough forward to go comfortably over its front edge, and so high that his legs and feet dangled down but could not reach the floor. The chair had immense wooden arms upon which, securely fastened with great hammered bolts, were metal restraints which had the general demeanour and character of thumb-screws. The Clerk raised Toad's unresisting arms to these and fastened him so that he could not, had the thought come to him and he been tempted to turn it into action, make a run for it.

"Is the prisoner comfortable?" asked the High Judge.

"As much as he's likely to be," said the Clerk.

"Are you?" asked the High Judge.

"Yes," said Toad hoarsely, faintly hoping that if he was polite and agreeable his punishment might be a little swifter, and a little less harsh.

"We know each other, do we not?" said the Judge.

Toad squinted through the dusty beams of light and saw that they did indeed: this was the Judge who had been at His Lordship's House when Toad was there; the same Judge who had once, as a mere Chairman of Magistrates, sentenced him so severely for a trifling offence. Toad's head swam with despair as he saw he could expect no mercy here.

"Do we not?" pressed the Judge.

"We do," whispered Toad forlornly.

"You are then Mr Toad, of Toad Hall?" the Judge said with resignation.

"Yes," bleated Toad, for it was no use lying.

"The infamous Toad of Toad Hall?"

"I suppose so," said Toad.

"Not a good beginning," said a different Judge, "not good at all. He only supposes so!"

"I am then," said Toad very, very politely.

"Hmmmm," said the Judge and, with the others, fell into a silence which deepened by the second and quite robbed Toad of any hope.

But then he dared have a thought.

"Sirs, Your Honours, Your High Lordships," he cried, "is there a lawyer who might represent me?"

There were seven sharp intakes of breath, and seven more sighs of disappointment, and a sevenfold pursing of lips.

But worse was to follow: finally, one by one, they smiled, ghastly smiles as it seemed to Toad, like fiends offering poisoned crumpets and butter to a teatime guest, and one of them said, "Toad of Toad Hall, why should you need a lawyer when you have us?"

This was followed by another long silence, which itself was followed by a dry interrogative noise: "Eh?"

"Am I to answer?" faltered Toad.

"You are, and much may depend on your answering correctly! Why should you — ?"

"I don't need a lawyer, or counsel, or help at all!" cried Toad. "I am happy, very happy, with you all."

"Let that be noted!" said a sharp voice. "The prisoner thereby expunges, exterminates, obliterates, and dismisses by his own admission all his rights, privileges, prerogatives, powers and perquisites to be represented here by another or himself and agrees forthwith to be interrogated, assessed, tried, considered, examined and judged without recourse, help, respite or care by us in the sole, exclusive, inalienable, immediate and eternal duty vested in us by their Lordships, the Bishops, all five of the Police Commissioners themselves answerable, though that is now too late and beyond possibility, to the Monarch himself and all his heirs and issue for ever more. Eh, Mr Toad?"

"Yes," said Toad who understood nothing but that all hope was now gone forever.

"The prisoner agrees!"

At this, and rather to Toad's surprise, the seven Judges rose to their feet to shake hands and congratulate each other before resuming their seats once more and their general sombre demeanour.

"Bring forth the List of Charges, Clerk!"

The list, which was so lengthy that it had been bound between leather covers and had various markers in it for ease of reference, was brought past Toad from somewhere behind him, and placed upon the table.

One of the seven Judges – Toad could never be quite sure which was to speak, or which had spoken – opened the book and pored over it before reading, "Toad of Toad Hall, whereas it is known that you did on the eighteenth day of –"

The horrid words charged towards Toad like so

many wild horses and overwhelmed him, and trampled him where he sat, so that his head was dizzy and he saw stars before his eyes. On and on they went till, like grey light at the end of a long, dark night, he heard this: "Therefore, Toad of Toad Hall, you are here charged as miscreant, felon, and common criminal with –"

The horses came galloping back again and charged him down once more, so that, breathless and beaten, Toad could only whisper his reply, when finally asked, "How do you plead?"

"Guilty, My Lords."

"To all one hundred and sixteen charges – ?" began another of the Judges.

Toad gulped.

" – including the attempted abduction of the said sweep's wife, and her five children," continued a third Judge, "and the damage, extensive and absolute, to property internal and external of His Lordship the –"

"Yes, yes, yes!" cried Toad, unable to sustain the awfulness of sitting in so terrible a place.

"Not to mention, though we must and should, the theft in the second and third degrees, and attempted manslaughter in the fourth degree –"

"It was all me," said the abject Toad, "all me."

"It is a pity," said yet another Judge, "that you have shown no remorse or shame for what you have done, for we have some power to mitigate. Some small token of regret, and pity for your victims, or a sign that you could learn from your mistakes –"

"I do feel shame," cried Toad, "I do feel regret, and

not only for those victims you have mentioned, but for others too. O, I do!"

"Others?" whispered the High Judge in the centre. "Did you mention others? Are they not all listed?"

"O no," said Toad, weeping real tears of contrition (and hoping that the sight of them might ameliorate a little the sentence that was soon surely to be passed), "for I also let down Mole, and I may have been the cause of Rat's death."

This unexpected confession produced a sudden silence, but of rather a different temper than those that had gone before. It was a silence of puzzlement, even of dismay.

"Mole? Rat? Who may they be, pray?"

"Friends of mine," wailed Toad. "O, I did not mean to leave Mole to die," wailed Toad, "or to have Rat fall out of the flying machine, but you see there was something so magnificent about it all that I got carried away for a moment and so without knowing what I was doing, and quite without any premeditation or forethought, I –"

His confession came tumbling forth and went on a very long time, yet they heard him out and when he had finally finished they sat once more, staring at him in silence.

"Clerk, bring forth the evidence that we may re-examine it for inaccuracy, and a tendency towards undue leniency," said one of the Judges, "or find some support for these claims the prisoner has now made."

"Hear! Hear!" cried all the others, falling into jovial and cheerful chatter among themselves while they

waited for the evidence to be brought. The evidence –
all twenty-one quarto volumes of it, close printed, and
each leather-bound like the List of Charges – eventually
arrived, pushed in by the Clerk's Assistant and neatly
stacked upon a silver trolley, as if it was roast beef all
cooked and ready to be carved up in the private
restaurant of the Royal Courts of Justice.

The re-examination of this material took some
considerable time, during which Toad wilted yet
further, the only relief being that the shaft of light that
had been upon him at the beginning shifted somewhat
to his right side.

"No mention of the Water Rat here," said the High
Judge with a terrible sigh, "nor any of the Mole either,
it would seem. Nor of the flying machine you make
claim to have flown."

The High Judge looked up at Toad and frowning the
deepest and most thorough frown yet said, "This is
grave, Mr Toad, grave indeed. To the one hundred and
sixteen charges already brought and officially listed must
forthwith be added eighteen more of false claim, of
impersonation, of subjugation of mechanical property,
namely a flying machine, of –"

There was something about this mention of the flying
machine – his flying machine, his beautiful bright red
and glorious flying machine – that stirred in Toad's
breast some last faint spark of rebellion. For if he had
understood aright, they were daring to suggest –

"But –" he began in protest.

"But?" thundered the Judge.

Toad blinked and struggled to raise himself a shade

from the semi-supine posture into which his chains and restraints, combined with fatigue physical and emotional, had forced him.

"I wanted to say —"

"He wants to say something voluntary and gratuitous!" cried the Judges in concert.

Toad looked at them and continued, quietly it is true, yet with a growing resolve and spirit which would not now be stopped.

" — to say," he continued, "that it was *my* flying machine, and I *did* fly it, and I'm sorry if it careered about the Town somewhat and disturbed people, but —"

But Toad could say no more, for he had no more strength, no more hope. Two great tears coursed down his cheeks. They could take his liberty, his life even, but they could not, should not, take away his memories of that great and glorious flight, a memory that was all he had to sustain him in the hard times to come – whether through the long years of incarceration, if that were to be his fate, or in those final moments when they took him down that cold passageway that led to his last moment in the sun, and the hangman's noose.

But then, when he had done, there came into the dusty and disbelieving silence that followed his final faltering claim (or denial as no doubt they saw it) a new sound: the Clerk coughed.

"Ahem!" he went.

Then "Ahem!" again.

But if this was meant to draw the attention of the Judges to some point of procedure they had over-looked, it failed, for with a suddenness that took even the now passive and resigned Toad by surprise, and caused him to start up, the High Judge declaimed the following: "The prisoner having been examined, con-sidered and found utterly wanting on all counts and probably several more, the verdict will now be given, and the sentence served and the consequential punish-ment (for we may reasonably pre-empt matters by assuming on the strength of the evidence and the pris-oner's paltry submissions that guilty it will be) brought forward to the earliest opportunity, unless there be any here who –"

"Ahem!" coughed the Clerk once more.

"Yes, Clerk! Have you anything to say? Should I have put on my black cap already, is that it?"

"My Lord, there are the depositions on the accused's behalf."

Nothing, not even an earthquake, could have had more effect on the seven Judges than this simple reminder from the excellent, and orderly, Clerk of the Court.

Yet the High Judge retained his composure (though the others gasped for air, and mopped their brows, and undid their legal collar studs and, in two cases, removed their heavy wigs) and said with admirable understatement, "Depositions in the plural?"

"Three, My Lord, or rather, as I am given to understand, two associated pleas on the accused's behalf, and a query concerning his identity."

"Are they ready?"

"And bound in leather, Your Lordship."

A last tome was brought in, this one so light and thin, so inconsequential-looking in all respects, that it was carried by the Under Assistant to the Clerk's Assistant.

"Just for the record, Your Lordship," said the Clerk, to cover himself.

The Judges eyed the slim volume with distaste till one of them, with an "I suppose we must at least glance at it", opened it, and glanced.

"But – !" he declared, visibly nonplussed at what he read inside.

"But – !" said another, passing it to the third.

"But," said he, "*this* deposition from no less a personage than –"

The clear and mighty lettering at the head of the thick white notepaper of the document that had caused such a stir was unmistakable, and put awe into all their hearts, for it was from the Editor's office of that newspaper so august and mighty that it could be said that it was to truth what the Bank of England was to sterling.

"Need there be more than *this*?" it asked of the seven rhetorically.

The deposition was read, followed by the two other documents, and Toad was astonished to hear two names whispered by the Judges, in the same breath as that of the Editor of the greatest newspaper in the world. One of the names was Badger, and the other was Mr Prendergast.

"Impressive indeed," muttered the High Judge.

"Things are beginning to look good," whispered the Clerk into Toad's astonished ear, "and there could be a turn-up."

Toad stared, his future now in the balance once more.

"It comes down to the issue of identity then," said the High Judge finally. "Though is he not Toad and therefore guilty? Has he not said as much?"

"Ahem!"

"Yes, Clerk, speak if you will."

"The last document by the aforesaid Prendergast is ill-writ, but it does say, if I may paraphrase for Your Lordships, that the accused is more than a Toad, he is more even than a pilot. He is *the* pilot. He is —"

Seven pairs of beady eyes examined the last-named document once more, seven pairs of lips pursed, seven pairs of brows knitted, seven pairs of eyes narrowed and, having read whatever it was that was ill-writ, looked up and gazed on Toad.

"Is this witness Prendergast to hand, and ready to identify the prisoner?"

"He is, My Lord. He awaits your order."

"Well then," said the High Judge almost indifferently, "our hands are tied, and sentencing cannot and should not commence till this matter is cleared up. But then, if the accused proves to be the Toad we think him to be, well, that will as it were put the seal on his fate, will it not? Eh, Clerk?"

"Yes, My Lord, I think it will."

Bemused and bewildered, and yet caught once more upon the carousel of hope, Toad was unshackled and made free, his body given up to the four gaolers who had brought him there, and dragged off.

"It's to be a parade then, like I said," said his gaoler.

"Couldn't they have done it before?" asked Toad.

"Due process, Mr Toad, due process," said his friend, as if that explained all.

Toad was taken down some steps and up some steps, and round one corner, and back round another, then along and down and up and between, each step of the way involving the opening and closing of gates and barred doors, till he was ushered forth into a courtyard.

"Stand in the line!" he was harshly told.

The line was of eleven other brutal, hardened, desperate criminals much like himself, except that all were much bigger of leg, arm, back and foot than Toad, though their heads were not so swollen as his. He did his best, which was not much, to raise himself up, to puff himself out and to generally make himself look as much like them as he could, for plainly, it would be better not to stand out. He feared that if he was identified, he was done for.

Then another door opened and in came two policemen accompanying a tall man in a morning coat: the butler Toad had not only duped, but endeavoured to bribe. Whatever hope Toad had dared harbour was gone in that moment.

"Have pity on me!" he cried in despair.

"Prisoners be silent!"

"Do not choose me!" cried Toad in the very vale of self-pity and terror, falling to his knees and grasping his hands together as if in prayer. "I never meant it! I got carried away."

"Sir," said one of the policeman to the butler, "is there anyone present whom you recognise? You need say nothing – merely raise your hand and point. Take as much time as you wish."

Slowly the butler's hand came up, slowly his forefinger was extended, and slowly and unerringly it pointed at Toad.

"O!" cried Toad, swaying in his distress, and swooning into the arms of the brutal felon who stood next to him.

Toad awoke in the loathsome chair once more, but this time he was not manacled, chained or restrained, and someone had thoughtfully placed a cushion or two under him, and behind his back.

"To help me face the worst," he thought.

"Prisoner," began the High Judge, "the scales of justice have rarely had to weigh so wretched and hopeless-seeming a case as this. Where do we begin when so many laws have been broken, when so many precedents for wrong-doing and malfeasance set? First –"

He droned on, and on, so long that Toad grew weary, and could not even react when finally he said, "For which the sentence is in each case that you be taken from here to a place of execution and there –"

But Toad no longer cared. He was, he now believed, a lost cause. His life was run, his time nearly over. He would –

" – but on the other side, upon the other scale as it were, we must put the fact, indubitable in the face of the evidence of a witness so full of sobriety as His Highest Lordship's Butler, that this extraordinary Toad, this master criminal, was also the hero of that flight upon which the fate of thousands was to turn."

Toad's ears pricked up.

"Alone, ailing, with nothing but his own courage and intelligence to rely on, faced by a choice of his own life or others', he wrestled with that flying machine and succeeded – we may say triumphed – where all others would surely have failed. Leaping from it only when he was sure others were safe and no damage would be caused, he –"

Toad sat up, enthralled.

" – he who is a hero yet made no claim to be one. Modest, retiring, risking his life a second time, and a third, and a fourth, he sought to escape public notice by

254

a series of brave escapes and stratagems the like of which we have rarely seen. Then, when this brave hero was brought before us here, did he lose his composure? Did he strive to wriggle free and escape in body, spirit or intellect? He did not! He successfully pretended to the part of vile criminal and felon."

"Yes!" cried Toad, truthfully.

"But friends who knew him well came forward and pleaded for him, knowing he was too good and honourable to plead for himself. Of the Editor of the august organ whose letter we have seen we shall say no more: that great citizen demands a veil of secrecy and we shall respect it, and we need not ask from what source of truth and rectitude he first heard of Mr Toad's connection with flying, and so pursued the enquiries whose happy outcome we now know. Yet, since crimes *have* been committed, the law of the land demands a surety in such a case as this, and by good fortune we have it on the good name of the wise and retiring Badger, than whom we understand there is none to be held in greater respect. That detail satisfied, we can rest assured that Toad will return to a good home. Therefore the scales are in balance, and his evil crimes are exactly matched by the greatness of his actions. He shall go free and our judgment is that, unheralded before, he shall go unheralded now, just as he himself would wish it —"

"But —" protested Toad, who was beginning to wonder whether to bring the charge of wrongful prosecution right there and then, or bide his time till he had retained the best counsel he could find, and had enjoyed his triumphant procession through the Town, where he might find a suit of clothes to replace his prison garb –

"Therefore," continued the High Judge, "take him hence beyond the city walls, put him upon the high road that leads back to where he came from, and let no man or woman pursue him more."

"I am free?" whispered Toad, utterly exhausted.

"Free to go, but not to come," was the reply. "Commit no more crimes, or all those sentences of execution eternal will be put back on the list from which they have not been fully expunged, and can never be, and we fear there will be no second chance."

Toad was escorted from the courtroom, bundled into the black and windowless automobile once more, and taken far beyond the Town walls, where he was put out upon the road beneath a road sign pointing south.

"There!" said his gaoler. "Duty done!" With that he placed a shilling in Toad's hand and said, "From His Lordship's Butler, sir. Says he never had so much fun in his whole professional career as serving Toad of Toad Hall in the Master Guest Bedroom."

"He knew me!" gasped Toad.

"Moment he saw your headgear and goggles, sir."

With that his gaoler climbed into the automobile, which turned and left.

Toad stared after it, utterly nonplussed.

Then he looked about him, just to see if there were any Bishops, or Lords, or policemen, or Judges, or butlers about. But there were none.

Just the last of the winter wind, a grey sky, an endless

road and a sign which pointed southwards. It read: TO THE RIVER.

Toad said not a word. He put one foot in front of the other, and set off home without a backward glance.

· XII ·

Winter's End

Winter returned to the river and all along the bank, and into the very heart of the Wild Wood, and with it harsh winds, long days of snow that quite swallowed up every snowdrop and aconite that had showed and other nascent signs of spring, and replaced them with that bitter cold which sends all animals back into their homes once more.

Even the stoats and the weasels accepted with good grace the further postponement of the party at Badger's that had been so long promised, and for which, finally, the precious invitations had gone out.

Yet, for all the disappointment, it would be idle to think that the party, despite the postponement, or even the prospect of spring, was uppermost in animals' minds – though greatly looked forward to those events undoubtedly were.

No, it was of Toad that most thought, and of him for a time that all talked.

Of the Badger's letter, and the mission of the stoat who delivered it, but little was known. The Badger was never inclined to talk of such things, and braggart though the stoat was tempted to be, there was really little that he could say. It was enough that he had earned one of the few invitations that had gone out to his kind, and enough that he knew that the Badger would honour it.

But with his return, a great deal of news came back to the river: news of Toad's heroic struggle with his flying machine to prevent it crashing upon the Town (as it was reported); of Toad's subsequent escapades and crimes and achievements (as his follies were variously described); and of Toad's incarceration and hearing before the Seven Judges ("It was a hearing, *not* a trial!" Toad's defenders insisted).

So too did the news, more important still, that Toad, by his own brilliant representation of himself and with a mite of Badger's influence and that of Lord Prendergast (the butler had been elevated ever higher with successive telling of the tale), by these and other devices as yet unknown, Toad had been given his liberty and set upon the road back home.

Such matters had served to preoccupy all those along the river before winter's ill-timed return.

Then, when Toad had not come, and the days had grown dark with winter once more, and there was still no sign of him, the discussions grew more worried, and more grim. Some said his experiences had been so terrible that he had been driven mad and was even now wandering the countryside not knowing who he was or where to turn; others were certain that Toad was now bored with the river and Toad Hall, and had set off for pastures new never to return. Perhaps, too, he had heard of the ruin of Toad Hall and had not the heart to return.

A third group, and in this must be counted the Mole, the Water Rat and the Badger himself, was more silent, and more worried. For the winter *had* grown severe once more, and it seemed quite impossible that Toad could survive long in such weather. True, he would no doubt have found somewhere warm and comfortable to see the bad weather out – but he had surely had opportunity enough to send a message to them.

More than that, of his own accord, and without either the Mole or the Badger knowing, the Water Rat had taken advantage of the days before the weather worsened to journey the open roads searching for Toad. But he had failed. Wherever he went there was neither sight nor sound of him.

The Rat had come home disconsolate, almost caught up himself in the renewed wintry blizzards, and had reluctantly reported what he had found – or rather, not found. So there was little enough cheer about the river in those hard long weeks, and one by one the animals became silent on the subject of Toad, and fearful, including Mole, and Rat – and even Badger.

Winter's attempt to thwart the spring finally began to peter out in April, and the party, long awaited, could no longer be delayed. The Badger's honour was at stake, as the Rat had said before, and if there was any more procrastination then with the warmer weather now on the way, who would have time for a get-together in the Wild Wood?

Certainly not the river animals, for already the river was astir with the gentler and more positive life of spring, and there was much to do, and much to see.

"It's this weekend or never!" the Rat told the Badger firmly, having brought the Mole and his Nephew, as well as the Otter and Portly, along for support. They all nodded grimly, though the two youngsters were nervous of this role which the Water Rat had thrust upon them, and would certainly have turned tail and run if the Badger had growled loudly and expressed his irritation.

But he did not.

He knew not only when he was beaten, but when the timc had come to do the right thing, and he gave in with good grace.

"We'll have it this weekend, just as you say, Water Rat – and the rest of you! We had better send out a new set of invitations after all this delay – Mole, you can help me check the list and you, Nephew, can organise the distribution. We have to be absolutely certain that the right animals get the right invitations or there'll be all sorts of trouble.

"Now, Otter, I've had a word with you already about the food, and I believe —"

The Otter nodded enthusiastically. He was liked and respected all along the river — probably further afield than any of them — and had long since readied his troops for the preparation of a feast the like of which the Wild Wood was unlikely to see again.

"The helpers are all just waiting for you to give the word, Badger, and I tell you, those involved are looking forward to it, though it beats me why. But some people positively like baking and cooking and basting and steaming and —"

The Badger raised a hand to stop him.

"My dear chap, no doubt they do, but I prefer not to know. If you start telling me what's involved I'll take fright and postpone the whole thing again —"

"Say no more, Badger; all you need to do is to take the place of honour and declare the feast begun! We'll do the rest!"

"Now," said the Badger, turning to the Water Rat, "I want you to attend to details in my home — it goes without saying that with stoats and weasels about the place we had best lock all my valuables away. I regret to say this but I really think we had better search animals as they leave, so —"

The Rat laughed and said, "I have to thank Mole for a suggestion that may deal with that matter *most* effectively, Badger. Mole, perhaps you can —"

The Mole came forward to address a meeting that was

rapidly beginning to sound like a war council, and said, "You'll remember that I had to deal with those untrustworthy fellows during that time some years ago when we had to wrest Toad Hall back from their power?"

"None of us have forgotten, Mole," said the Badger appreciatively; and while the Mole brushed this aside with a modest gesture, his Nephew's snout went pink with pride and pleasure on his uncle's behalf.

"That's as maybe," said the Mole, "but the fact is that I learnt that the weasels and stoats are driven by twin evils – greed on one hand, and vanity on the other – and we must use the second to control the first!"

There was a quality in the Mole – firmness combined with common sense, with a dash of ruthlessness as well – which only emerged in situations such as this. He was indeed a friend upon whom an animal could rely.

"Go on," said the Badger.

"Well then, I suggest we issue attendance certificates to those who come, and let them know that we shall be doing so – certificates suitably inscribed in copperplate upon vellum, which they can frame and put upon their wall. We shall let them know these are to be issued – but that since we shall be using Toad's crockery and silver we are honour bound to protect it to the last. Which being so, if so much as one sugar spoon goes missing, then *no* certificate will be issued to *any* animal. That should keep them in order!"

The Badger laughed heartily and said, "Mole, behind that quiet and self-effacing exterior, do you know what you are? A brute!"

For a further two hours the plans were laid, the orders given, and the guest list revised and checked.

"And now," said the Rat finally, "there's only one thing left for you to do, Badger!"

"And what's that?" growled the Badger, who had been showing signs of impatience once again, for the planning had gone on rather longer than he had expected, and he had learnt that various females would be coming in to his quarters to spruce things up a bit – and he did not like it, not one little bit.

"I'm not going to ask you to do it," said the Water Rat very firmly, "I'm going to *order* you to do it, for your good and everybody else's."

This was bold indeed, and a hush fell over the Badger's parlour as they waited for his reply.

"Well?" he said in a low and dangerous voice.

But the Rat did not falter. He stood up, he faced the Badger square on, and said, "You are going to take a little holiday, Badger. If you stay here while the preparations are made you'll grumble and grouse and nothing will get done and everybody will get irritable. Therefore – and I have already discussed this with Mole – you are going to live in his home for the days till the party itself."

"I –" began the Badger in protest.

"And while you're there you will help me inscribe the certificates!" said the Mole quickly.

"I –"

"Won't you, Badger?"

The Badger's mouth closed slowly and then opened again. "When?" he said.

"Now," said the Water Rat. "Pack a bag and off you go!"

"Well —" said the Badger, out-thought and out-manoeuvred for once, "well —"

He frowned. He growled. He thumped about a bit. The only thing he did not do, before he gave up his home to the tender care of Rat, and allowed Mole to lead him triumphantly away, was to let them see that despite his frowns and grumpiness there was in his eye the light of good humour, and the pleasure and satisfaction of knowing that few animals had such friends as these.

Yet as he left with the Mole at his side he turned impulsively back and said in a voice full of emotion, "Water Rat! And you others! Let's make this party one that no animal is likely to forget! Let's do so in memory of one who cannot be with us, and may never now be. One who for all his faults will be sorely missed! Let us make such a celebration of friendship and the winter's end that all who came to it will say, 'Had Toad been there, *that* was a party *he* would have enjoyed.' "

It was a very touching moment, for it was the first time since Toad's disappearance that the Badger had expressed so clearly the true loss he felt. Indeed, if by the end of his rousing words his voice was a little rough, a little choking even, and his eyes moister than they had been – so much so that when he turned once more to leave he took the opportunity of brushing aside a tear – then it was all no more than the others felt; and, yes, this *would* be a party that Toad might have enjoyed.

The next few days passed rapidly, and if the weather stayed inclement, and winter would not yet admit defeat and be gone, the spring-like mood among the animals of river, of bank and of Wild Wood made up for it.

Before long it was as if every animal alive was involved one way or another with the coming festivity. What with the preparations of food (in which the rabbits took a leading part) and the choosing of drink (wherein the weasels and certain of the stoats could not be excelled) and the decoration (and here certain of the Otter's female friends emerged from an anonymity in which he might rather they had stayed), the highways and byways of those parts were busy with the comings and goings of those with tasks in hand.

The Water Rat, relying heavily on Mole's Nephew as his second-in-command and general factotum, kept close watch from his headquarters. which is to say the Badger's bedroom. Here he had placed all Badger's valuables and most-treasured possessions, along with Toad's silver till it was needed, and to the door he had affixed a padlock for which he had the only key.

At the same time, when it became known that numbers were strictly limited – and in this respect alone the party differed from any of Toad's, to which any Tom, Dick or Harry was inclined to be invited to swell the numbers – there was a certain amount of rancour. There were even claims that one or two of the invitations had been traded on the black market, though these were so scarce that the going rate was very high indeed. But in fact, those unable to attend had long since decided to hold their own celebrations, and to invite their own particular friends and neighbours, and many said (though these, needless to say, were only those not going to the Badger's party) that *personally* they felt that the party *they* were going to was definitely the only one worth attending.

Quite what the original purpose of the party had been was now forgotten, and the general feeling was, as the Badger himself had said, that the celebration was in memory of Mr Toad, and all that Toad Hall had once represented; and in addition to that, it *had* been a long winter, and why not raise a glass or two in celebration of its end?

But what of Toad Hall? Was it as ruinous as people said? Sadly it was. The harsh days of winter's renewal had caused more pipes to freeze and more flooding, and now the wind had forced its way behind some of the shutters, windowpanes were broken and the place was growing more derelict by the week.

It was only in deference to Toad's memory – now a wholly revered and heroic one in the popular imagination, if not yet in that of his closest friends – that none had yet despoiled the place further, or sought to loot it, or occupy some corner of it. But then, everybody knew what had happened in years gone by when the weasels and stoats had taken advantage of another of Toad's enforced absences, and none could doubt that if such advantage was taken again, then the wrath of the Badger, and of the Water Rat, and of the Mole would know no bounds.

Added to which, and here the cunning Water Rat was the culprit, there was a rumour abroad that Toad Hall was haunted, and not a place to go near at all.

"That'll keep 'em away like nothing else!" declared the Rat with satisfaction, when he told the Otter of his clever ruse to keep Toad Hall safe till the proper authorities could come in and seal it, or whatever they must do, when spring finally came.

"You're a clever animal to think of that," said the Otter. "But – are you sure it isn't really haunted?"

"Of course it's not. Never was and never will be. But don't let on, Otter, just spread the story about a bit."

By the party's eve all the preparations were done, and the Rat went to bed, with Nephew tucked up beneath one of the tables already laid in the parlour and ready for the morrow afternoon, both feeling that theirs was a job well done.

The Rat could do with some sleep, for in addition to his other duties he had felt it best to find time to cross the river in his boat to visit Mole End, just to see that all was well with the Badger, which indeed it was. The Certificates of Attendance were all done, and the Badger had enjoyed some days of unwonted peace, made all the easier and more enjoyable by the hospitable Mole's attentions.

So when, with the Rat already asleep and Mole's Nephew nearly so, and the night advanced, there was a rat-tat-tat at the door, the Rat was not well pleased to be woken up.

It was one of the senior stoats.

"Sorry to disturb you, Water Rat, but there's trouble at Toad Hall. One of my own youngsters saw a ghost —"

"But it's not —" began the Rat impatiently.

"I know it's not haunted, you know it's not haunted," said the stoat with a knowing wink, "but fact is 'e saw a light, and if 'e says 'e did, 'e did. Intruders, likely as not."

"Well I'm not fool enough to investigate anything in the dead of night," said the Water Rat decisively. "If there's time, I'll go and have a look in the morning. Now I suggest you get back to bed just like I'm going to —"

Later, when the stoat was gone and Badger's front door securely bolted once more, Rat said to Mole's Nephew, "Might be true, might not be. Hard to say. Could be one of their little schemes to get us both out of here. Well, it hasn't worked."

"Will you go over in the morning?"

"I will," said the Rat, "and Otter can accompany me, for you'll be needed here."

The next day, the day of the party, was fine, and guessing that once it began he would get little rest till the following day, the Water Rat decided to investigate the stoat's claim with the help of the Otter, and to get some fresh air while he did so.

It was a pleasant walk, for the day was warmer than

any previously and spring really was in the air. The mallards were back on the river, and in the water meadows on the far side many of the wintering geese had already departed, and the others were testing their wings. While all along the bank was a sight that never failed to stir the Rat's spirit, and warm his heart: the willows, in bud so long, were showing signs of leaf at last. Not much, it is true, but there were enough touches of green to hint at the gentle, swaying glory that would soon be theirs.

They approached Toad Hall with some misgiving, for it was a forlorn place now, with broken windows and here and there curtains blown out of them, lying bedraggled and untidy on the sills. Yet for all that it was an impressive sight, vast and grand, and all it might need was resolution to put it right once more.

"And money, plenty of it," said the Rat. "Come on then, let's have a quick look about and then be gone."

They took up what sticks and wood they could find as weapons, lest they disturb intruders, and quartered the ground floor.

"Shall we bother with the floors above?" asked the Otter.

"Just the next, perhaps," said the Rat, "though there seems to be no sign of life that I can detect."

"None at all," said the Otter.

They searched the first floor, but no more than that, for time was passing by and the Rat was anxious to get back to the Badger's home to oversee the final preparations.

"You had better come with me, Otter, for if any of

the guests come early we'll need an extra pair of sturdy hands to keep order. Mole's bringing Badger over this morning as well. Come on then, let's leave this dreary place."

They returned to the daylight once more, threw down their weapons on the lawn, and were off along the bank, finding it all too easy to forget what lay behind them now, in anticipation of the pleasures that lay ahead.

Of the start of the Badger's party, and its progress into the clear mild night, little need be said, but this: some parties have all the ingredients for success – the food, the drink, place, the occasion and the company – and yet do not quite come off. It is as if some extra ingredient, mysterious and unidentifiable by anyone, yet whose absence is recognized by all, is missing. This is how Badger's party was.

The Badger tried his hardest to play the affable host; the Rat positively danced about in his determination that all and sundry should have a good and memorable time; the Mole's courtesy to even the rudest and most brutish of the weasels should have melted the heart of all, and been enough to make the party swing.

But it did not. There was a solemnity about the occasion which none could seem to find a way of lifting. However good the food – and it was lavishly inviting; however excellent the drink – and it was more than that; however eager all were to have a good time – and all were very eager indeed, a good time was had by none.

Smiles were strained, laughter cracked, jokes ill-timed, and that black spot that marks a party doomed was upon it well before midnight.

"What," whispered the Rat to the Mole, "are we going to do? This is, well —"

"Desperate," said the Mole feelingly, "that's what it is, and the Badger's reputation will be sorely dented tomorrow, if it is not already tonight."

"Desperate is the word," said the Rat with resignation. "I just don't know what's wrong, or how to put it right."

"There's no way to put it right," said the Mole sorrowfully, "for what's wrong cannot be put right."

The Rat looked at him with surprise and interest. The Mole rarely spoke thus gloomily, and in the Rat's experience once you knew what was wrong with a thing it *could* be put right.

The Mole shook his head, as if he read the Rat's thoughts.

"Not this time, Ratty. You know what's really wrong? We're missing Toad, every single one of us. *That's* the trouble, isn't it?"

The Rat heard this and thought about it for a very long time till he finally said, "Yes, old fellow, I'm afraid it is."

Desperation would have been too mild a description of the mood that had overtaken another creature that night. The only creature, indeed, who had received no invitation to any party, whether it was the Badger's, the weasels' and stoats', or even the rabbits'.

All he could do was wander abroad in the night shadows of the bank, and the Wild Wood, and down by the river, and listen to the sounds of fun he could hear, and peer in unseen at others' windows and wish that he too might be one of them. That creature was Toad. He had come back the previous night, skulking along ditches, hiding among the river reeds, and in the Wild Wood's undergrowth; and retreating for a long time under the bridge while some festive souls conversed above his head – so happily, so cheerfully, so excitedly, so generously.

It had taken him many long weeks to get this far, weeks when he had skulked across country and down dale, under hedge and by old rough surface root, as he skulked now by night between river and Wild Wood, with only the cold stars and a risen moon for company.

In that time Toad convinced himself that he was neither villain nor hero any more, but just Toad, almost Toad with a small "t", so sorry did he feel for all he had done, and all he was.

It was not the flying machine, or the scrapes into which he had got himself – these things he could bear the memory of easily enough. No, it was the friends he had betrayed.

"Mole, Ratty and Badger!" he had fallen to whispering to himself ever since he had been left upon the road outside the Town. "Why could I not see how fine and worthy they were? Much finer and much more worthy than anything I could ever be! Why was I so dazzled and deluded by machines and flight and seeking the attention of others

273

when there, on my doorstep, I had all I could ever really want?

"Friendship was mine for the asking! And companionship! But all I could do was take, and dupe, delude and cheat. All I strove for was to show how clever I was, and how —"

When Toad got into this kind of vein he was inclined to go on for a very long time, and he did so now, ending much later thus: "I see it all now, far too late. I duped them all! I failed them! I caused them trouble, and upset and grief, and in return what do they do — or what does the Badger do? He stands surety for me! He — O, but it is too much to think of, too much to bear."

It is true to say that Toad had come home because he had nowhere else to go. Along the way he had frequently been recognised and either reviled as a villain (which he did not like) or cheered as a hero (which irked him in his mood of new-found remorse). What he wanted was the friendly acceptance that he used to have, more or less, from those who lived near Toad Hall, and for this he had finally come back.

He had timed his arrival the previous evening so that he would not be observed, but it had been light enough for him to see at a glance the derelict state into which the Hall had fallen. When twilight came it looked even worse, and at night, by the solitary candle which was all he dared light, it looked yet worse still.

Peering out from the attic windows, or from the huge holes he found in the roof tiles, he looked upon a night-time scene he had forgotten that he loved.

274

For there was the river by starlight, there the Wild Wood, there the river bank and beyond the meadows.

There too, in their burrows, conversing with each other no doubt, content, their homes filled with life's best and simplest pleasures of food and conversation and conviviality, there would be friends he now knew he did not have the courage to call on, friends he would probably never see again.

How pathetic would his sad face have seemed to any able to see it, as he gazed from the portals of his ruined home upon a landscape wherein he felt he might never again be at home.

"I'll stay a night or two, for old times' sake," he told himself, "and then I'll be gone! I shall be a wanderer without a home and leave all this trumpery, this vainglory, behind me. I shall dedicate my life to a search for the inner contentment that has always eluded me. Unsung, shall I be; unremembered; unknown, a toad without a name."

Toad soon fell asleep to the sound of his own lorn voice, and it was his candle then whose light the young stoat had seen, and which had duly been reported to the Water Rat.

Indeed, it was the visit of the Water Rat the following morning that had woken Toad and sent him scurrying for cover. But used to hiding as he was, it was not so hard as it might once have been for him to lie low while his old friends searched the place below.

But at least he had seen that Rat was alive – that much he could clear from his conscience; and when he heard Rat mention that Mole was alive, and Badger staying with him, Toad could deduce that both were well.

"Farewell, Rat! Goodbye, Otter!" he whispered after them when they left. "I shall remember you. And you, Mole, and Badger, so wise and forgiving – you will never know that this night a reformed and altered Toad thought of you, and wished you well!"

So they left, and Toad spent the day of the party alone in his own home. Feelings of remorse apart, he quite enjoyed himself, for the sun was shining and, never able to dwell on reality for long, he began to imagine what the Hall might be like if it could be refurbished some-what, an opportunity presented by its present state in a way never presented before.

"I'm bored with red and scarlet," he declared impa-tiently, "and those velvet drapes! It is a good job they've fallen down! As for all this furniture, why, it's been get-ting me down for years! Hmmm!"

Then Toad ventured into the kitchen, and found cer-tain provisions still intact, as well as some claret laid down by his father decades before, and made him-self a little feast – just to keep the wolves at bay. He made do with a writing bureau in his study as a table, choosing the sunniest spot he could find, and ate and drank his fill, ending with a little speech to the empty room on the subject of change, remorse, interior decoration, and the pleasures of a well-stocked cellar.

This done, Toad slept once more – taking the precaution of retiring to one of the lesser bedrooms in the south wing, where the bed was but a small double, yet comfortable for all that.

But when he woke up at dusk his gloom returned.

He tried to cheer himself up, but the high spirits of the afternoon — for that was what they had been — had quite fled, and he suddenly found the empty dereliction about him too much to bear. Toad therefore went out onto his lawn and paced about, wondering if he might play croquet by moonlight, or declaim a poem about his coming lonely struggle with life and proposed search for inner peace, perhaps making his address from the balustrade that commanded the best view of the lawn and river beyond.

"From there," he thought, "I might be heard to best effect, if there were an audience. It is a pity there is not."

Feeling hungry again, he went inside, rummaged around the pantry, fed himself by candlelight on an upper floor and said, "It is enough! I shall sleep for the last time in the Hall, and by dawn I shall leave. Then —"

But these good resolutions were interrupted by a stirring at the window where, the panes broken, a light wind fretted the curtains. Somewhere a stair creaked, and a door seemed to slam, and Toad was suddenly overtaken by that irrational sense of fear that any alone in such a great place might feel.

He left the candle where it was, for he had no wish for it to be seen at the window, and went to look out upon the advancing night. The moon was bright once more; a solitary cloud drifted towards it, across it, and away once more, and then another loomed.

Impulsively Toad decided he could not stay one moment more where he was.

"Moonlight will see me down the stairs! I must go —"

Then he was gone, before the moonlight was clouded out once more, down the great stairs, across the ruined ballroom and out onto the safety of the terrace.

There he might have stayed, and slept perhaps, had he not heard some distant shout, or moment of laughter, and the sounds of the conviviality he missed so much.

"That must be the party Rat referred to when he was here earlier," he thought, little knowing what a dreary affair it had so far proved to be.

"It would do no harm," thought Toad, "if I ventured over — though it is rather shadowy by night — and got near enough to Badger's place at least to hear what is going on. A last look at those familiar faces, and then I shall really go!"

With an objective at last in mind, Toad was an animal

renewed. He darted back into the gloomy, creaky Hall, gathered together his few needs – two bottles of wine and several cheeses and water biscuits and suchlike, in case he felt like supper later on – and was on his way.

Here and there he stopped to eat and drink, lest the cold get to him, and to give him courage, for the Wild Wood is not an easy place at night, even to those who walk along its edge.

He went by way of Otter's house, and seeing he was not at home, he took the liberty of popping in – to eat and drink in a little more comfort than was possible along the bank, which did not have the chairs and tables he liked to use if they were available. Toad even slept a little in the Otter's armchair till, waking with a start, he remembered his purpose, which was to get as near to Badger's house as he could.

The path into the Wild Wood looked forbidding, and Toad took an extra tot of the richer of the two wines he was carrying to give him strength and courage.

"I shall do it all at one go, show to shpeak," said Toad, whose enunciation was deteriorating. "I shall – "

Toad paused, and swayed, and frowned, and seemed to think.

"I shall," he said very slowly, "*not* shkulk! I shall not peer and peek! I shall –" and here he took a straight swig from the bottle and nodded his head in agreement at his own words before, wiping his mouth with the back of his free hand, he continued, "I shall *speak* to the Badger! What I shall say I do not know, but say it I shall. Then, that done, I shall turn and leave these parts forever. Now then, letsh be off as besht we can up this

279

dark and sha – shaow – doshowee – shady bath!"

Tottering a little, and seeking support from the occasional tree, Toad began to make his way through the Wild Wood, looking to neither left nor right, and thinking only that when he got to Badger's he hoped he might find courage to knock upon his door.

Midnight had come and gone when Rat whispered to Mole, "No need for you to linger on, old chap. Badger and I will do the honours and see the night out till our guests have gone."

"I thought this was going to be high tea, Rat, not an all-night affair. I wouldn't mind if –"

The Rat smiled and said, "It's what the stoats and weasels expected, a good night of it."

"They don't *look* as if they expect anything at all any more. They look as dull and gloomy as I feel," said the Mole with feeling. "Why, this is the dreariest affair –"

"Off you go, Mole, and take Otter with you – for company and protection. No one will even notice you've gone."

The two slipped away from the table and headed for Badger's front door. They were in the very act of raising the latch when they heard a loud and confident knocking from outside.

Anything was a welcome distraction from the social gathering within, and the Badger himself rose up and said, "A late caller then. A reveller on his way home from some other party, no doubt! Open the door, Mole! Open the door!"

Mole did so and stood back; and there *he* stood: Toad.

He had a half-empty bottle in one hand and upon his face was a look of feigned cheer and jollity.

"I happened," he declared to his dumbfounded audience, "jush 'appened, show to shpeak, to be parshing by and –"

His voice, like his jollity, subsided, and his hand lowered the bottle to his side.

"Ish Badgsher at home, or do I need an invis – invish – ivinashun?"

Alone of them all, the Badger retained his composure. He pushed forward till he was in the midst of the gathering and said, "Toad, you are drunk."

"I have drunk, that *ish* true, Basher old fellow, and I may be merry, very, bu –"

"Toad," growled the Badger in a most terrible way, looming higher than any about him, "you are incapable!"

"I am –" began Toad, his inebriated mind searching for the right words, "intoshicated, but as for –"

"Toad!" said the Badger, his voice low and unforgettable. "Toad –"

"Yesh, Badgsher, I am –"

What was it he was trying so hard to say, for trying he now was? Indeed, he went so far as to place the bottle upon the ground, nearly falling over as he did so, before straightening up again with a strange wild look in his eye, made the stranger by the light that shone on him from within, and the starry night sky behind.

"Badsher," said Toad, frowning, "what Toad wanted to say, to try to shay, to –"

Behind him the Wild Wood suddenly seemed a visible presence – though only the outline of trees could be seen against the night sky, and here and there a branch caught in moonlight. But there it was, and beyond it, a presence too, seemed a great wild and desolate world out of which, so unexpectedly, so typically perhaps, so bravely it was beginning to seem, Toad had come.

Now he stood, still swaying, with that great hostile world behind him, and he sought words he could not find.

"Toad —" said the Badger once more.

"What am I, Badger?" said Toad, with terrible, painful clarity, his swaying stopped now, his head high, his face worn with the trials of a long journey, his eyes lost.

"You are *home*, Toad," said the Badger with a sudden gentleness, "and none is more welcome here than you tonight."

"Home," whispered Toad, "and welcome."

Then something stirred across that tired face and he said, "I shall be good now, Badger, I shall —"

But Badger raised a hand to silence him.

"No, Toad, you will not be good tonight. You will be bad, very bad."

"I will?"

"You will."

"I might," said Toad gratefully, his face suddenly losing years.

"You will," said the Badger, coming forward and ushering Toad in, "and you will tell us about all your adventures."

"Will I?" said the relieved Toad.

"You will!" "He will!" "You must!" cried many a voice, among them Rat's and Mole's and Otter's and many of the weasels', and all the stoats', who now crowded out to welcome Toad home.

"But you won't be wanting a speech about myself, will you? For I have not prepared one, you see, I hadn't thought that —"

"Speech?" cried the Badger. "It's speeches we *want*, speeches we're lacking, and you're just the chap to get us started, keep us going, and finish us off!"

"I am!" cried Toad enthusiastically. "I mean. 'Am I?'"

"You are," said the Badger, "you are – now come in, sit down, and tell us – everything."

It is strange how when a gathering is gloomy the drink and the food and the talk are gloomy too. Then, when it is gloomy no more, the drink sparkles, the food entices, and the conversation is scintillating. So it was then, at Badger's party, when Toad came home.

And the night seemed young, and after but a short time invitations, attendance certificates, and all the rest mattered no more. For whether it was from a weasel who had seen Toad rollicking earlier along the bank, or a sharp-eyed stoat rather later, staggering through the Wild Wood, the word soon got out that Toad, *the* Toad, Toad of Toad Hall, was at the Badger's, and it was open house.

Yet, memorable though that party became, it is not quite for Toad's homecoming that it is now remembered. Nor for the speeches he gave, and the merriment he caused by his vain and conceited account of his adventures and escapades; nor even for the ribald songs he sang of sweeps' wives, and young brides, and butlers.

Nor even for his demonstration on Badger's high table, using his own silver as instruments of navigation, and the Rat's pyjamas as a parachute – and all as the sky began to streak with the light of dawn – of how easy it was to fly a flying machine.

No, Badger's party, the most memorable ever given in the history of the river and the Wild Wood, is remembered for something more.

For as the dawn rapidly advanced, and the entertainment had spilled over onto the clearing outside the Badger's front door, the Mole was heard to say to the Rat, "Old fellow, tell me, have you heard the expression, 'Red sky at night, shepherd's delight; red sky at morning, shepherd's warning'?"

"Why?" asked the Rat.

"Because," said the Mole, "the sky is red, and growing redder. Over there —"

And he pointed, and all fell silent as he did so and looked in the direction he indicated.

"But that's over Toad Hall way," said the Otter slowly.

But it was rather more than that: it *was* Toad Hall.

The shouts of "Fire!" were useless. The general rush down to the bank and thence over to Toad's estate held no hope that it would be in time to serve a useful purpose other than to be spectators at an unstoppable conflagration.

The only practical action came from the Rat who, guessing at once the way things must be, cried out to the weasels and stoats, "Bring whatever food and drink you can; no point in leaving it!"

Finally they stood staring dumbly at the flames that shot up the length and breadth of Toad Hall. At a little distance from them, and as close to the Hall as he could get in the heat, stood Toad, alone, silhouetted against the flames, almost demonic before the fire.

"Let him be," suggested the Badger, "for I think no words can console him."

Then Toad slowly turned to them, stared at them where the flames lit up their faces, and cried out

285

suddenly, "Don't look so gloomy, you fellows! Isn't it just magnificent? Did you ever see anything like it? I haven't! My!"

"But, Toad," said the Rat, "it's your ancestral home!"

"*Was*, you mean," said Toad excitedly.

"But, Toad," joined in the Mole, "you'll have nowhere to live."

"Ha! Ha!" cried Toad, dancing about as parts of Toad Hall began to crash and crumble beneath the inferno. "I had decided to get rid of it anyway."

"Toad," said the Badger with something of his old sternness, "you didn't —"

"I did not!" protested Toad. "It may be that I carelessly left a candle burning, but do not use the word premeditation, Badger, for it is a word that reminds me of things I prefer to forget. No, this is a careless accident from which much good will come. A new Toad Hall, bigger and better, finer and more splendid –"

"Not just a little smaller?" wondered the Mole.

"I may have one room less over there perhaps," said Toad, turning back to the flames and waving in the general direction of where a scullery had once stood, "or perhaps the ballroom might be more homely than it used to be –"

"But the money," said the Rat, "what of that?"

"Lloyd's will pay for it. Their word is their bond!" said Toad with satisfaction, before dancing about some more. "My father thought of everything."

"I think," said the Badger in a measured and careful way, "that perhaps I will after all have that additional glass of wine that I refused earlier."

"Give him the bottle!" said Toad.

So the party continued into the morning, as Toad Hall burned down before their eyes, its Lord and Master the least worried of any of them there. Indeed, by midday, when all was but a heap of smoking ruins, Toad was already pacing about the lawn with the Badger, both deep in conversation about the drawings, plans and schemes that Toad already had in mind. While the weasels and the stoats, sensing that the party was over, began to drift back to the Wild Wood, and their homes.

Standing on the bank, by the river, where the last of the food and drink had been spread upon the grass in the springtime sun, the Rat said, "Mole, do you know what I think? I think we might perhaps venture out in my boat today."

"Now!" cried Mole, who was the worse for wear. "Right away!"

It did not take the Water Rat long to collect his boat, which was moored up by Otter's house, and bring it up-river to where the Mole waited so impatiently for his first trip of the season.

"Just a short one, mind!" said the Rat. "Just to whet our appetite for more!"

Then they were off, leaving Otter and Portly and the Mole's Nephew to wave them on.

"Well, spring's here, all right," said the Otter after a short time, "and we've things to do. Portly, don't be long!"

The two youngsters were left sitting wearily on the grass, for the night had been a long one, with so much to take in. Yet Mole's Nephew felt suddenly at peace.

"Look!" he said to Portly, and pointed to where Toad and the Badger went busily about the blackened balustrades, pacing, measuring, conferring.

"And there!" said Portly, pointing to the little blue boat in which the Mole sat so happily, being sculled about the river by the Water Rat.

"And —"

They spoke together, one for the river perhaps, the other for the bank, where the spring had started now, and winter fled away.

"Mole," said Portly suddenly, "it's —"

"I'm not Mole," said Mole's Nephew gently, "not yet,

nor ever, I hope. But yes, it *is* as it should be. I think that this – all this – is what I came to see. Now you had better –"

But Portly was already off, wandering along the bank and humming as he peered at the water, as otters will, to try to catch a glimpse of all the River promised through the season that had just begun.

While Mole's Nephew looked about him once again, and heard the murmur of the Badger's voice in the distance, and the more excitable tones of Toad; and from the river the soft laughter of his uncle, and the plashing of the Rat's oars across the water.

Mole's Nephew nodded and sighed, and he lay back on the soft new grass and closed his eyes with sweet content, as the Mole himself might have done, and listened to the joyful growing sounds of spring.

THE END

Author's Note

In the winter of 1992 I acquired several of E H Shepard's famous illustrations for Kenneth Grahame's *The Wind in the Willows*. One of them was of the Mole, nervous and alone, trekking fearfully through the blizzardy Wild Wood.

I knew, of course, what errand the Mole was on, for Shepard's illustrations displaced all others after they first appeared in 1931, and provide the images most of us associate with the River Bank characters. This very drawing had been used to illustrate the edition I originally read so I knew that the Mole was looking for Badger's house.

But the Mole alone in the Wild Wood in a book was one thing; on my study wall he was rather different. As the months went by Shepard's drawing became part of my own imaginative landscape and Mole's original errand to find Badger faded as the great trees of the Wild Wood loomed larger before me, and the blizzard winds of winter surged and blew.

One day, quite unexpectedly (though the drawing had not changed at all), it seemed to me that Mole was off on a journey rather different from his original one. True, he had set off from the same comfortable home he loved so much, but now he was no longer heading towards the comfort and safety of Badger's house, but instead towards the River – the frozen River – and towards disaster. The story of *The Willows in Winter* had begun.

So it was that just as Grahame inspired Ernest Shepard in 1931, sixty years later Shepard inspired me. No doubt he has inspired many other writers, though whether they have had the same connections with Oxford, where Grahame went to school, that I have had, or with the River Thames, where I learnt my rivercraft, or with moles ... I do not know.

I do know that once the Mole had set off in my mind on his new journey there was no stopping him, nor any way of not writing the adventures that he and the Water Rat, the Badger and Toad subsequently have in the novel you have just read. I did not think much about whether or not it was wise to write a sequel to a classic; not then at any rate. Only afterwards, when people said, "But *should* you have?" did I really think about it.

Those who are familiar with my work know that I tell stories in a broadly oral tradition. Before there were books I would have been one of those who wandered in from the shadows beyond the stockade, went to the communal fire, and sat down and began to tell stories in return for food and drink, and somewhere to rest. It is something one cannot help doing if one is made that way. Out of that living tradition have come all the great myths and folk tales, stories passed on from one generation to the next, not always from adults to children, but often so. Indeed, Kenneth Grahame, then Secretary to the Bank of England, began to tell stories about moles and water rats to his son Alastair on the occasion of his fourth birthday, May 12th 1904. It happens that May 12th is also *my* birthday, not the least of many coincidences of birth, place and spirit that make me feel an affinity with the life of Kenneth Grahame.

As for the storytelling, it seems that most artists, whether painters or composers or writers, have always borrowed from others' work and probably always will. We re-tell, re-form, borrow and transmute. Shakespeare's *Hamlet* is based on an earlier version of the same story; Malory's *Morte D'Arthur* is a great re-telling and re-packaging of the myths of Arthur and the Holy Grail; James Joyce's *Ulysses* could not exist in the form he wrote it but for the Greek epic upon which it is based.

So my novel, *The Willows in Winter*, arises out of Kenneth Grahame's *The Wind in the Willows,* and with "his" Mole upon my study wall now transmuted into my own, I am content to be part of a continuum of storytelling and to write the sequel. If the story is good it will live; if not it will die.

But in fact it is less the issue of writing a sequel that has interested me than the deeper level of meanings that may, or may not, exist in these Willows stories. It is through such meanings that stories gain their continuing resonance, and live on. Grahame himself was a modest and retiring man who was disinclined to attach deeper meanings to his work, but this is not to say there are none. Even a minimal knowledge of English social history suggests to readers that something of the clubby bachelor world of Edwardian England (particularly of the Edwardian City of London Grahame worked in) informs the four central characters of his story. Then too there is the strong pantheistic element in *The Wind in the Willows,* which was a popular view of nature in his time, and which gives rise in the original work to the much remembered, and sometimes ridiculed, chapter entitled "The Piper at the Gates of Dawn". It has intrigued me that so many people remember so well passages they read as children which, as adults, they feel uncomfortable with. But it does not surprise me, for I have written passages like that myself in all of my Duncton books and I know that many readers share with me – and with Grahame – a sense of mystery about nature and life forces to which we prefer not to give religious or sectarian names.

But finally what has given me most pleasure in the re-creation of the world of *The Wind in the Willows* is the discovery – obvious to many readers and critics before me – of the universality of the four great characters Grahame first created in those stories told to his young son: Mole, Rat, Badger and most of all Toad. It is for readers to work out their own meanings for these characters, and to call one loyal, another resourceful, a third stern but wise and a fourth, well, exasperatingly lovable.

What I have learnt in writing *The Willows in Winter* is that the characters' profoundest universality lies not in them as individuals to which we can give such easy labels, but in them as a small community in whose giving and taking, laughter and tears, exasperation and love, and final acceptance, we find something we may hope to touch in our own communities.

As the Mole says in the first chapter of *The Willows in Winter*: "Liking Toad doesn't come into it at all. Toad *is,* that's the thing about Toad. Just as the trees are, and the river, and summer ... without Toad there would be nothing much to live for." Which, were they given to reflection as the Mole is, any of the other characters might well also say about each other.

For me, the greatness of Kenneth Grahame lies in this creation of characters who are at once complete individuals *and* mutually dependent, and so make up a true community. One might add – for without an audience to listen to his tale a storyteller is nothing at all – that the greatness of succeeding generations of readers since *The Wind in the Willows* was first published in 1908 has been to recognise the real depth of Grahame's tale by continuing to read and remember it so that it has become not just a story but a cultural tradition. To be part of that, as both reader and storyteller, seems to me as pure a pleasure as there can be.

One day, of course, I shall retreat from the firelight back into the shadows, as Kenneth Grahame has done, but the River Bank characters will live eternally on. *Especially* Toad. He wasn't really finished off at the end of *The Wind in the Willows,* and he seems to be thriving still at the end of *The Willows in Winter.* And the terrible truth is that even as I write, there on my wall, not far from Mole, is Patrick Benson's brilliant new Mr Toad ... and he seems to be rubbing his hands in gleeful expectation of some other wild adventure yet to come.

William Horwood
Oxford
August 1993

Publisher's Note

Readers who have enjoyed *The Willows in Winter* and would like to be informed about William Horwood's future work should write to:

Department Willows
HarperCollins*Publishers*
77–85 Fulham Palace Road
Hammersmith
London
W6 8JB